W9-CMB-811

OPEN DOORS

AND THREE NOVELLAS

OPEN DOORS

AND THREE NOVELLAS

LEONARDO SCIASCIA

TRANSLATED FROM THE ITALIAN BY
MARIE EVANS, JOSEPH FARRELL,
AND SACHA RABINOVITCH

ALFRED A. KNOPF

NEW YORK

1992

THIS IS A BORZOI BOOK
PUBLISHED BY ALFRED A. KNOPF, INC.

Published in the United States by Alfred A. Knopf, Inc., New York,
and simultaneously in Canada by Random House of Canada Limited,
Toronto. Distributed by Random House, Inc., New York.

Originally published in Italy as four separate works by Adelphi Edizioni
S.P.A., Milan, in 1986, 1987, 1988, 1989.

These translations were originally published in Great Britain as *1912 + 1*
and *The Knight and Death and Other Novellas* by Carcanet Press, Ltd.,
Manchester, in 1989 and 1991.

Library of Congress Cataloging-in-Publication Data
Sciascia, Leonardo.
[Cavaliere e la morte. English]
Open doors and three novellas/Leonardo Sciascia; translated from the
Italian by Joseph Farrell, Marie Evans, and Sacha Rabinovitch.
p. cm.
Translation of: Il cavaliere e la morte and 3 other novellas.
ISBN 0-394-58979-3
I. Title.
PQ4879.C54C3413 1992
853'.914—dc20 91-52805
CIP

MANUFACTURED IN THE UNITED STATES OF AMERICA

FIRST EDITION

CONTENTS

OPEN DOORS

TRANSLATED FROM THE ITALIAN BY

MARIE EVANS

INTRODUCTION

Nineteen thirty-seven might be seen, with hindsight, as a point of suspension in Mussolini's Italy, when the temporary euphoria inspired by the seizure of Abyssinia in spring 1936 was giving way to unease about Mussolini's other major initiatives of the same year: his prompt and lavish support in war matériel and troops for Franco's attack on the Spanish republic, and his instigation of the Rome-Berlin Axis, which would soon lead to the subservience of Italy to Nazi Germany. These events were seen by many as the beginning of a universal conflict between fascism and democracy.

After 1938 Mussolini's popularity would go into an irreversible decline.

But in 1937 he had been in power for fifteen years and a total dictator for more than a decade. Corporativism, perhaps the only theory that an opportunist movement might be said to have elevated to the status of a political philosophy, was established in 1926 by the Rocco Law, named after the minister of justice, independent trade unions having previously been outlawed. However valuable the theory of corporations of employees and employers, in practice it was merely part of the power structure, providing jobs for the party faithful and abundant opportunity for corruption and for labor exploitation. Unemployment was always high—possibly as high as two million in 1932—real wages fell by about eleven percent between 1925 and 1938, and there was a decline in standard of basic foods and of general health among workers.

Total obedience was demanded from Italians of all ages. Membership in the various Fascist youth movements, starting with the Balilla at the age of four, became compulsory. Out of twelve hundred professors, only eleven refused the loyalty oath, and they were forced into retirement. Standard punishment for political offenders was *confino*, sometimes on a penal island but often under surveillance in a remote mainland district, where life could be extremely primitive. Culture and intellectual pursuits were scorned, except as a means of glorifying fascism under the aegis of the Fascist Institute of Culture and the School of Fascist Mysticism. Mussolini was a powerful journalist and demagogue, and he poured money into his propaganda machine. Press censorship was imposed early and Fascists put in charge of the well-known liberal papers.

Mussolini's was not a murderous regime compared with Hitler's or Stalin's, but violence was rife in the early years, abating after 1925, partly for lack of opposition, since most dissenters had either been variously silenced or chosen to leave the country. One murder in 1924 caused such revulsion that it rocked Mussolini's power. A Socialist deputy, Giacomo Matteotti, protested eloquently in the Chamber of Deputies against the Fascist terror tactics in the April elections; on June 10 he was attacked by five men and taken off in a car; in August his body was found, with multiple stab wounds in a shallow grave. By the end of the year Mussolini's "consuls" compelled him to reassert himself by a return to force. A secret police force was created in 1926; its arbitrary procedures included torture, together with Special Tribunals for the Defense of the State. The death penalty, which had been abandoned in Italy forty years before, was reintroduced and became identified with fascism and its boasted law and order.

It is within this system of fear and oppression that Sciascia's "little judge" conducts a murder trial in Palermo in 1937.

> The fact is, it is not the legislator who kills, but the judge, not the legislative ruling, but the judicial ruling. Thus the trial stands with total autonomy before the law and its injunctions, an autonomy in which and through which the injunction, as an arbitrary act of authority, melts away and the trial, imposing itself on both the object and the originator of the injunction, and without any revolutionary implication, finds its "moment of eternity."
>
> —Salvatore Satta
> *Soliloqui e colloqui di un giurista*

MARIE EVANS

You know my thinking," said the district prosecutor. The perfect opening for the man whose thinking you don't know, or if he has a "thinking," or if he thinks at all. The little judge looked at him gently, sleepily, a lingering, indulgent look. And the prosecutor felt the look on his face, just as once, as a boy, he had felt the hand of an old, blind relative who wanted—he said—to see which of the older members of the family he resembled. The hand of that relative, whom he'd never met before, moving over his face as though modeling it, had aroused in him a certain repugnance, disgust. And now this look caused him irritation and anxiety. Who was the little judge likening him to? And he regretted the sentence, which had been meant to open a confiding, almost friendly discussion. But he could think of nothing better than to turn it around. He said: "I know your thinking." But still that look, increasing his irritation and anxiety. He skipped the whole argument he had carefully prepared and, as if grasping at air, said: "It must be admitted they have never asked anything of us. Even in this

7

case—let's be quite clear about this—they have made no demands."

The prosecutor's imposing stature, and the imposing chair he usually sat in, made the little judge uneasy and embarrassed, and in their rare conversations this unease always turned to indifference and boredom. His mind wandered, or gave an ironic twist to the phrases it caught: His thinking, my thinking: what a silly, tedious game. I don't know his thinking, and I don't want to know; but I don't have a "thinking" at all: I just think. And his mind dwelt on the phrase whose essence no grammar or dictionary would register as a substitute for the thing you don't want to name, the thing you don't want to think: especially when the possessive pronoun precedes the thinking and nothing follows. A phrase that, for Italians, belonged to the Catholic religion, the governing party, Freemasonry, anything that had—obviously or, worse, obscurely—force and power, anything to be feared; and now belonged to fascism, its rulings and its rituals. "You know my thinking, I know your thinking: so let's not think about it. That's the best thing."

Like a landscape out of the mist, the prosecutor's words floated to the surface of his mind. He was saying: "They set up their special tribunals, they kept us outside and—why shouldn't we say it—above politics, their politics: and we still have judges, functioning without any interference, who have not only passed sentences that were unpopular with some official, or even with the regime, but have quite openly and firmly ignored the pronouncement of some official or some group or of the entire party, on certain cases or certain interpretations of the laws . . ."

"Yes, outside or above: but their special tribunals . . ."

"We couldn't oppose them: we would have lost what we have managed to hold on to."

"We went along with it."

"Yes, we went along with it," the prosecutor admitted. A sigh of resignation turned into a yawn. He yawned frequently: because of something going on in his body that he chose to ignore; but also because of the life he led, caught between the huge power his office gave him, which he exercised with obsessive caution and concern, and that which his family utterly denied him, caring only for his salary. "But you know my thinking," he said again. And again he yawned, this time for the tedium of having to work out his thinking, if only on a matter of detail, losing sight, as always, of the whole. But all at once he lost sight of that detail too, descending to another, more concrete. He opened a desk drawer and pulled out a red folder. He held it between his hands to surprise the judge at the right moment. "The police," he said, "sent us all the papers found in the defendant's house. All except this one. It was included in the list that accompanied the others, but was held back at the police station. To get hold of it, I had to insist. Why, I said, and wrote, why send us so many papers, even useless ones—agendas, letters, postcards, family photos, butcher's bills, baker's bills—and not this one? It seems they had orders from above not to give it to us. If I ask myself why, one answer does occur to me; but perhaps it's not the right one. So I'd like to hear your opinion. Yesterday, at last, they gave way." And he gave way, holding the folder out to the judge.

The judge took it, and as he glanced at it he gave a start: it was an image that, thirteen years before, newspapers, manifestos, even postcards, had as it were hammered into the memory of Italians with a memory, into the feelings of Italians with feelings. This very image: a serene, severe countenance, broad brow, thoughtful gaze with something sorrowful, even tragic, about it; or perhaps with the tragic touch conferred upon his living image by his tragic death. An image that took the judge back to that summer of 1924 (he was a *pretore* in a little country district in Sicily, where there were few Fascists and fewer Socialists), when the fate of fascism seemed to hang in the balance but, as the summer waned, to reassert itself and get the upper hand. And in his memory the sense, literally the sense—colors, smells, even tastes—of the dying summer was associated with the waning of the passions that tragic case had kindled even in ordinary homes. A passion he, too, had felt, but within a passion for law, justice, and right. And he thought: A feeling like that was never meant to die.

Beside the photo, spattered with dots and exclamation marks, was the passage in which, attributed to Giacomo Matteotti, were phrases addressed "to his executioners": "kill me, but you will never kill the idea that is in me ... my ideas cannot die ... my little ones will glory in their father ... the workers will bless my corpse ... long live socialism." And from these ingenuously solemn and heroic phrases (which nonetheless, he remembered, proved effective not only in encouraging the opposition but in moving the hearts of housewives) the word "corpse" stood out starkly, and the image in front of him dissolved into another: the photograph showing the "mortal remains" being carried from the Quartarella woods to the cemetery at Riano Flaminio; the white wood box, the four carabinieri carrying it; and the first one (on the left in the photo, he recalled with terrible precision), closest to the camera, holding a handkerchief to his nose and mouth. For years now, whenever certain facts at certain moments had reminded him of the murder of Matteotti, he had thought of it only in words belonging to subsequent history and its verdict; but this red folder had thrown him right back into visual memories, surprising in their clarity and precision, that were steeped in those words and that verdict. Photographs from the weekly magazine that printed more than any other at the time: the women of Riano carrying flowers to the place where the body had been found; the funeral at Fratta Polesine, the coffin carried on the shoulders of relatives and friends (the baritone Titta Ruffo, a cousin, was singled out in the caption: had he paid dearly for that relationship and that devotion?); and the most remarkable image of all, which said more than a whole chapter in a history book, of those Socialist deputies kneeling near the parapet of the bridge where Matteotti had been seized. They had laid a wreath and knelt down: eyes eager to pass into history turned toward the camera; some at the back had got to their feet, fearing the lens would miss them. And he thought he would search out the photograph: he remembered two or three of the kneeling men and was curious to know what had become of them all.

One thought led to another, and he found himself saying rashly: "One thing nobody paid much attention to at the time: he was a qualified teacher of criminal law at the University of Bologna."

"Who?" asked the prosecutor.

"Matteotti," said the judge; but the prosecutor's guarded, almost pitying look suggested not only wariness but a suspicion of muddled thinking, of talking in non sequiturs: what had the detail of being a qualified teacher to do with such a thorny subject? But that detail had told the judge something: that Matteotti had been considered the most implacable of all the opponents of fascism, not because he spoke in the name of socialism, which was then an open door that anyone could pass through, but because he spoke in the name of the law. Of criminal law.

The prosecutor gave him time to switch back to the topic he had invited him there to discuss; then he asked with a yawn: "What do you think? I mean, about the fact that they didn't want to send us this particular document."

"Delicacy," said the judge.

"Quite so," said the prosecutor, irritated as he always was when he suspected sarcasm or irony. "It seems to me that in drawing attention to the omission, and persisting in it, they were telling us: we don't want to confuse the issue and accuse the defendant of a crime of a quite different order, although it might be necessary to bear it in mind as a detail that completes the whole wretched picture; besides, you have plenty of evidence on which to base the harshest verdict."

"Indelicacy, then," commented the judge.

"Never mind delicacy and indelicacy, let's take it for what it is: a warning. The fact is, they expect a swift, exemplary sentence."

There was a knock; the prosecutor said: "Come in"; the usher came in with a bundle of mail and put it on the table. As soon as he had gone out again, shutting the door behind him, the prosecutor said: "A spy: I suspect a high-ranking one and well paid; I got the carabinieri to inquire very discreetly: he lives way above his salary. Or mine ... At this moment he'll certainly have his ear glued to the door. But only for art's sake: you can't hear anything; I've checked."

The judge longed to cut short this conversation, in which he felt uneasily he must either reveal his true feelings or lie. Or worse still: fail both to conceal his feelings and to lie. He tried a shortcut: "So you say they expect a swift, exemplary sentence. But they're not the only ones: I am well aware that everyone expects it."

The prosecutor looked relieved. "Let's speak quite clearly about it, then," he said; but instead he fell silent for some time, as if waiting for a slow-dawning light to clarify what he had to say. At last, like a hunting dog returning from some distant trail: "The prosecutor's office and the judiciary: it's almost a commonplace to believe that the judiciary, to which you belong, has nothing to do with political power and has remained absolutely independent these last years; while people think quite the opposite about the prosecutor's office. But I could quote as many cases of submission on both sides. Cases, I may say, which cannot be assumed to prove real dependency on either side. But let's admit the truth of the commonplace, and that you, too, at this very moment, believe it to be true and see in my words some sort of message, an oblique threat, that the political powers have charged me to convey. It's not true; but go ahead and think it, if you like . . ."

The judge moved his right hand in a gesture of denial: the gesture of a boy wiping something off a blackboard. And he really did not believe it: the prosecutor was not a bad fellow; almost always boring but never underhanded; outside the corporate body arrogant at times, but within the confraternity capable of only small, fairly harmless deceptions.

"If you don't believe it at this moment," the prosecutor went on, with his inveterate pessimism, "you'll end up believing it tomorrow or next year. Anyway, the point is this: I remember, about ten years ago, a discussion we had about the death penalty. We were not alone, if you recall. An article by His Excellency Rocco had just come out, in *The Empire*. Here it is: I read it through again this morning . . ." He pulled the review out from under the bundle of letters and opened it at a marker. "Here it is: 'On the Reintroduction of the Death Penalty in Italy.' I don't remember the arguments you used to refute it, but I remember your tone of extreme irritation. And I grant you, his introduction is rather irritating: " 'The return,' " he read, " 'of the death penalty in Italy demanded by the national conscience, invoked by the Chamber of Deputies, decided by His Majesty's Government, satisfies an ancient wish of Italian wisdom': which is a bit much, I admit. But I was and am entirely in agreement with the arguments developed in the article." He waited for the judge to say something. Disappointed, he went on. "Believe it or not, out of the respect I feel for you and, if you will permit me to say so, out of a feeling of goodwill, of friendship . . ."

"Thank you," said the judge.

". . . I merely ask you to think twice about this trial, which is due to come up in your court; and above all, if it poses problems for you, assuming your opinions on the death penalty are unchanged, to turn it down or—it's not my field—get together with the president of the court of appeals to find the most convenient, least prejudicial way of transferring it to another session . . . least prejudicial, I mean, to your career: a brilliant one up to now, it seems to me . . . I said it before and I say it again: I am entirely in agreement with the theses of His Excellency Rocco"—he never forgot to give the title he boasted to anyone else with a claim to it— "and therefore in agreement with the law, since the death penalty has been a state law for ten years now: law is law; we can only apply it and serve it. And this, of all cases, would seem to call for capital punishment, since capital punishment is now the law of the land; these are cold, brutal crimes; the man is the lowest of the low. The whole town is up in arms, appalled: in a lynching mood. But I seem to recall—I say it without irony, indeed with regret, almost with pain—that you would prefer lynching . . ."

"I would not prefer it. I said at the time, I recall, that a band of fanatics or drunks who think they are making their own justice in fact corroborate the law by contravening it: in the sense that the action imposes on its agents the indemnification of the law, an affirmation that must not, cannot be. But surely the instincts that erupt in a lynching, the fury and madness, are less atrocious than the macabre ritual that activates a court of justice in pronouncing the death sentence: a sentence that, in the very name of justice, law, reason, of the king by the grace of God and the will of the nation, consigns a man, the way it is done here, to be shot by twelve rifles: twelve rifles aimed by twelve men who were enlisted for the good of the people, the ultimate good being life, but who at a particular moment in time have responded eagerly to a call to commit murder, not only unpunished but rewarded . . . a vocation to murder fulfilled with the state's gratitude and remuneration."

"Let's not exaggerate," said the prosecutor. He was quite thrown; the "at the time" with which the judge had begun, distancing into memory the opinion he had held ten years before, had led him to expect a different, changed opinion now; but the ensuing vehemence accorded ill with the "at the time."

Generally a taciturn man of few and well-honed words, the little judge seemed a prey to uncontrollable eloquence. "Do you know," he went on, "how a firing squad is formed? I don't mean by the military and in time of war, when there's an obligation to take part: I mean here and now, in peacetime, in the system we administer. Have you ever seen the men in a squad? Black uniforms, black capes when I saw them; faces that lend conviction to Lombroso's theories on the physiognomy of criminals, faces that in a barracks of the *guardia* or the carabinieri, where they are performing the duties for which they were enrolled, we might say showed atavistic deprivation and brutality: but looking at them, and knowing that these are the faces of men who have chosen to kill, who have been chosen to kill ... They call them *metropolitani;* they arrive like a flock of crows, a flock of death, from the capital: a curious association of the capital city with capital punishment."

"Never mind that," said the prosecutor, irritated by the judge's emotion and a little by his own. And he thought: I wash my hands of it: and thought it so intensely that he made the gesture. "Never mind that. But whatever your thinking and whatever my thinking on the matter, we must consider ..." That phrase again: but this time it was a technical, a "shop" matter, a more or less pointless debating matter within a confraternity, since the law was stronger than any opinion: "... we must consider that no novelistic fancy could confer the slightest doubt or the slightest ambiguity on this case, not the faintest echo of pity or mercy: unless for the victims, of course; nor project it in such a way as to arouse regret for the old state or criticism of the new. Impossible to turn it into anything like the Sergeant Grischa question, believe me." Arnold Zweig's novel had been on the prosecutor's latest reading list: it wasn't really relevant, but the prosecutor was keen to show himself a man of literary pursuits, and besides, he wanted to change the subject slightly. And indeed, the judge asked: "What question is that?"

"I don't know what historical or documentary basis it has. A novel. By a German. Very interesting: the old Prussian state with its princes, its rules, its scruples, losing out in the clash against postwar Germany and its petty tyrannies, disregard for law, total lack of scruple, its inhuman abstraction ... the Germany of today: and let's hope ours will stop in time, that they won't get us too compromised in that liaison ..." But he realized he was getting too compromised himself, and said "Let's get back to the point. You know it's generally felt here that since fascism, you can sleep with open doors ..."

"I always close mine," said the judge.

"So do I: but we must admit that for the past fifteen years conditions of public safety have improved considerably. Even in Sicily, in spite of everything. Now, whatever we think about the death penalty, we must admit that its reintroduction serves to hammer home the idea of a state totally dedicated to the safety of its citizens; the idea that from now on people really can sleep with open doors."

"I wouldn't deny it," said the judge.

"So we agree," said the prosecutor, with the haste of a man afraid to find they don't agree in the least. He got up, the judge got up, they shook hands. "May I ask you," said the judge, "to lend me this review? I should like to reread the article by His Excellency Rocco." The prosecutor gave it to him, led him to the door, opened it; the usher was standing outside, a false obsequiousness making his real expression even more disagreeable: greedy and ferrety. Looking at him, prosecutor and judge remembered they had doubly infringed the Fascist party code: they had used the formal "you" to each other and shaken hands. They took leave using *voi* and giving the Fascist salute.

The prosecutor went back into his office and returned to

his lofty chair. He yawned wearily. "Whatever his thinking, he will have to reflect, weigh the pros and cons. After all, it's his career!" But we are often wrong to judge our fellows as our fellows in every way. Some are worse, but some are better too.

The conversation with the prosecutor had lasted a very long time (much longer than it will have seemed to the reader). When the judge left the Palace of Justice it was already evening; streetlamps were lit, the great trees on the square formed dark masses, their branches monstrously articulated. Every time he crossed the threshold of this palace, the word "inquisition" flashed through the judge's mind. For a couple of centuries it was here that blasphemers, witches, heretics, often of no known heresy, were judged; from this portico the auto-da-fé processions had wound through the town to the fire that would be lit not far away, though the plan of the route and the slowness of the cortege made it seem very far indeed. The state—the Bourbon state, the state of Savoy—was obviously fated, given the shortage of public buildings, to inherit this palace from the Inquisition; but by a choice made law, it had also inherited the conduct of fiscal proceedings against the heretics, appropriating the estates of the condemned and disputing interminably with the legitimate heirs. One dispute had lasted until about 1910, over the estate of a Quietist heretic, a woman (the transgression had been sexual rather than doctrinal), who had been burned in 1724. Money has no smell, not even of the living flesh burning at the stake, which spectators at autos-da-fé maintain has a powerful and quite peculiar smell. "When all's said and done, it attaches tremendous weight to one's own opinions if a man is roasted alive for their sake." Grand words; everything is a matter of opinion, of relative or derisory value, except the opinion that you cannot roast a man alive because he does not share certain opinions. And except the opinion, here and now in 1937 (1987) that humanity, justice, law—in short, the state, which the idealist philosophy and the doctrine of fascism at the time called *ethical*—must not answer murder with murder.

Speaking of those years, perhaps of that very year, Vitaliano Brancati says of a poor man who felt a strong aversion to iniquity that he could find no words to explain: "Why did a canto on liberty by Milton or Leopardi, or a book by some outlawed philosopher, not fly to the help of this poor man, suffering all the torment oppression can inflict upon an honest soul, yet incapable of explaining his suffering?" But the little judge was not lacking in such help. There were these indelible words: "When I saw how the head split away from the body, and how each landed separately in the crate, then I realized, not with my intelligence but with my whole being, that there is no theory of the rationality of life or of progress that can justify such an act, and that even if everyone on earth since the world began, arguing from whatever theory, were to declare it necessary, I know that it is not necessary, that it is evil and therefore that neither the words and actions of men, nor progress itself, can judge what is good and necessary, but only I, in my own heart." Words that, in our pursuit of the judge's thoughts, we failed to find in the translation he had acquired as a boy around Christmas 1913 (he remembered it exactly, because only at such a time, thanks to a gift from a relative in America, did he have the one and a half or two lire needed to buy it); so we have used another, more recent one, knowing that no translation, neither the clumsiest nor the most beautiful (the most beautiful could be the most dangerous), will ever succeed in translating a great Russian writer. In the judge's mind, too, was another page, by another Russian: "But the Prince was a half-wit—the lackey was quite sure of this": that is, the Prince who is telling of an execution he has witnessed (again by the guillotine in Paris) and who pours out the most inspired attack on capital punishment that has ever been made. And the judge seemed to recall that the lackey had been moved at one point, but it could not have gone very deep, for lackeys are always in favor of capital punishment, those who are lackeys by their function and those who are lackeys in their soul.

Now, here (he had arrived home, put on his slippers, opened the balcony windows, lit the lamp on his desk, and begun to read the article "On the Reintroduction of the Death Penalty in Italy"), here's this poor Rocco—and he really felt a sort of commiseration, almost pity for him—who starts with a long list of the great names of Italian and foreign "wisdom" who have approved, or even invoked, the death penalty. Wisdom, wisdom. Poor Rocco, professor of criminal law in the Royal University of Rome, minister of justice (and grace), His Excellency Rocco: titles perfectly suited to the garb of a lackey, but the title of lawyer, which he liked to put before his name—no, the judge really could not grant him that.

His Excellency Rocco: the prosecutor was always referring to him. A good fellow, the prosecutor, but good fellows form the base of every pyramid of iniquity. "In fact, I'm one of those good fellows too." And even if the prosecutor thought otherwise, the judge could not bring himself to believe, not even remotely, that the cautious admonition he had received was prompted by anything but a sense of corporate concern, by a hope of satisfying an almost universal demand for justice in this case, and perhaps by some personal esteem bordering on friendship, although there had never really been a proper friendship between them. According to his parents, his brothers, and his wife, the judge's chief weakness was this: believing until direct evidence to the contrary, and even then viewing the evidence in an indulgent light, that there was more good than bad in everyone and that in everyone the bad might suddenly prevail because of some absentmindedness, a false step, some fall of more or less vast and deadly consequence, both for oneself and for others. A weakness that had prompted his calling to become a judge and enabled him to carry out the task. Not that he did not feel touches of unkindness and spite, prickings of amour propre, but he sublimated them—at least he thought so and took comfort in the fact—in a sphere we might call literary and that he called innocent, in the sense that he considered they hurt no one. But we will use *literary*, giving it another, although not too serious, sense, since literature is never wholly innocent. Not even the most innocent.

He had come to the end of Rocco's article: "As for cases involving the death penalty (whether this should be limited only to the gravest political crimes or only to the most brutal common crimes or extended to both and to those that lie between the two), likewise as to the mode of execution of the death penalty, and the judicial body to which it should be entrusted, the forms of procedure and judgment and so on, these are particular questions of criminal legislative policy which I consider must be left to the political wisdom of government and parliament. For they will know how to act in this as in other matters as sure and faithful interpreters of the juridical conscience of the Italian Nation." And "in this matter, too," Rocco's expectations had not been disappointed. How could they be, since he was the prime contributor to their realization?

He had failed to wax indignant in rereading it, which had been his intention in asking the prosecutor to lend it to him. Whereas the latter had thought he wanted to find in it reasons for rethinking his ideas, changing his mind. A good fellow, in favor of the death penalty as of something remote, willed by others, carried out by others, abstract, almost a piece of propaganda and, ultimately, aesthetic. He had never been required to call for it in a trial; and if it was called for by his substitutes, perhaps he thought it was their business, of no great weight since calling for it was quite different from carrying it out. And to give him his due, the judge thought, if he had been required to carry it out, at least the perception that it had been reintroduced to deceive the citizenry about improved law and order under the Fascist State, this dawning perception would have touched and troubled his conscience. Which would never have happened to Professor Rocco, who knew perfectly well the reason for the reintroduction.

He had failed to work up a fresh sense of indignation. As his chemistry professor used to say, the solution was already saturated. Saturated with indignation.

Open doors. Supreme metaphor for order, security, and trust: "You can sleep with the doors open." But in that sleep would be a dream of open doors, corresponding in everyday, wide-awake reality, especially for those who liked to stay awake and scrutinize and understand and judge, to so many closed doors. The newspapers, above all, were closed doors, but the citizens who spent thirty centesimi a day to buy them—two out of every thousand in the densely populated south—were unaware of this closed door, except when something happened before their own eyes, something serious or tragic, and they looked for news of it, and either did not find it or found it shamelessly impostured (the word is not considered good usage, we know, but we are sure the reader will forgive it if we offer in its justification the definitions that persuaded us to use it: "*Falsity* directly concerns things, insofar as they do not correspond to the concept in the mind; *falsehood* concerns words, insofar as they do not correspond to the heart; *imposture* concerns facts, insofar as words and actions and silence are directed to deceiving someone, that is, to making him believe untruths to the advantage of the deceiver and to the satisfaction of some ignoble passion of his": definitions, I need hardly say, to be found in the great Tommaseo dictionary).

In the case that was about to come before the judge—a man who had killed three people in a matter of hours—

imposture had reached its apogee and toppled over into the grotesque or comic. The victims had been, in chronological order, the murderer's wife; the man who had taken over the murderer's job in the office from which he had been dismissed; and the man in charge of the office, who had decided upon his dismissal. But as far as the paper was concerned, there had been no murder: There was no mention of the wife, and the other two had died, albeit suddenly, a natural death. For two days, reports had spoken of them, their sudden deaths, the funerals, the grief of the townspeople. So, as journalism moves onward and upward toward the magnificent destiny it must surely achieve, if it has not already done so, we thought it might serve as a model to offer the report as it appeared, the day after the tragic events, in the paper with the widest circulation in Sicily:

The news of the sudden death of Municipal Advocate Giuseppe Bruno, president of the Fascist Provincial Union of Artists and Professionals and secretary of the Legal Syndicate, has spread rapidly throughout our city, causing a general sense of profound grief in every area of life in which the deceased was so highly esteemed for his noble qualities of heart and mind.

In Giuseppe Bruno, Palermo has lost one of its most active representatives, whose generous contribution to public life was always wide-ranging and invariably marked by balanced judgment, rectitude of feeling, and nobility of intention.

The outstanding qualities that so widely endeared him to all unions of artists and professionals in our city made him a distinguished syndicate chairman and administrative head. President of the Union of Artists and Professionals from its foundation, secretary of the Legal Syndicate, vice-secretary of the Federation of Fascist

Branches in Palermo, he was a wise organizer and promoter of every institution entrusted to his leadership.

In the Palermo law courts in particular he will be remembered for his exquisite sense of justice, which made his presence a guarantee of harmony in every decision taken.

In the administration of public affairs, as municipal assessor, commissioner of the Water Board, chairman of the governing body of the hospital, member of the governing council of the Bank of Sicily, he displayed at all times the energy and passion with which he espoused the highest causes, born of a scrupulous and lofty sense of responsibility.

The unfailing trust he earned among party leaders for his dignified conduct of the most delicate Fascist and Syndicalist functions in the province was to him the cherished reward for his disinterested and devoted work as a party official.

The grief of his afflicted family is therefore shared by the great family of Artists and Professionals in Palermo, by whom he will always be remembered as an example and a guide.

Around his mortal remains today are dipped the banners of fascism and of syndicalism in Palermo, just as around his memory are gathered the grieving thoughts of all who knew him and were enabled to appreciate his noble qualities.

The solemn honors which will be rendered to Giuseppe Bruno today will be a fitting testimony to these feelings.

The body, lying in state at the Union of Artists and Professionals, has been since yesterday evening the focus of a devoted pilgrimage on the part of the principal Fascist and Syndicalist leaders and officials, as well as a wide range of representatives from the various categories of professional people and artists.

Conveyed late yesterday afternoon to the headquarters of the union, the body has been the object of an all-night vigil by Young Fascists, and from nine in the morning all the representatives of the Unions of Artists and Professionals will take turns in mounting guard until the cortege moves off.

The funeral will be attended by the party leaders and officials, and all the unions, led by the flag bearers, secretaries, and presidents of the individual directories.

Party members will attend the funeral in Fascist uniform.

Starting from Via Caltanissetta at 16 hours, the funeral cortege will proceed along Via Libertà, Via Ruggero Settimo, Via Cavour, and Via Roma. At the home of the deceased in Via San Cristoforo, the hearse will pause a few moments for those present to pay homage to the birthplace of Giuseppe Bruno. The cortege will disperse in Piazza Giulio Cesare (at the Central Station), with the Fascist salute.

On receipt of these fatal tidings, the Union of Artists and Professionals wished to give immediate expression to their profound grief, and arranged for General Officer Gennaro Vitelli, president of the Union of Artists and Professionals in Messina, to represent them.

The ceremony in honor of the late lamented Advocate Giuseppe Bruno will be combined with the funeral of Antonino Speciale, accountant to the secretariat of the Legal Syndicate, who yesterday was also suddenly taken from his loving family and from all those in the legal world who so highly valued his work.

The body of Accountant Antonino Speciale is also lying in a funeral chamber in the Union of Artists and Professionals, watched over by Young Fascists and by the police.

The judge had placed this report, together with the next day's describing the solemn "obsequies," in a file labeled "Nonexistence of the Crimes for Which Judgment upon the Man Accused of Them Is Entrusted to the Second Session of the Superior Court of Palermo"; and he would have liked to take the sad jest further and insert the file among the documents of the trial, fantasizing about a possible, or impossible, incrimination of the newspaper and the reporter. To what legal "dictum," properly or by analogy, could one resort to incriminate them? Fantasies, to which the judge often succumbed, juridical daydreams in a scheme of things that, while leaving the letter of the law intact, destroyed its substance.

In the report that we have extracted from this file there was only one point you could call a wink and a nod from the reporter to the reader, from the voluntary slave to the involuntary slave: and this was the word "fatal," which, strictly in its dictionary meaning, might be defended to the hierarchy simply for its sense of grievous and doomed undeniability, for pleonastically, every death is "fatal"; but not one of its readers would have failed to recognize its sense of the dark, violent, and bloody deed they were choosing to hide.

W hen the trial began, in fact at the very first session, in a flash of childish fancy born of the many fairy tales that had marked his childhood, some funny, some frightening, the judge kept thinking what a good thing it would be to possess the power, some magic gift, to make the defendant invisible. To be precise, he did not think it: it was as if his thoughts were brushed, even suffused, for a moment by something vague and fleeting from a world of memory and dream, memory melting into dream. Sometimes it was only the flash of an object—a ring. Turn it around on the finger, and the man would vanish from the witness box, where he stood talking calmly with the two carabinieri at every pause in the proceedings. So that at times the judge was annoyed to catch himself twisting his wedding ring on his finger.

The man made him terribly uneasy; almost as if, while unconsciously soliciting and at times unbearably stimulating it, he prevented the dialogue with reason to which the judge was accustomed. And his instinct was to rub him out, as if from a drawing in which an allegorical representation of life— of the terrifying side of life: passions, violence, pain—became unbalanced by the excessive realism of this figure. An incongruous note. An error.

But the drawing from which to erase him and the magic ring to make him invisible were, as he knew to his great irritation, a transference, an alibi, an attempt to escape from the word and the judgment upon this man that the law expected of him. Therefore to yield to this instinct would be to take on the mantle of the Rocco doctrine, an acceptance that is total and unhesitating in those who demand the return of capital punishment and, when they have got it, want it to apply not only to murderers but also to rapists, pickpockets, and chicken thieves, especially when they are the victims of the theft. But it could also be that those in favor of capital punishment were prompted by a sort of primordial, larval aestheticism. Aesthetic in two ways: because they wanted life cleansed and liberated from all extreme human degradation, that is, from those who have killed for degrading passions and degrading motives and in degrading ways (deceit, betrayal) and must be considered unfit to live; and because, sometimes having witnessed it but usually in their imagination, they see the ordered ritual violence of this death-dealing, with its savage but considerate rules, as a pure spectacle, almost a fiction, assuming the death-dealers are concerned only to *perform it well* and the recipient only to accept its inevitability and *behave well.* In short, what Stendhal called the sublime conceived by ignoble minds, when likening the torments depicted by Pomaráncio and Tempesta in a church in Rome to the spectacle of the guillotine in action. And indeed, at every session, the judge felt an occasional stab of something ignoble, a contraction, pause, suspended animation as in a dream, the vertiginous horror and fascination of the void or abyss. It never lasted, but the uneasiness lingered. He had been allotted a case in which even the most just and serene of men, those most illuminated by what the theologians call Grace and laymen Reason, must come to terms with the darkest, most secret part of himself: in fact, the most ignoble.

And then he was disturbed in a sort of gut reaction, a

horror of the flesh rather than the mind, by the dagger lying on a corner of the table at which the clerk went on and on writing—never lifting his bald head, spectacles thick as bottle glass—as if it were not he producing the writing but the writing producing him, like an excrescence. Placed on a sheet of newspaper—from his high seat the judge could read the banner headline: THE DUCE TO FRANCO ON THE FIRST ANNIVERSARY OF HIS NOMINATION AS HEAD OF THE SPANISH STATE—the dagger, rusty with traces of blood, reminded him of the defendant's words at the first interrogation, the one with the police commissioner: "I had already envisaged the rash acts I committed today, in that, at the time when I was no longer receiving my salary, I bought fifty cartridges for the revolver. I also bought a hunting knife ... and in the same period I took a bayonet I had in the house to be sharpened by a knife sharpener in the Via Beati Paoli" (the right name, thought the judge, for a street in which to sharpen a dagger, a weapon of which that legendary sect made frequent and, according to people of the same persuasion as the accused, perfectly justified use). Determined to carry out the punishment he had "envisaged" (all his experience with lawyers and magistrates failed to alert him to the fact that he was confessing premeditation), he had collected the bayonet that morning, paying the knife sharpener one lira for sharpening it and shortening it to the size of a dagger, and had put it into the belt of his trousers, in the pocket of which he already had a pistol and twenty-five cartridges. But he had chosen the dagger as the murder weapon; he said he meant to use the pistol to kill himself.

Why the dagger? Looking at it on the clerk's table, then looking up at the defendant, the judge answered his own question with a definition that was already in a book, but one that he would never read, by a writer whose name he would hear, perhaps, but only his name at the very end of his life: "It is more than a simple metal object; men conceived and forged it to a precise end; in a sense it is eternal: the dagger that killed a man last night in Tacuarembó, or the daggers that killed Caesar. It is meant to kill, to strike without warning, to shed blood still pulsing." Exactly what the judge was thinking, but he extended the thought, opening it out into a fan of somber images and memories that were part of him, just as suffering the consequences of a whole year of malaria was part of him: the Arditi shock troops arriving at the front for some night sortie demanding silence and surprise, armed only with daggers. The snipping of shears at barbed wire seemed to expand and echo like an alarm in the darkness of the night, and sometimes the alarm was really sounded in the enemy trench, so that the Arditi crawling toward it were met by a sudden burst of rifle and machine-gun fire. But the actions were usually successful, and when the Arditi returned and the infantry moved forward—a hundred, two hundred yards—to occupy the conquered enemy trench, there were the beardless Austrian soldiers stabbed in their sleep or in their sudden, alarmed awakening. It was like a vision, slowly revealed by the dawning light, those soldiers lying on their backs, blood trickling from their mouths: one of the worst atrocities of the war for the beardless Italian soldier called up in the autumn of 1917. And what of the song of the Fascist squads that ended with a promise of "bombs, bombs and the dagger's caress"? And the multiple stabbing of Matteotti.

"The dagger's caress": how can you accept, help, applaud a faction that promises such things to those who reject it?

One might also formulate a "detective story" hypothesis, which on the one hand aggravated the notion of premeditation, on the other gave the benefit of the doubt about the wickedness of the defendant, which seemed so profound, stubborn, and unfathomable. It went like this: that his use of the dagger was prompted not by perversity but by a wish to experience the pleasure of killing close up, in a sort of deadly intimacy. Having "envisaged" three killings, at different places and times, he may have reckoned that shooting, at the first or second, might have attracted attention that would prevent him from completing the slaughter "envisaged." He could have used the pistol for the third, but granted that he had also "envisaged" the place where he would commit suicide, then he needed a little time to get there. But the judge had only to glance at this hypothesis for it to evaporate. Perhaps he had thought that nothing remained but suicide, once the slaughter was consummated. But without conviction, as if judging someone else's actions and fate, something quite apart from him, his being, or his being there. For someone else who had done what he had done, the only open door would be suicide; but maybe he saw himself standing over the three bodies as if in one of those foolish photographs of a day's hunting: the slaughter was fulfilled, and in the great hereafter his victims knew the price of opposing him—or at least they had found out at the moment of death. In the dock, between the two carabinieri, he was forever assuming expressions and attitudes that were both swaggering and servile. And these expressions and attitudes moved the judge to seek something in his case akin to what the penal code called "extenuating circumstances of a generic nature." In his swaggering, servile way, the man might be considered the product of an ambience, almost of a whole city, in which servants were allowed a more swaggering style than their masters. "Capital city of Sicily, seat of the King, distinguished by the title of Archbishopric, renowned among all authors, both ancient and modern, for the amenity of its spacious position, the excellence of its citizens ..." And this was the snag, the false note, the impasse: the excellence of the citizens. About two thousand noble families, and many of improbable nobility, were concentrated in Sicily in the eighteenth century; and out of 102,106 "souls," if you take away the masters, what souls do you expect the rest to be, if not servants?

In the legal and judicial undergrowth in which everything, in such a city, is indefinably entangled—as a coefficient, pure number, eluding all measure and measurement—the defendant had undeniably wielded a certain power. In those days when accounts and matrimony were both held sacred, his life could not be called irreproachable; and among his peers his temperament was far from gentle. But he had been awarded the cross of Cavaliere della Corona d'Italia, and he enjoyed the esteem, one might even say familiarity, of magistrates, lawyers, and artists. When called to testify in his favor, most of them maintained a cautious approach: they had no complaints, he had always behaved "with deference" toward them. The mayor of Palermo, however, had more to admit, so he pleaded the burden of his office, or offices, to avoid testifying in court. But the court issued an order for him to appear: and this was the first sign that they were not going to be impressed by the hierarchy, from the mayor up, or what the Russians apparently call the *nomenclatura*. So the mayor climbed into the witness box, swore the oath, and admitted that he addressed the defendant as "my dear fellow," called him *tu*, and had insisted on his being included in the roll of honor of NOMI, the National Organization for the protection of Mothers and Infants: which had a rather macabre ring in the courtroom, considering that the defendant had stabbed the mother of his children. And the defendant had been an associate not only of NOMI, at the express demand of the mayor, but also of the Society for the Protection of Animals, of the Italian Red Cross, of the National Artistic Institute of Fashion, of the Fascist Colonial Institute, of the National Tenants' Association, of the Azzurri di Dalmazia, a national association of war volunteers: all this either to satisfy people, like the mayor, who wanted him on their side; or because he had a mania for joining and holding membership cards. We don't know if he really was an associate of the Sicilian Society for the History of the Fatherland, whose president had nominated him inspector of the Risorgimento Museum: "In view of your evident patriotism, I beg you on behalf of the board of directors to accept the appointment." In short, he had been involved in so many activities; he had had so many friends. And out of the many documents in the investigation, the judge remembered one that stressed his active and ardent pursuit of friendship, presumably not unprofitable, since the real open doors of the city were those that only friendship could open: perhaps it was a report by the carabinieri. The carabinieri! Those ungrammatical reports of theirs, with their shaky spelling and the curiously "posh" courtroom language that seemed to have evolved from memories of Dante or the opera (with words surfacing every now and then from the southern dialects they were trying to disguise and smother): those reports, thought the judge, were the only truths current in Italy. Not all of them and not always, of course: but you could trust almost all of them, almost always. Just to look at the carabinieri gave him a certain childish sense of security. Perhaps it went back to that childhood game in which the world was divided apodictically between cops and robbers, and nobody much wanted to be the robbers. And in the squalid, ill-lit courtroom, where everything was so worn and damp that you feared some sort of contagion, and the stale smell made you think of the lives of Inquisition victims that had macerated there, or the macerating and moldering of documents macerating other human destinies—even in this courtroom the two carabinieri in their grand uniforms standing at his shoulders gave him a sense of security and, whenever he glanced around at them, of repose and visual refreshment. Blue, red, and silver: vivid colors in this dead and dusty air. And he privately acknowledged a weakness for their grand uniforms: again, a childish weakness, but the adult and judge added the bitter rider that it would be difficult—or at least difficult to imagine—for carabinieri in grand uniforms to set about torturing their fellowmen.

F rom the many friends he had had, from the many relatives he had helped, from the many people who had shown their esteem for him and who, especially of late, had tried to help him hold on to his job, the defendant now listened to cautious testimonies that so distanced him from their lives that they seemed to be making an effort to remember ever having known him. And in this attitude, according to each man's social standing, two sentiments were at play: one was rather ignoble, dictated by the fear of compromising themselves politically; the other an instinctive repugnance and recoil from a man who, in these three murders that had all the appearance of cold premeditation, had proved to be a "beast," as the prosecution lawyers thundered ("The Man-Beast of Palermo" would later be the title of Lawyer Filippo Ungaro's protest to the court of cassation calling for a review of the verdict). It hardly needs saying that the first of these two sentiments prompted the people who had something to lose by compromising themselves politically; and the second, almost to the exclusion of the first, those who had little or nothing to lose and simply felt a horror of the "beast."

Although the newspapers gave no information, the time, place, and manner of the three killings were known in minute detail, and more besides: things said to be certain that, on the contrary, if not imaginary were at least dubious.

In the murder of the wife, one detail that seemed to the judge dubious and, however he resolved it, extremely disturbing, to the general public had become a terrible certainty: before stabbing her, the defendant had made his wife say her prayers, for a good death, so to speak. But the facts should be reported, briefly at least.

After collecting the dagger from the knife sharpener, the defendant had hired a car, a Balilla to be precise, and had returned home to tell his wife he was going to Piana degli Albanesi (the Fascists had foolishly changed the name Albanians to Greeks) to collect the children, who were staying with relatives. His wife, the defendant maintained, chose to go with him—but according to the prosecution, it was he who invited her to come, which seemed quite probable, if he had already "envisaged" the slaughters and had the dagger with him. During the journey they quarreled as usual; and since, in his nervous irritation, he had jerked the wheel and bumped a mudguard, they got out of the car, and as his wife went on nagging, the "rash" act occurred. But just as it seemed unlikely that the wife had insisted on accompanying him, so it seemed quite incredible that things had happened as the defendant maintained: the car owner testified that there was no trace of a bump on the mudguards; and a peasant from Piana had recognized the dead woman as the lady he had seen praying at a roadside shrine. He had been struck by this well-dressed lady on her knees, praying, while a well-dressed man, a little way off, was strolling about near a car; then, hearing of a body that had been found in that area, he had gone to the police station at Piana to report what he had seen. The defendant denied it: either because he really had behaved as judge and executioner, pronouncing the death sentence upon his wife and giving her a chance to put herself right with the hereafter (he was a very devout man; years before, he had had his family dedicated to the Heart of Jesus by a *monsignore*, a sub-cantor at the cathedral); or because he felt that this detail, of a lady kneeling at prayer on a country road, suggested submission on her part rather than a resumption of their quarrel; or because he felt that killing her immediately after seeing her at prayer somehow made his act seem more solemn and barbarous. Or for the last two reasons together. And the judge oscillated between them, desperately wanting to exclude the one the public took to be certain: that he had cruelly communicated the sentence to his wife, cruelly offered her this celestial chance, then cruelly stabbed her.

A striking feature of the second murder was the cold hypocrisy, the lying, the treachery with which poor Speciale, the accountant, had been drawn into the fatal trap. The defendant had called for him at home, with a friendly smile and a credible pretext to go to the office together: and there, face-to-face, he had stabbed him, then, according to the charge, contrived to lock the office door from inside and get out by some other door or window (the topographical description in the report was rather confused), thus delaying the discovery of the body long enough for him to strike down Lawyer Bruno, who was still unaware of what had happened in the office. But in the defendant's mind, as well as a calculated plan, killing Speciale in the office where, he thought, by sly pimping and prodding the man had coaxed Lawyer Bruno to give him the defendant's job was part of an almost symbolic design, a rite. However, although the offices were deserted at that hour, someone was about: hearing a cry as the man was stabbed to death, he had run up the stairs and bumped into the defendant on his way down; asked what had happened, the latter had answered casually: "A joker," like Hamlet saying as he killed Polonius: "A rat."

The incident had been included in the police report, but it was when he heard it spoken in evidence that this sudden automatic, and in a sense gratuitous, surfacing of Hamlet's riposte seemed to draw the judge almost unconsciously closer to the defendant. The sordid matter of the trial, the brutal and bloody misery of the facts, began to lift and take on the guise of tragedy. And why deny it the name of tragedy, if such passions were involved, revealed to the defendant by a ghostly apparition of despair that cried out for vengeance?

Except that the law does not admit such phantoms; it would not even have admitted them in Hamlet's case, if he had found himself on the level of the law and not above it: which, the judge recalled, was the difference one of his teachers, speaking of Alfieri, had postulated between tragedy and drama: tragedy was what took place in a sphere where law was powerless, drama what was subordinated to the vigor and rigor of the law; not an exhaustive definition, but quite useful academically. The law admits only one phantom, which is madness. Only then does it stand back from the crime, refrain from judgment, leaving it instead to the psychiatrist and turning the punishment, in theory (for in fact it is quite another matter), into care.

L awyer Bruno enjoyed considerable authority and prestige in Palermo, as well as being a popular and respected figure. The spectacular pomp of his funeral, to which the coffin of poor Accountant Speciale was admitted but from which the first victim's was carefully excluded, had been a demonstration of the unanimous affection and grief of the city, and of their unanimous loathing of the author of these atrocities. So when called upon by the Public Prosecutor's Office to undertake the official defense of the accused, some lawyers had refused, pleading the ties of friendship and grief that still bound them to the late lamented Lawyer Bruno. But when the defendant did manage to find a "family lawyer," as they say, why on earth did the latter not make an immediate appeal that the trial should be transferred to a superior court away from Palermo, on the grounds of *legittima suspicione* that he would not get a fair hearing at the scene of the crime? And granted that it was late to plead *legittima suspicione,* why on earth did they not call for psychiatric assessment of the defendant at the start of the proceedings? In his submission to the court of cassation Lawyer Ungaro was later to say: "It should be noted that not once in the proceedings did the defense request psychiatric assessment, clearly indicating their conviction that the defendant had throughout retained the ability to understand and to will his actions." A fine argument for the prosecution, but it really does nothing to explain why an appeal so obvious and basic in a trial of this kind was overlooked or omitted. Whatever judgment a lawyer may nurse in his heart of hearts about the man he has accepted to defend, his duty is precisely to defend him by all the means the law allows.

Considering that the defendant felt he had gleaned a fair sprinkling of the law from his time spent in the judicial and notarial mill, the fact that psychiatric assessment was not requested as the hearing went on more or less convinced the judge it must be the man's own decision. Fierce, twisted, and desperate self-love that had gone beyond control. "Amour propre lives by all extremes ... it even crosses over to the side of its enemies, enters into their designs, and—in a wonderful way—joins them in hating itself, plots its own destruction, works for its own ruin: in short, is concerned only to exist and, in order to exist, adapts to becoming its own enemy." *In a wonderful way,* says La Rochefoucauld: and taking away from the wonderful its sense of wonder and amazement, the judge gave it the sense of wondering, examining, scrutinizing—which is precisely the role of the psychiatrist. If, then, in his madness, the defendant refused to be relegated to the sphere of madness, the defense could, indeed should, have put forward the request, at the risk of his opposition. But perhaps the defense, too, had only a common, banal notion of madness: madness without method, without calculation, inconsequential; while there is a sort of madness in which only the first link is faulty and all the rest is methodical, calculated, and consequential, and the first is usually the link of self-love in relation to an enemy.

One must also bear in mind, thought the judge, that whether it was refused by the defendant or neglected by the defense, the very fact of applying for psychiatric assessment at this stage, even if the court accepted it, would provoke a storm of derision in the prosecution ranks and in public opinion, which might prejudice the result. But the fact remains that this man lacks the two elements that should have been the mainstay of the defense: *legittima suspicione,* which defense lawyers often prefer to call "an atmosphere of raging passion," and psychiatric assessment. And so, thinking over the technicalities of the trial and linking certain moments in it with things he had read, or thought about things he had read, the little judge drew imperceptibly closer to the defendant, to his fierce, twisted humanity, to his madness: in short, as was his duty, seeing him with painful clarity.

One thing that troubled him somewhat was the part played in all this by his own aversion to fascism (even if he refused to consider himself an anti-fascist, merely opposing to fascism his personal dignity in thought and action). He could not fail to recognize that if, instead of Lawyer Bruno, one of the three victims had been a cousin of the defendant (they had always hated each other) or just any other clerk in the office, the trial would have proceeded aseptically in a more or less routine way, though still involving for him, of course, the problem of not leading to the death penalty. But Lawyer Bruno belonged to a corporation and was its chief representative in the provinces: the corporation must inevitably rise up with all its might and means to bring down the maximum penalty upon the guilty person, fascism or no fascism. Any corporation will react with exasperation against any threat to its security, even in the sphere of opinion; just imagine the reaction to a criminal attack against a corporation of lawyers (or judges), whose natural habitat is law. So

the corporate closing of ranks against the defendant was perfectly natural and spontaneous and would have occurred even
in a free system. But in fact it was a fascist idea, at the core
of fascist thinking, that the death penalty was, so to speak,
an innate part of its existence, its security and its defense,
suspended over any possible opposition and ready, before or
beyond judgment, to fall upon anyone who offended the party
in any way. Thus, after about forty years, the death penalty
had been reintroduced in Italy, in defense of the Fascist State,
and had been imposed upon those intending, simply intending, an attempt upon the life of Mussolini. Then it had been
extended to the most serious nonpolitical crimes, but the
political stamp remained, so that the solemn funeral ordained
by the Fascist organizations, and by the party itself, then the
appointment as counsel for the prosecution of the honorable
Dr. Alessandro Pavolini, in the name and interests of the
Fascist Union of Artists and Professionals, these were already
a death sentence for the defendant, the superior court being
summoned only as a matter of form and ceremony. And in
all this the judge recognized that his aversion to fascism
played a part, and rightly so; but he tried to contain it, telling
himself it was not altogether true if, as judge in this trial, he
was consulting only his own conscience and his own "dignity." But each day increased a sense, like an indefinable (all
too clearly definable) threat, of isolation and growing solitude. A question from his wife had made it painful to the
point of obsession. They had never discussed his work, that
weight of papers and scruples he carried with him even at
home, in the hours he spent shut away in his study among
his books. So he was startled by the sudden question, one
day at table: "Will he be condemned?" She certainly meant
would he be condemned to death: fearing he would, he chose

to think. But the suspicion that she, like all the rest, felt it was right that he should die, and that any other verdict would be an absolution, gnawed at him insidiously, especially as she looked reassured and appeased when he replied: "Of course he will."

There was, however, in the jury drawn for this trial, in a few of the jurors (the law at that time required that they be called assessors), some scarcely perceptible sign of human tenderness. Not toward the defendant—none could rise to that—but toward life, the things of life, its order and disorder. As with the homosexuals in a famous page of Proust—though here it had nothing to do with homosexuality—it is given to some happy or unhappy men, in sensitivity, intelligence, and thought, to meet, recognize, and choose one another.

Five selected jurors, one substitute. Three were tradesmen and betrayed their anxiety for the business they had left with others for the sake of the trial; occasionally they lamented the fact. Of the others, one was a municipal clerk, one a teacher of Latin and Greek in a grammar school, one a farmer. These three were selected members, as were two of the tradesmen, one of whom, despite an absent look apparently intent upon following from afar what was going on in the "colonial grocer's," as they were then called, which his wife and son were running in his absence, also had a sharp ear and a quick understanding for what was going on in the court. But the other four were attentive, too, quietly attentive, and shrewd. The substitute, on the other hand showed a certain inattention and impatience, and an occasional spasm of boredom; he felt useless and as if trapped there by a whim of the presiding judge.

With three of them—the "colonial grocer," the farmer, and the teacher—the judge had established a rapport, an afflatus, an understanding; over and above the few words they exchanged every day and one might even say through the silences their eyes exchanged every now and then, during the hearings and in the meetings in the council chamber. Especially with the farmer. He had the tanned face of a peasant, large peasant hands, a peasant's proverbs and metaphors: but one day the judge heard him talking to the teacher about the codex of *Daphnis and Chloe* at the Laurenziana and the blot of ink Courier had left on it. Sometimes, for some people, the name of a writer, the title of a book, can ring out like the name of one's homeland: this was the effect on the judge of the name of Courier, in whose *Complete Works,* found in the lumber room of a relative who did not know what to do with them, he had begun to spell out French and logic, French and law.

One day toward the end of the trial, when he got home, the doorman gave him an envelope that seemed to contain a card: a large sealed envelope, with neither his name nor that of the bearer or sender on it. "He told me it was for you, but he wouldn't say from whom. I insisted, but he said you knew." And as if by way of apology: "He looked a decent Christian fellow, tall, face like a peasant; dressed like a farmer in his Sunday best." Like all those born in a back alley in Palermo, the doorman felt a certain scorn for country people, even if he considered them, more for the simplicity of their minds than for the piety of their lives, decent Christians. The judge knew who it was. And when he opened the envelope and looked inside, good Christian seemed a fair definition of the bearer: between two pieces of card was an old popular woodcut. Nothing else: not a note, not a word. It was a picture of a Madonna, crowned by two angels, between two saints, one of whom was clearly Saint John. The group was ethereal, radiating shafts of light, held up by clouds that, to tell the truth, looked like shapeless lumps of stone. Below were a little church, a bridge with two small trees, four figures praying in the flames of purgatory, a guillotine, a gallows with a man dangling from it, and the words: "The Society of the Souls of the Beheaded." The judge remembered: the image referred to one of the most obscure and spontaneous cults that had grown up in the Catholic Church in Sicily at a certain time: never officially encouraged, perhaps, but certainly widely tolerated. Tolerance for the souls of the beheaded had reached the point that the word "holy" had slipped in, and the cult of the souls in purgatory had merged with that of the souls of the beheaded: "the holy souls of the beheaded," an expression not admitted and not seen in writing, but predominant in common speech and common worship. Indeed, in the village where he was born, and to which he returned on holidays, the judge remembered the little Church of the Holy Souls, very much like the one in the woodcut. It must have been built for the holy souls in purgatory—all the inhabitants of the village through the centuries, since nobody would admit that even the most distant of his forebears could be anywhere in the hereafter but in purgatory; but at some point the souls of the beheaded had begun to take possession, so that the little church, at the end of the inhabited world, inspired those who approached it after dark with terrifying visions of beheaded (head in hand) and hanged men, and the fact that these specters were guardian spirits, preserving passersby to whom they appeared from all violence, did not prevent their causing such terror as to make the hair stand on end or even turn white.

The movement toward such a cult must have started in the second half of the sixteenth century, when the White Company was formed to comfort the condemned, praying with them to the last, then continuing to intercede for their souls with prayers and masses. Considering that the condemned were at first denied any religious consolation, the history of religion had taken a step forward. As had the history of Reason, since one Palermo writer, like Guicciardini leaving "memoirs" to his children, particularly recommended a son who was entering upon a legal career not to prescribe torture or flogging, and never to condemn to death "for anything whatsoever."

And now the judge had gone searching in the disorder of his many books for the little volume of *Christian Admonitions* by Argisto Giuffredi, written five or six years before his tragic death in 1591. He found the passage at once, as he had folded down the corner of the page about ten years before. "I know full well," said Giuffredi, "that this will seem to you an extravagant opinion"; and it certainly must have seemed so, two centuries before Beccaria. How had Giuffredi arrived at that "extravagant" idea? Speaking of the most common torture of the time, the rope, he states his reason quite clearly: "for that, apart from the danger a man is put in, by confessing, of dying, he is also put in danger of breaking his neck, by, as I have sometimes seen, the breaking of the rope or the beam to which it is attached: and be advised that today this use of the rope has come to such a pass that, where formerly it was not applied unless with those evidences or testimonies which today, as if certain proofs, incur the ultimate penalty: the rope is now ordered for such shallow evidences that it is a disgrace ..." Giuffredi evidently feared the effects of torture on the innocent: perhaps because he, too, had been an innocent victim of torture, we do not know on what accusation, and had been on the point of confessing guilt; and as for the disgrace of resorting to it too freely, the judge thought: "just like today, in the squads of the *polizia giudiziaria:* and it is a disgrace for us judges." And Giuffredi's radical aversion to capital punishment followed naturally upon his aversion to torture and flogging, but perhaps there was another reason, private and more anguished: the condemning to death, perhaps innocently, of a beautiful lady who held a sort of literary salon in the town, and with whom Giuffredi, as a young man, may have been in love (if not, why had the other Palermo poets dedicated to him the verses they wrote upon the death of the beautiful lady?).

He left his reading of Giuffredi to look for another book he had suddenly remembered: by Pitrè, on the cult of the souls of the beheaded. He had always loved to unravel a thread of spontaneous curiosity through his books and in his thoughts, ever since he had had dealings with books: which was why his brothers, whose relations with books required will power and effort, thought him a time-waster. But he knew how much he had gained from those wasted hours and days; and anyway, he had always taken pleasure in it.

Here was the Pitrè: twenty pages, all about that cult. But he gave no answer to the questions why. Why in Sicily, why in that century, why the contradiction of flocking to the so-called judgments as if to festivals, then conferring sanctity on the condemned? He began to answer his own questions: but we leave it to each reader to seek his own answers.

A few years before, a grand celebration in honor of great Sicilians had been ordained by the regime: one of those contradictions forced upon fascism by its need in some respect to come to terms with the reality, the history, and the habits of the Italians. They were opposed to regionalism, but so that certain regions should not feel forgotten—as indeed they were—they set about exalting the men who were born there and who in spite of being born there, great and less great alike, had been blissfully indifferent to the birthplace or had held a distinctly low opinion of it. Sicily had not realized she had so many great sons: visiting academics from mainland Italy came to remind her. But she continued in ignorance of Argisto Giuffredi, whose greatness consisted chiefly in a private "memoir" against torture, public corporal punishment, and the death penalty: a "memoir" that had emerged in 1896 from an archive manuscript, but that must certainly not be remembered at a time when Italy was full of such pernicious nonsense as this by an idealist philosopher: "even death may be considered not in vain, if it has given or restored to the guilty man one hour, one

moment, of that contact with the infinite that he had lost.''
A stupendous notion, that might perhaps have suggested to
a tyrant like Falaride (see Diodoro Siculo) the murderous
whim of putting that philosopher in contact with infinity right
away; but Mussolini's tyranny consisted of less murderous,
quite modest caprices. It is worth remembering the pun on
Plato and platoon by the sculptor and wit Marino Mazzacur-
ati, when he dubbed an idealist philosopher who had gone
over to Marxism (without ever, I suspect, losing sight of his
contact with the infinite) *Il Platone d'esecuzione*. And he,
alas, was not the only Plato turned executioner, nor could
one say the line of such philosophers has ended.

But to return to the judge: the day after the anonymous
gift of the woodcut, as he was donning his robe and the jurors
their tricolor sashes, he asked the farmer in an absentminded
way: ''Do you know Giuffredi's *Christian Admonitions*?''
Looking slightly embarrassed and confused, the juror said he
did. And to make the signal more explicit, the judge added:
''I reread some passages yesterday, and then a chapter of
Pitrè's *Customs and Usages*.'' The juror nodded, as if ap-
proving his reading matter.

That morning there was to be some excitement in the
courtroom. As we have seen, the Public Prosecutor's Office
had insisted that the police produce the picture of Matteotti
found in the defendant's house. But now that they had it,
the very fact of their insistence upon having it put them in
the thorny position of having to confront the defendant with
it. And he was perhaps more frightened of this than of the
impending penalty for three murders confessed in all their
''envisaging'': clearly, and with the most damning effect, he
could think of nothing better than to lie.

The minutes on the interrogation had already been

closed, but the prosecutor, who had vacillated about it, obviously decided at the last minute to go ahead, which meant that the clerk, after writing "read, confirmed, and signed," had added: "and before the signing, the defendant stated in answer to a question: 'It is true there may have been a photograph of Giacomo Matteotti in my house. It was passed on to me by Bruno long after the Matteotti episode was closed. In fact, this is how it came into my hands: from time to time he used to give me all the magazines and papers he no longer needed, which might include anything sent to his office: advertisements for hotels, invitations to conferences, etc. One day this photo of Matteotti was in the bundle. I took them home and forgot all about it.' " The prosecutor did not pursue the matter; he had achieved his objective: that the politicians should not say he had failed to understand the gravity of keeping a picture of Matteotti in the house, and those still attached to legality should not say he had failed to understand the law. As if to say: I have taken note of the matter but cannot turn it into a charge; the superior court judges can deal with it as they choose, or as best they can. Just two links in the chain of transferring and off-loading responsibility, which, for people whose lives are entangled in the Italian judicial system, tends to be an endless one, coming to resemble, in some cases, the idealist philosopher's contact with infinity.

The superior court dealt with it according to the law; the picture of Matteotti could not be considered criminal evidence; moreover, the fact that the defendant kept it at home had not even been mentioned as a crime in the case for the prosecution. It was as if the prosecutor had asked for it out of some personal, private curiosity. That it added a further count of grave and offensive amorality against the defendant was an opportunity the prosecution did not let slip. But judges, lawyers on both sides, and spectators at the trial alike had no doubt about the truth of the matter: in his mania for joining, belonging, siding with anything that was, or might shortly become, powerful, the defendant, like the keen lotto player he was, had played the number of fascism on the wane and socialism on the rebound; and in his mania for hoarding, he had kept the picture of Matteotti when it had become not only a losing card but dangerous enough to ruin a man and cost him his freedom and his job. Political exile; instant dismissal by the state authorities, without gratuity or pension. The judge remembered a case very close to him: a distant relative who had lost his job as an elementary school master and had been unable to get another because he gave a lira toward the Matteotti monument in the summer of 1924 and had been given that photo as a sort of receipt. A man of fifty, he would drift silently around the house, and only the name of Mussolini would provoke, as a conditioned reflex, the exclamation: "That murderer has ruined me."

All the jurors wore the Fascist badge in their buttonholes, but if you had asked any one of them in confidence if he felt he was a Fascist, he would have answered with a hesitant yes; and if you had asked again, even more confidentially, among friends, and added "really," it is likely that one of them would have given an outright no, while the others would have avoided a yes: not out of caution but in all sincerity. They had never faced up to the problem of judging fascism as a whole, just as they had never judged Catholicism. They had been baptized and confirmed, had arranged baptisms and confirmations, had got married in church (those that were married), and had sent for the priest for dying relatives. And they carried a Fascist card and wore a Fascist

badge. But there were plenty of things they disapproved of
in the Catholic Church. And plenty in fascism. Catholics,
Fascists. But while the Catholic Church stood there, massive and firm as a rock, so that they could always call themselves Catholics in the same way, fascism did not: it was
always in a state of flux, changing, and changing their—
ever-decreasing—sense of being Fascists. It was happening
all over Italy for most Italians. Acceptance of the Fascist
regime, which had been solid for at least ten years, was beginning to crack and weaken. The conquest of Ethiopia was
all very well: though they couldn't understand how on earth
a conquered empire meant, for the conquerors, a growing
shortage of things that had been plentiful, at least for those
who could afford them. And then why on earth had Mussolini
got involved in the Spanish war and in an ever-closer friendship with Hitler? Although they went on repeating, more and
more wearily, the hyperbole about sleeping with open doors,
it was the open door of the Brenner Pass that was beginning
to worry them: even if armies were not about to pour through
it, looting and laying waste, it seemed as if veritable flocks
of ill omen were already sweeping through. The fact was,
things were going from bad to worse. And the "quiet life"
to which people had anxiously aspired for centuries was beginning to appear ever more remote and unattainable. The
Fascist party was becoming more and more obliging to its
insiders and harsher to outsiders. And this impatience, wide-
spread throughout Italy at different levels of awareness, was
active at different levels in the six jurors, too, although it had
little to do with the trial, except, somewhat tenuously, for the
fact that the death penalty had always been considered Fascist, and, more tenaciously, for the fact that it was required
in this case, for this man, not only because his crimes were

punishable by death by also because one of the victims had represented municipal fascism and an important section of the Fascist corporations—the most important in Palermo for prestige, if not in number. The corporation, and fascism, were summed up in one name: Alessandro Pavolini, who had accepted the role of plaintiff for the corporation in his trial and was one of the best-known figures in fascism, after commanding an air squadron called the Daredevils in the Ethiopian war. We cannot know if Pavolini felt a shiver of presentiment as he followed the Palermo trial from home—as it seems he did—then in the court of cassation, and then in the appeals court: a presentiment that he, too, would find himself standing, as he wished the defendant to do, before a firing squad.

But, with one quite certain exception, at the beginning of the trial all the jurors were in favor of capital punishment in the abstract: for reasons, as the prosecutor had seen so clearly, of open doors. But in each man this abstract consensus underwent modifications and moderations in the course of argument, which, if they did not end up in a denial, came quite close to it. Common to all was the affirmation that some people, for certain crimes of peculiar savagery or for despicable motives, *deserved it.* But between the consideration that they deserved it and the necessity of carrying it out began the divergence of opinions, particularly in relation to judicial error. Those who remained in favor, either considering error to be unlikely, seeing how such trials were bound to get at the truth, or accepting the risk fairly cynically, nevertheless stopped in perplexity at the sort of borderline where the problem ceased to be abstract and general and became quite concretely particular and personal. The death penalty is law, there are criminals who deserve it: "but is it really my business to decide whether they deserve it and then to impose it?" To those who experienced it, this perplexity seemed to imply they were only one step away from questioning the very existence of lay juries: but only where the death sentence was concerned; and an assurance by the professional judges, in their robes, that the penalty was necessary and inevitable would have sufficed to appease it. And it should be said at this point that for southerners, of any southern clime, a judge, a man who chooses the job of judging his fellowmen, is a comprehensible figure if he is corrupt but a man of unfathomable sentiments and intentions, as if detached from common human feeling—in short, incomprehensible—if he does not allow himself to be corrupted by material things or by friendship or by compassion. As Don Quixote said as he freed the galley slaves: Let everyone answer for his sins in the other world (up or down), but it is not right that down (or up) here, men of honor should appoint themselves judges of others who have done them no harm; but we may add, setting aside Don Quixote, if there are men who, beyond or above the matter of honor, have chosen to judge other men, let them answer for their sins or merits in the other world (up or down): but a man who did not choose to judge and who, all unprepared, relies upon the judges' knowledge and expertise has nothing to answer for in the hereafter, up or down. A state of mind that may apply, from a minimum to a maximum according—Savinio would say—to the thickness of their overcoats, to all juries: but certainly to most of the jurors in the trial we are talking about. Not that such a state of mind made them inattentive to the proceedings; indeed, in their preoccupation with the responsibility they would ultimately have to assume, they would have been more inattentive if they had felt themselves to be judges, as in fact they were, on a par with the ones in robes.

They had reacted indignantly to the defendant's lie about

the picture of Matteotti; as a prosecuting lawyer put it, it was a second stab in the heart of poor Lawyer Bruno: in the heart of his sure and limpid fascist faith; but the opinion of the judges in their robes that the detail of the picture was irrelevant to the trial calmed the fears of some that outside the courtroom, in the eyes of the party they belonged to, it might appear extremely grave and that their dismissal of the fact that the defendant, in hatred of fascism, had kept this portrait for more than ten years might have serious consequences for them.

The jurors who had wives were questioned about the trial every day by their wives, and their evasive answers, broken phrases, and incomprehensible mutterings led to resentment and reproofs. The jurors kept the secret they had sworn: it cost them to remain silent with friends, but in their heart of hearts they approved the law that bound them to silence with their wives. The two berobed judges and the public prosecutor also had to adopt a shield of silence, or resort to vague replies. And all the ladies' questions, insinuated or direct, could be summed up in the one asked by our judge's wife: "Will he be condemned?"—that is, to death, since any other sentence seemed to them inadequate for a man who had so cruelly killed his wife. The other two crimes were terrible, it's true; but murdering his wife ... Housewives at that time, who really stayed at home, bound by rules and habits that a girl of twenty today could not possibly imagine applying to her and to her life, felt in a vague sort of way that everything outside the home was fascism, that spies and informers were lying in wait on all sides, starting from the doorman's station in the apartment house, to catch the lukewarm, the grumblers, and, a category particularly hated by the regime, the indifferent. And since almost all Italians, and therefore their husbands, belonged to one of those three categories, or to all three, according to the mood and the moment, they feared this trial was a sort of acid test to find them more or less lacking in zeal; and then inscrutable sanctions would descend upon them, ruining the whole family. So frustrated curiosity mixed with apprehension prevailed in the minds of the jurors' wives, equal curiosity but greater apprehension in the judges' wives: but the wife of the public prosecutor settled for curiosity, certain as she was that her husband would call for the death penalty. For her, therefore, no anxiety that this trial would put an end to her husband's career and bring him into such disfavor with the whole party hierarchy as to disrupt his work, his social life, and the fairly serene course of his family life: which is what the two judges' wives more specifically feared. But it is only fair to say that the ladies, who were then kept out of so many things (above, below), saw the death penalty in images, words, and music that had more to do with the rare treat of going to the theater or the cinema than with reality and conscience: André Chénier, Mario Cavaradossi, Maximilian of Austria in an American film, and so on from guillotine to firing squad, from innocent condemned aristocrats to some convict on whom repentance and resignation conferred the nobility that the idealist philosopher called "contact with the infinite."

"Don't talk of rope in a hanged man's house, or even in the house of the hangman," a Polish writer would say about ten years later; and it could be said that talking about this case, for those who were close to it or felt close to it, was rather like being in the house of the hanged man and the hangman at one and the same time: whatever the intensity or awareness of such feelings, the direct or inverse ratio of the two terms. It was for this reason, too, above all others, that those standing close to the abyss shrank from discussing it, however vaguely, with anyone who could not see what an abyss it was—for their conscience and for their life. It was not only a problem of justice—administering it according to the law, or affirming it against the law; it was also a problem of inner freedom, which is the prerogative of anyone called upon to judge.

Outside the hearings, therefore, they tried not only not to talk about it, which was easy, but not to think about it, which was extremely difficult. And the fact that the jurors tried to meet, as if casually or upon pretexts connected with their regular activities, was the reverse side of the same coin. Of the two judges, ours also felt the need, one Sunday, to meet the juror whose occupation was farming and accept his invitation to spend a few hours in the country: "without a thought in the world"—which was impossible, since even letting your eye travel over the countryside, picking out a tree or a stone, is already a thought. Even if it is not *that* thought.

It was a mild, opulent, golden November, as always in Palermo. Although the Feast of the Faithful Departed was over, the pastry-shop windows were bright with gingerbread men and marzipan fruits, just as Indian figs, sorb apples in padding, date plums, and oranges brightened the fruit stalls. The gingerbread men and marzipan fruits were "gifts from the dead" that children seek and find in some corner of the house on the second of November: and in bed the night before they had stayed awake just a few minutes longer than usual, feigning sleep, in the hope of seeing the dead arrive with the gifts and hide them; not a bit afraid, for these were family dead, some of whom even the children had known quite recently. The dead bringing gifts; mass-produced killing among the living; the stalls offering bread and cheese as well as fruit on a Sunday, when selling was forbidden; the price tags on the goods that you thought meant kilos but, when you got closer, putting on your glasses if necessary, discovered meant half kilos; the police with a carton of fruit in their hands instead of a notebook for fines: all things that combined to give the judge the sense of a city beyond redemption.

The tram had reached the outskirts of the town. At the stop where the countryside began, open and green with orange groves, the judge got off. He had suddenly decided not to go to the juror's villa. There was no rule, written or customary, that disallowed personal contact or an exchange of visits between judge and juror; but he had suddenly made one for himself. When the trial is over, he thought, for he was curious about this country house, the library the juror had spoken of, his way of life. He walked home, in a city in its Sunday best, with bright dresses that were beginning daringly to reveal the flesh and outline the forms of the ladies walking arm in arm with their soberly dressed husbands and fiancés, and where cabs blossomed with ladies' cloche hats. "Daydreaming my dry-as-dust thoughts," he mused about himself, and about his thinking, on the contrary, the most fluid of thoughts. Dreaming, too, about this line of poetry, and failing to recall who wrote it.

T he trial went its predictable way, except for the defendant's adding to it an element seriously damaging to himself: obvious lies; expressions that slipped out, in references to his three victims, betraying inextinguishable hatred. Not a shade of repentance or remorse: he just went on calling his murderous acts "rash."

He had tried to cast on Bruno the suspicion that he had dismissed him not for petty thefts, which were the result of bookkeeping audits and which he himself had admitted as quite pardonable trivia, but in competition for the favors an office typist had granted him and denied Bruno: something he had once boasted of but that he now declared was a false impression on Bruno's part, swearing that the behavior of the typist in question was beyond reproach. He probably saw this as the conduct of a man of honor and a gentleman: but it did not stop the poor lady, now living her life in a small town far away, from being called to testify, resulting in such damage as the news, even if unreported by the papers in their general silence about the whole trial, must inevitably cause as it passed from mouth to mouth throughout the length of Italy from Palermo to the small town she was living in.

Then he tried to cast another suspicion on Bruno: that Bruno had attempted to seduce his wife, having gone to his house at least twice in his absence. And when asked if he

had also suspected his wife of responding to Bruno's somewhat sporadic attentions, he had replied that he did not think
so: but in the same style and tone of voice as when he denied
the relations he had boasted with the typist. Like a gentleman
who replied with a no that should be interpreted as a yes,
out of sheer generosity. Which aroused such indignation that
the president repeated, sotto voce, what the prosecution had
said of the Matteotti portrait he claimed to have had from
Bruno: that he was stabbing his wife all over again. And I've
just noticed that I have spoken for the first time of the president of the court: this was not the one I sometimes call the
little judge, or our judge. The judge we have been talking
about from the first was what is usually called—perhaps in-
accurately, as regards its meaning in the courts—the *giudice
a latere* or associate judge: but more formidable than the
president (or less, for everything is relative) in his expertise,
as a man of letters (which counted at that time in any profession), and for his acute and unfettered judgment. The president was a solemn, silent man, rigorous in his conduct of a
trial and of this particular trial, impenetrable in his thoughts
and feelings even about those closest to him; perhaps the
impenetrability was his answer to a certain awe he felt for
his *a latere,* to whom he was shrewdly giving plenty of room.

But even if, as he (you might well say rashly) hoped, the
defendant had succeeded in persuading people that Lawyer
Bruno had given him the Matteotti picture in a bundle of
papers, that he was jealous because the typist resisted his
advances, or that he had attempted to dishonor him as head
of a family, these were not the sort of things to impeach the
memory of the late lamented Lawyer Bruno. He might rather
be blamed for his prolonged indulgence about the cash leaks,
his long-standing tolerance of the petty but continual embez-

zling: indeed, if he were alive, the law would have gone beyond blaming him, but now that he was dead, at the hand of
the man who had long profited by his indulgence, there had
been a sort of tacit agreement to emphasize his kindness and
generosity as opposed to the monstrous and brutal ingrati-
tude of his murderer. But it was precisely his kindness and
indulgence—thought the judge—that had been his undoing,
unleashing the fury of the defendant when they came to an
end, as end they must: he had been tolerated so long, he
could not see why this tolerance should fail him at that particular moment. And Bruno had been warned of his under-
ling's viewpoint, and of his threats, by colleagues who
apparently tried to persuade him to go on ignoring and for-
giving. But Bruno had answered the more explicit threats
reported by one man with a careless: "What will he do then—
kill me?" either because he was resolved to do his duty or
because he thought the man too meek ever to do what, in
fact, he promptly did. Or for both reasons: and the defense
quibbled in vain about the second, for the man's meekness,
granted that he had been meek in the past, became quite
incredible in view of his determination, his weapon, and the
way the three crimes were committed; not to mention his
conduct in the courtroom, always an important factor in criminal trials, which could not be said to arouse the remotest
desire to understand or pity him.

And this is the reason—the judge's thoughts went on—
why things will always go to the bad in this world: personal
relations, friendly interventions and recommendations, compassion for the innocent who might suffer in the punishment
of the guilty, settling for the lesser evil in view of the greater
that might result from revealing it; in short (like Manzoni's
count uncle and the country priest in league with him), block-

ing and smoothing over anything that might involve the law, for fear of consequences that might prove of vast and serious import, but not so vast and serious in the long run as letting things be, tolerating, paying to friendship a tribute of silences and omissions. It all comes to this. Or almost all.

Only at the final stages, in the flood of "concluding statements," did the counsel for the defense launch his appeal for an assessment of the defendant's capacity to comprehend and to will his acts: and they were arguing not insanity but partial insanity: a man divided between sense and madness, with sense prevailing over madness at times or—and certainly at the moment of the crime—madness over sanity. "The man who commits a crime in a state of total insanity is not punishable. The man who commits a crime in a state of partial insanity must answer for the crime, but the penalty is diminished." But in the case in question it would have been easier to plead total than partial insanity: as in any criminal trial, in our opinion. For in every human being, partial insanity, or something technically indefinable of that kind (admitting that partial insanity itself is a valid technical term), is sleeping or lying in wait and therefore liable to start awake or to explode at the right moment (that is, at the wrong, most ill-fated moment); so to refer to it and recognize it in certain crimes of passion, and not in all, is ultimately to proclaim that inequality of the law that popular opinion considers intrinsic to its functioning, as opposed to the principle declaring it to be equal for all.

Anyway, it was too late. One might well ask if the defense lawyer should not have tried to persuade the defendant to agree to the request, entrenched as he seemed, and in his folly really was, in the belief that he had taken his revenge for wrongs suffered only a little too far. They were in the council chamber now, which in decor was no less disagreeable, in the visual and olfactory sense, than the courtroom. On walls that had been whitewashed before the law courts were established there, drawings and writings left by two centuries of victims of the Inquisition could be seen through the coat of lime or were revealed where it had flaked away. They were partly covered by wooden shelves with their serried ranks of pamphlets, but some writings and drawings could be seen in full. By now the judges knew them very well, some to the point of obsession; but the jurors looked at them curiously. And some felt a sense of dismay to find themselves administering secular law, albeit weighed down with ancient curbs and patched up with modern mysticism, in the very rooms in which it had been tenaciously and fanatically denied.

The council chamber. And as the judges donned and doffed their robes there, and the jurors their tricolor sashes, with the portraits on the walls and the moldy smell of old papers, it made one think of a sacristy. In a more fundamental sense, too, by virtue of the ritual they had come forth to celebrate each morning and of the final ritual they were preparing, which would sum up all that so many sessions had revealed about the defendant's life and actions. He had, as it were, been stripped bare. His cult of the family, which he displayed above all by insisting, against his wife's wishes, on bringing two unmarried sisters to live with them, was nonexistent. As a married man he had seduced a thirteen-year-old girl and set her up in a house in Palermo, where he kept her and had children by her. It was also charged to his account that as a young boy he had run away with the girl he had then married—the classic "flit" of poor youngsters—surrendering to marriage after being denounced by her father for abduction of a minor and unlawful sexual intercourse. As for his patriotism, he had kept out of the front line in the 1915 war, possibly by means of a self-inflicted wound. His meekness: he had been involved in violent quarrels, always carried a gun, and taught his sons that a pistol was more important than bread. His devotion to work: he stole from the petty cash and held back the subscriptions the lawyers paid to be included in the album of honor. And then there were the crimes that "fatal" day. The murder of his wife was totally premeditated, for in a testament—a letter to his sons, written at least a year before and found among his papers—he said he wanted to "put her down": a veterinary expression intended to refer to his wife's animality, which rebounded to suggest a bestiality of his own. And he had been able to carry out the three murders because the victims and the people around them had trusted him. He had invited his wife to go for a drive to pick up their children. He had called to ask Speciale, the accountant, to accompany him to the Palace of Justice to look for a file he needed urgently. He had been shown into Lawyer Bruno's house by the maid as a friend. Three times in a matter of hours he had taken the dagger, well sharpened for the purpose, from its case; and with a steady hand, presumably looking them in the eye, perhaps enjoying the moment of final torture he was inflicting on them, he had plunged it into the bodies of his victims. Twice, which seemed to the judges and jurors the most atrocious detail, he had put the bloody dagger back in its case, and the last time thrown it at Lawyer Bruno's niece, who was following him downstairs. That was the moment when he could have used the pistol in his pocket against himself, as he said he had planned: not only did he not do so, but meeting his wife's brother at the police station, where he was immediately taken, he warned the police to see if the man was armed, fearing that he might succumb to the urge to avenge his sister. Another detail that made a deep impression on the judges and jurors and seemed to sum up his character.

But after quite a short discussion, the court emerged from the council chamber with a verdict that was not the death sentence.

About ten days later, while most people were still in a state of shock and resentment about this verdict, and a few—colleagues, lawyers, and party leaders—raised a bitter, accusatory "I told you so" against the associate judge, meaning that he was not a Fascist and that he had shown contempt for the regime; about ten days later, then, the little judge decided he would go and call on the juror who had an old villa at the gates of the town. I see I have called him the little judge again, not because he was particularly small in stature but because of the impression I retained of him from the first time I saw him. He was in a group of men, and pointing him out as the shortest among them, someone said to me: "He had a brilliant career ahead of him, but he ruined it by refusing to condemn a man to death"; and he gave me a rather sketchy account of the trial. From then on, every time I saw him, and on the few occasions when I spoke to him, it seemed a measure of his greatness to call him small: because of the things so much more powerful than himself that he had confronted with serenity.

So he went to the villa, one December day shortly before Christmas: a day as warm as September. Even in the suburbs, the city already had a festive air, but of a Christmas still unaware of the northern fir tree and presents, content with the crib, the capon, dried figs, and roasted almonds.

He found the house easily enough: it stood as if within the walls of a little fort, and you could see the apex of its neoclassical pediment from a distance. But the building was not entirely neoclassical for there had been alterations, additions, and more additions; there was even a stupendous Chiaramonti two-light window, like the ones in the Steri, in which justice was celebrated.

The owner of the house greeted him like an old friend he had not seen for some time; and that is how the judge felt: that they had not seen each other for a long time. The days that had passed since the verdict, with all that had been said and all that they had thought, seemed to have expanded. And now they met again like people who had once lived through a dramatic experience together and escaped a danger; and they almost felt a sense of mutual gratitude for the help they had given each other in the escape. They had both been in the war, at the same age and almost the same places; perhaps they had met, even spoken to each other; so they felt as if they were coming out of it now as companions and friends, while the air still throbbed with resentful threatening comments about the verdict. But they both tried not to mention the trial. In fact, they talked about the war and their memories. And then about books, sitting in the fine library: a spacious, harmonious room, warm with the colors of the shelves and with a real grace in the decorations and the carvings, which touched upon the rococo and anticipated Art Nouveau.

The judge was fascinated by this man with the antique peasant face and great peasant hands, opening books and leafing through them with impressive delicacy, dressed in the corduroy that was the peasants' Sunday best at the time (but on a closer look proved to be of a different quality and cut).

While he was showing the judge one of the books lying on the table, the Bodoni from the Camera della Badessa that had arrived that morning, he said: "Perhaps you imagine that this house has come down to me through a long family line, yet the fact is I don't even know what my great-grandfather did; but he certainly lived in such miserly poverty that his son, my grandfather, thought of nothing but building up miserly wealth. All this comes from him, from my grandfather: he got it from some member of a great family who was deeply in debt to him. With the library as it stands, or almost; I've added maybe a sixth of the books that you see. Mostly nineteenth- and twentieth-century French, many of them in the fine editions the French are so clever at and that we are just making timid attempts at producing. Illustrated books, a weakness of mine: to make up for a childhood in which I longed for an illustrated *Pinocchio* or an illustrated *Cuore* with a passion equal to the obstinacy of my grandfather's refusal to buy me them. He was illiterate, he hated books; fortunately, he died before he could carry out his plan of getting rid of all these. Don't think I'm a cynic to say fortunately: I don't remember my father, and all things considered, I can say I was quite fond of my grandfather, in spite of the fear of him that I got from my mother. A rough diamond. As for the debts paid for with this house, the canon who was his father confessor assured me there was no usury involved; but I suspect the canon went in for it too. Better not dig too deep: we have quite enough on our consciences already. Besides, as the old Socialists used to say, there's some murky secret at the beginning of every great estate: by what usury and violence did this house and the surrounding land come into the hands of the great family whose debts brought them to ruin?"

"The eternal vicissitudes of families and peoples: in my opinion, nobody showed such a keen sense of it as Guicciardini, but in a gentle way; quite the opposite of our Verga, with his superstitions and fears," said the judge. He felt a sort of thirst to talk of books and writers, so rarely did he come across people with whom he could do so. And after looking at the Rosaspina engravings, he put down the book and said: "Splendid: it won't have escaped Stendhal, with his love of Correggio."

"Surely not; and if he ever mentioned it in a letter or a note somewhere, Trompeo will know for sure. But the trouble with so many books printed by Bodoni is that when you try to read them, you realize that the beauty of the printed page is worth much more than what it says. I have so many of them, but I think I've read only *Aminta* right through. It's a shame: it would be splendid to read one's favorite books in a Bodoni edition."

"I have only one: Monti's *Aristodemo.*"

"Beautiful, clear, but unreadable. And yet I like Monti; his contribution to the linguistic work of the Accademia della

Crusca are a joy. And then poor Monti, with his convoluted waltz steps, gains by comparison with the things we've seen since the war, that I must confess I've been involved in too. You will have noticed my Fascist badge at the hearings: I put it on out of ostentation. But the fact is, I am a party member. Do you know why, particularly? So they won't refuse me a passport."

From a door at the back of the room came a tall, dark young woman with very short hair, like a Diana dressed in riding clothes. "This is the lady who is living with me at present."

To the judge the sentence had an intriguingly detached and provisional ring, and while he was pondering the "at present" and startled by the apparition, staring at her face, full of cordiality and irony, he said almost inadvertently: "French."

"Yes, French," said the young lady, holding out her hand. "Of course, you guessed from my nose ... Oh, Lord— the French nose!"

The judge blushed, because it was true. As he was articulating a clumsy compliment, his friend came to his rescue: "A lamb's hoof is the rather rustic expression for it in Sicily."

"An exact description; I'll remember it," she said. The talk went from noses to physiognomy and to Della Porta's book, which was taken down from a shelf. The judge felt a sense of repose and refreshment. And as he marveled at the young lady's excellent Italian and her extensive knowledge of Italian writers and books, his friend explained: "Simone is *una francese italianizzante,* to Italianize one of their words. They form a sort of republic, as you well know, with Stendhal as first consul. They love what we most detest in ourselves. Think how Stendhal would have written up the wretched, sordid case we've been involved in. The trouble with Italophiles, not only the French variety, is that they love the worst in us and stop loving us as soon as they begin to see there is something better."

"Perhaps that's true," admitted Simone. "But I already know the best of this country, and I still love the Italians."

"It won't last," said her friend with a smile; but with a touch of melancholy, as if alluding to their relationship. "It's the same with all love. There's always some wrong assumption about the other. Just think of our love for any country not our own, and all the generalizations that leads to. The Germans are thus and thus, the Spaniards, the French ... and what are Italians like? Not to mention Sicilians and all the hasty, dogmatic definitions made about them, judgments that allow no appeal ... All things considered, I think generalizations might work more or less by negatives: what we aren't, what we wouldn't want to be, and by implication what we would like to be, roughly speaking. It would be amusing, and quite useful, to see European history in the guise of the Russians who would like to be Germans, Germans who'd like to be French, French who would like to be half German and half Italian while still remaining French, Spaniards who would settle for being English if they can't be Romans; and Italians who would like to be anything and everything except Italian."

"At this moment," said Simone, "all the Spaniards want to do is kill each other."

"With the moral support of Léon Blum," said the judge.

"Moral only, to the party he's supposed to belong to," added Simone.

"Blum the Socialist, Blum the Stendhalist: and what comes out of it but the masquerade of nonintervention," said their friend. "Mussolini sends telegrams congratulating Italian generals who conquer Spanish towns with Italian troops: and Blum goes on talking calmly of nonintervention in Spain as if he believed in it ..."

"Unless you accept that Mussolini has done so, nobody seems to realize that the war in Spain is the keystone of everything that is threatening the world," said the judge.

"And unless you accept again that Mussolini has realized it, with the buffoonery of his about the sword of Islam, while none of those directly involved have done so, it's the events in Tel Aviv that worry me," said his friend. "I often like to see history through some apparently insignificant detail, a shadowy figure, an anecdote—Napoleon goes into a synogogue, sees the Jews squatting at prayer, and tells them: 'Gentlemen, nobody has ever founded a state sitting down'; and now we've got bombs in the markets of Tel Aviv, an affair that will drag on forever ..."

This anxiety about news items relegated by the Spanish war to the small print, the terrorism of Jews wanting to found a state, and the way the English were handling their mandate in Palestine seemed quite excessive to Simone and the judge: to turn it into a debating issue bordered on the manic. However, their friend had traveled in the area and seemed to know more about it than they did. So after a while that topic died away, and a cheerful, spirited discussion ensued about France and about certain writers and books. And about fascism. But when it was discussed in that way, fascism seemed to recede, as if marked on an imaginary map of human folly.

It had been dark for a good while when the judge realized it was time, long past time, to go home. His friend (we can call him that now, from what we know came later) offered to take him in the car. Driving slowly, he talked about the woman who had come to live with him for a few months, as others had done in the past: ties that had left wonderful memories, partly because they had ended, as this one was destined to do. He talked of his travels. About his life in the country.

As they were saying goodbye, he said: "I felt a great admiration for you in the council chamber: you managed to pose the problem of the death penalty in the most terrible terms without ever referring to it directly."

"You too: I'm convinced that without your intervention, the result ..."

"I only followed your lead. You've probably realized it already, but I wanted to tell you why I took part in the jury—to make a gesture against the death penalty ... Giolitti said that no one in our country is refused a cigar and a mention on the honors list. Nor a false medical certificate, I would add; I could have got one too ..."

"I must admit I could have got out of this trial too; in fact, I was advised to do so by someone in authority. But I saw it as a point of honor—of my whole life—of living."

"So we did it. But how will it all end?"

"Badly," said the judge.

Since their conversation three months before, which he remembered as an ambiguous and painful one, the judge had often met the prosecutor, but only in the corridors, where they would exchange a brief, almost reluctant, nod. But meeting him in the corridor again after Christmas, and exchanging the usual sketchy greeting, the judge went on a few steps and heard his name. He turned. "If you have half an hour to spare," said the prosecutor, "come to my office for a chat." The tone was as cordial as the words.

"I am going to a hearing, but it shouldn't take long; I'll come, let's say, in an hour."

"Splendid; I'll be waiting for you."

He went punctually. As if he did not recognize him, the usher asked his name with some hauteur, then went in to announce him. Or perhaps he really hadn't recognized him and the hauteur was his usual way of protecting the prosecutor from nuisance calls: but of late the judge had noticed many people behaving toward him as the usher had.

The prosecutor came to meet him at the door with an effusiveness that seemed to impress the usher. Instead of sitting at his desk and putting the judge on the other side, he chose the two armchairs in a corner of the room, with a round coffee table in front of them, and an ashtray on it. The prosecutor pointed to it, saying: "Do smoke if you like."

The judge was a little thrown by the reception.

"I hope," the prosecutor began, "you didn't take amiss what I said to you some months ago. I must repeat that it was said with goodwill and respect; as well as (I'm sure you realized at the time and now I can say so) out of—how can I put it?—a sort of professional concern: I didn't want any misunderstandings, friction, petty points of order, that might make for awkwardness between us, things being what they are. But it's all over now. Believe me, I don't feel the shadow of a reproach toward you, not in my heart of hearts: if I am to be perfectly frank, partly because the resentment has focused on you and not upon the Palermo magistracy in general . . ."

"So I've noticed," said the judge.

"I'm sorry, believe me, very sorry: but that's how it is. Look: yesterday I received a copy of Lawyer Ungaro's protest to the court of cassation. I asked for it so that I could compare it with the one from our office: Ungaro is a great lawyer. Well, the verdict of the superior court in which you served is presented as the result of misguided scruples of conscience and attributed to the distress and perplexity of the jury. The gravity of the penalty, it says, made them lose sight of the gravity of the crime, thus leading to a violation of the law and a miscarriage of justice. You know I am in complete agreement with him; but I know, as everyone does, and perhaps he knows too, that the lay element, as he calls the jury, gave way to the opinion . . ."

"To my opinion, you mean. But they didn't give way at all: they already had what you call an opinion and I call principle. And the principle of opposition to capital punishment is so strong that you can feel quite sure you're in the right, even if you're alone in maintaining it . . . so I can't

complain if people choose to believe that I convinced a reluctant jury by specious arguments against the death sentence. Only, to the credit of the jury, I can assure you that
they were not reluctant."

"I'm glad," said the prosecutor.

"Why?"

The prosecutor hesitated, closed his eyes as if concentrating on his search for a reply. Then he seemed suddenly
to crumple into weariness and old age, the network of wrin-
kles on his brow seemed closer and deeper, and he said: "I'm
finishing in a few months; I'm leaving this office and this
job. Retirement: a terrible prospect—why not admit it?—for
someone who has had the power I've had. But I'm adapting:
I'm starting to think things I haven't thought till now. For
example: that I have been a dead man who has buried other
dead men. Furthermore: that that's what we all are, in this
trade of accusing and judging. And then again: I wonder if,
as dead men burying the dead, we really have the right to
bury them by means of capital punishment. Don't misunder-
stand me; it's only a question, and I still think the answer is
yes, we have the right, if the law requires it. But when I told
you just now that I am in complete agreement with Ungaro,
as I said last time I was in complete agreement with Rocco,
well, 'complete' does not express what I really feel. There's
something that disturbs me, and worries me, about affirming
the law to that point. On the threshold of old age, retirement,
perhaps of death"—his hand went to his chest, his fingers
moved as if pressing something; angina, thought the judge,
remembering his father, who died of it, making the same
gesture—"I want to understand. That's why I wanted to talk
to you this morning, to understand what's happening to
you now, what you feel, what you fear. Not about your ca-

reer, which you already know you have gambled away, and you knew from the first; but about your conscience, about life ..."

The judge would never have imagined a conversation with the prosecutor turning into a confession—in fact, a plea for help. He said: "I'd be lying if I told you I felt quite calm."

"That's what I thought."

"I mean, I'm convinced I did my duty as a man and as a judge; I'm convinced I did my best, technically, with the legal arguments. The chief argument for the defense should have been insanity; without it, I chose to adopt the tactic of including the three murders in one single criminal intention. Now I think with horror of what will happen. What do I feel? Fear."

"I can tell you exactly what will happen: the court of cassation will annul your verdict and assign the trial to the superior court at Agrigento, where, I'm sorry to say, there's a president who has a weakness for the death penalty. There's also an old Socialist lawyer at Agrigento; I think he was once a deputy: a good lawyer and, needless to say, marked down as anti-fascist. This lawyer will certainly take on the defense, which is all that's required to present this trial as a clash between fascism, which comes down inexorably upon crimes of violence, and anti-fascism, with its squalid defense of them; which will no doubt have a secondary, retroactive effect on you and on your verdict. It will end with the death sentence; the defendant will be shot. So what will your verdict have achieved, except to prolong the agony?"

"*Ab uno disce omnes* ... I mean, knowing myself as I do, and presuming from this that I know other men, and this man in particular, I am almost certain that, condemned to

imprisonment without hope, in the time that will elapse between the protests, the new trial, the death sentence, and the
appeal, he will manage to spin a thread of hope for himself,
however tenuous. Until the moment when they come and
wake him one night to tell him the appeal has been rejected
and that he will be shot before dawn, he will simply play out
this thread, the more successfully if madness still comes to
his aid. And from that moment, with the chaplain beside him,
he will spend two or three terrible hours in agony, what we
commonly refer to as the death agony: that is, the feeling
that life is over for him, that he'll never see the sun rise
again, that he is about to cross the bounds of earthly night
to enter into boundless night; not to mention all the terrible
visions his mind will conjure up of the moment when death
will explode in his body."

The prosecutor mopped his brow, almost as if he were
sweating in that chilly room.

"But agony, in the true sense of the word," the judge
went on, "is really a state in which life has more part than
death; so I will concede that the verdict has prolonged it for
him. But it's like this: either this life of ours is just chance
and absurdity, meaningful only in itself, in the illusions in
which it is lived, falling short of any other illusion, and therefore living it a few more years, months, or even days would
seem to be a gift: just as it would to people suffering from
cancer or tuberculosis, absurdly, in all its absurdity; or else
our life is part of an inscrutable design, in which case the
agony will serve to deliver this man up to some sort of hereafter, with more thoughts, more reflection, perhaps with more
madness, if not more faith."

"But all this, more thinking, more faith, as you say . . .
It's my feeling that it will come to him with an intensity no

doubt more painful but at the same time—how can I say?—
more liberating in the two or three hours when he knows he
is about to go to his death.''

"No, death is no longer a thought at that moment; indeed, there's nothing, at that moment, that can be called a
thought. Try as you may, there's no way you can identify
with it in the remotest degree.''

"But don't you think you are finding an alibi for yourself, for the vanity, to be quite frank, of your protest within
a context that allowed it only by heaping even greater suffering upon the human being upon whom you concentrated
your defense of a principle; in short, that in defense of a principle
you failed to take into account that man's suffering?''

"It's true that for me the defense of the principle counted
for more than the life of the man. But it's a problem, not an
alibi. I saved my soul, the jurors have saved theirs, which
may all sound very convenient. But just think if every judge,
one after another, were concerned to save his.''

"It won't happen; you know that as well as I do.''

"Yes, I know: and that's the counterpart, the horror and
fear that I feel not just in connection with this trial ... But
I'm consoled by this fantasy: that if all this—the world, life,
ourselves—is nothing but someone's dream, as has been said,
then this infinitesimal detail in his dream, the case we're
discussing, the condemned man's agony, mine, yours, may
yet serve to alert the dreamer that he is having nightmares,
that he should turn over and try to have better dreams: at
least, dreams without the death penalty.''

"A fantasy," said the prosecutor wearily. And wearily
added: "But you go on feeling horror, and fear.''

"Yes.''

"So do I. Of everything.''

DEATH AND
THE KNIGHT

A SOTIE

TRANSLATED FROM THE ITALIAN BY

JOSEPH FARRELL

An old Danish bishop, I remember, once told
that there are many ways of reaching the truth
and that burgundy is one of the many.

KAREN BLIXEN
Seven Gothic Tales

E ach time he raised his eyes from the paperwork, and even more each time he leaned his head against the top of the high, unyielding chair back, he saw every detail, every outline in all its clarity, as though his gaze had newly acquired a subtlety and a sharpness, or as though the print were being reborn before his eyes with the same meticulous precision with which, in the year 1513, Albrecht Dürer had first engraved it. He had purchased it many years previously, at an auction sale: one of those sudden, rash cravings for possession that at certain times, in the presence of a painting, an etching, or a book, took hold of him. He had competed for it with others who had themselves set their hearts on it, reaching a state of near hatred for the most tenacious of his rivals, who then casually abandoned it to him. The price corresponded to two months' salary, and when it came to handing over the money, the sum involved took him aback. At the time, it was sizable, and not only in relation to his ability to pay; but now, with soaring inflation and the tenfold increase in the value of works by Dürer and the other great engravers, it seemed derisory. He had taken it with him from one workplace to another, from one office to the next, always choosing to hang it on the wall facing his desk, but of all those who, over the years, had passed through his office, only one (a talented swindler who genially accepted the destiny that would see him taken from that office to become for a period of years the guest of some inhospitable prison) had taken the time to look at it and appreciate it: to appreciate it fully, in the light of the most recent catalogues of the print dealers of Paris and Zurich.

This appreciation had alarmed him somewhat; in an initial impulse of meanness or avarice, he had decided to take it home, but the decision was forgotten almost as soon as it was made. He had long grown accustomed to having it there before him, in the many hours he spent in his office. *The Knight, Death, and the Devil.* On the back, on the protecting cover, there were titles written in pencil in German and French: *Ritter, Tod, und Teufel; Le Chevalier, la Mort, et le Diable.* And mysteriously: *Christ? Savonarole?* Had the collector or dealer who had wondered about those two names perhaps thought that Dürer wished to symbolize one or the other in the figure of the Knight?

Time and again, gazing at the print, he had asked himself that question. But now, leaning back in the chair in exhaustion and pain, he stared at it, groping for some meaning in the fact that he had purchased it all those years ago. Death; and that castle in the background, unattainable.

With the many cigarettes he had smoked during the night, the ever-present pain had lost its heaviness and density, changing shade to a more diffuse agony. It was undoubtedly possible to give the names of colors to the different qualities and shifts of pain. At the moment, it had changed from violet to red: flame red, in probing tongues that quite unpredictably pierced every part of his body, either lingering there or fading away.

Automatically, he lit another cigarette, but he would have let it burn out in the ashtray had not the chief, on entering, launched into his customary tirade against the destructive habit of heavy smoking. A senseless vice, a death vice. He, the chief, had given up smoking within the last six months and was extremely proud of himself, but he still experienced, together with a certain pain, pangs of envy and rancor when he saw others smoke; both were nourished by the fact that, at the very time when the memory of smoking was to him like a paradise lost, the smell of smoke occasioned a discomfort that came close to nausea.

"Don't you feel suffocated in here?" said the chief.

The deputy picked up the cigarette from the ashtray and inhaled slowly and voluptuously. It was perfectly true. The atmosphere was suffocating. The room was full of smoke, which hung thickly around the still-burning lights; like a transparent curtain, it veiled the glass of the windows, through which, flickeringly, morning was beginning to shine in. He inhaled once more.

"I can understand," said the chief in a tone of superior tolerance, "that certain people may lack the will power to kick the habit entirely, but to pursue a death of this kind with such stubbornness and self-indulgence ... My brother-in-law ..." He employed his brother-in-law, a chain-smoker deceased a few months previously, as a blind, in a delicate effort to avoid having to refer directly to the illness of which, plainly, the deputy was intent on dying.

"I know. We were friends. You, I imagine, will have already chosen your own style of death. I must get you to talk to me about it one of these days. Who knows, you might even persuade me to choose it too."

"I haven't chosen it, and it is not a thing that can be chosen; but now that I have given up smoking, I hope to die a different death."

"You are no doubt aware it was the converted Jews who invented the Catholic Inquisition in Spain."

He was not aware. And so: "I have never had much time for the Jews, strictly between you and me."

"I know, but I would have expected you to have some interest in converts." They were almost colleagues, having known each other for years, and so could indulge, but always without malice, in the occasional ironic, pointed, or even sarcastic remark. The chief let them pass on account of the unease occasioned by the incomprehensible loyalty of the deputy toward him. Never had he met a deputy of such loyalty; initially he had left no stone unturned in his efforts to locate a hidden reason; now he knew there was none.

"Converts or not, I've no time for them. You, on the other hand . . ."

"I, on the other hand, have no time for converts, Jewish or not: every convert opts for something worse, even when it seems better. The worst, in someone who is capable of conversion, always becomes the very worst of the worst."

"Conversion to not smoking has nothing to do with it: granted that conversion is generally an abomination."

"It has everything to do with it: because the tendency is to become persecutors of those who still smoke."

"How can you say that? Persecutors! If I were a persecutor, these offices would be filled with huge notices screaming No Smoking at you: it might be an idea—in spite of you and for your own good. Because I am saying this for your good: my brother-in-law—"

"I know."

"So let's say no more about it. As regards your philosophy on converts, I could produce arguments to annihilate you, just like that." The snap of the thumb and the index finger indicated the lightning speed of the act of annihilation. It was a gesture he employed frequently, because there was no limit to the number of things he planned to annihilate; and the deputy, who sometimes attempted to imitate it, but without ever managing to produce the slightest snap, was prone to a childish envy on this account. "However, we have work to do. Come with me."

"Where?"

"You know already. Let's go."

"Isn't it a bit early?"

"No, it's already seven o'clock: I was deliberately killing time with your philosophy."

"Early, always early." He hated the police custom of executing warrants, carrying out house searches, routine investigations, and door-to-door inquiries in the early hours of the morning or, more often that not, in the dead of night. Both fellow officers and the lower ranks considered it a pleasure to be savored whenever the slightest opportunity or the remotest justification presented itself. The thunderous knock at the door behind which unwitting families were enjoying their rest, their sleep, at the very hour when sleep, once the weight of exhaustion has been lightened, becomes less dark, more open to dreams, more blissful; the terrified "Who's there?" and the solemn, booming reply: "Police"; the door held barely ajar, the eyes, distrustful and sleep-filled, peering out; the violent shove at the door, the rush of bodies; and inside, the agitated awakening of the whole family, the voices of fear and bewilderment, the crying of the children . . . For such a delight, there was not a man in the force, whatever his rank, who would think twice about his own lost sleep. The deputy, however, loved to sleep, after at least an hour with a book, right through from midnight to seven o'clock, and on the rare occasions when—invariably because of the division to which he was attached—he had to take part in such operations, he was always tormented by a personal sense of anguished shame.

"It's seven o'clock," said the chief, "and it takes at least half an hour to get to Villaserena. After all, in the circumstances, I can hardly allow any special consideration, not even for him."

"We have already allowed just that," said the deputy ironically. "If it had been anyone else, we would have been there three hours ago and already had the house upside down."

"No doubt," said the chief, stung to the point of cynicism.

The black car waited for them in the courtyard—a beautiful, harmoniously colonnaded Baroque courtyard. There was no need to tell the policeman at the wheel where they were heading: everyone in the building—which, buzzing as busily as any beehive, was even then coming back to life—was fully aware. How many calls, wondered the deputy, had already gone out from that building to alert the president of the visit he was about to receive? The president: there was not the slightest need to add "of United Industries," because in that city, anyone referring to "the president" without further qualification had only one person in mind; for any other president, not excluding the President of the Republic, some specification was essential.

They remained silent for the entire half hour of the drive, or race, in traffic that grew more frantic by the minute. The chief cast and considered, recast and reconsidered what he would say to the president; concern was written on his face like a toothache. The deputy knew him well enough to be able to decipher every detail of that concern almost word for word, with each and every erasure, correction, and replacement that he judged suitable for the case: a palimpsest.

They arrived at the villa. The officer at the wheel (I have been overcome by a sudden inhibition against using the word "driver," with a sense of regret over having used it on other occasions; but will it ever again be possible to say, as was common in my childhood, "chauffeur"?) got out and rang the bell at the gatehouse long and imperiously. The chief's toothache gave him a visible stabbing pain: Not like that, for God's sake! There are ways and ways. But he said nothing, out of deference to custom.

The chief gave only his own name to the gatekeeper who came forward. Not to mention the word "police" seemed to him the first act of consideration due to the president; but the gatekeeper was sufficiently quick-witted and experienced to grasp that he should announce "Two gentlemen from the police," even if, as a southerner, he felt the word "gentlemen" stick in his craw; he made up for it with the contempt he put into the pronunciation. Coming back without saying a word, he opened the gate and signed to them to proceed along the avenue toward the villa, which could be seen at the end of the tree-lined driveway, in all its enchantment, in all its song. ("When a building sings, it is architecture.")

Everything—entrance hall, staircase, corridors, library, and the president's studio—was a fragile, musical rococo, as though indeed a burst of song.

They had not long to wait: the president glided in silently from behind a curtain. He was clad in a velvet dressing gown, but was already shaved and on the point of dressing with that severe and sure elegance which the fashion journals— now of each and every fashion—attributed to him. There hovered in the air around him an irritation at being compelled to delay his customary, almost legendarily punctual, morning departure for the offices of United Industries, from whose top floor, as though in confidential familiarity with heaven, he took the daily, invariably correct, decisions that kept the whole country on the road to affluence and well-being, even if it was besieged on one side by the specter of poverty and on the other by that of plague.

"To what do I owe the pleasure of this unaccustomed visit?" asked the president, taking his time over shaking the chief's hand and almost ignoring the deputy's. He uttered the word "unaccustomed" as though watching it materialize in italics.

The chief spluttered, as everything he had prepared fled from his mind, like hydrogen from a punctured balloon. He said: "You knew Sandoz, the lawyer, well, and—"

"We are friends," replied the president, "but as for knowing him well . . . you don't even know your own children well—in fact, you invariably know them badly, very badly indeed. In other words, Mr. Sandoz is a friend of mine, we see each other a lot, we have interests that are, if not exactly common, at least closely related. But you said, I think, *knew*: so . . ."

The chief and the deputy exchanged understanding glances. There flitted into those minds trained in distrust and suspicion, trained in the setting of word traps or in picking up stray words that could be converted into traps, the certainty that the president already knew—and it hardly came as a surprise, since there was no shortage of his acolytes in their offices—of the death of Sandoz. The chief immediately put the thought aside, in the belief that for his part the president had a mind trained in not compromising his informers. He said: "Unfortunately, Mr. Sandoz is no more: he was murdered this evening, probably sometime after midnight."

"Murdered?"

"Murdered."

"Unbelievable! I left him just before midnight. We said goodbye at the door of La Vecchia Cucina ... Murdered! But why? And by whom?"

"If we knew, we would not be here taking up your time."

"Unbelievable!" repeated the president, but then he corrected himself. "Unbelievable? What am I saying? Nowadays, in this country, everything is believable, everything is possible. I myself ..." He was unable to make up his mind, thought the deputy, between pretending he wanted to show them out and admitting that he understood there was more to come and that he had other questions to answer. By placing his hands on the arms of the chair as though to raise himself and see them to the door, he chose the pretense: ill advisedly, because the chief sensed it instinctively and, quite unconsciously, freed himself of the unease to which he had been prey until that moment. As was normal when beginning an interrogation, he settled into his armchair as though taking up residence in it. His voice trembled with the customary: *Say what you please, but I won't believe a word of it.* The well-prepared attack was launched. "We had to come and disturb you, at this inopportune hour, to ask you something that might be entirely meaningless but could just as easily provide the starting point for our investigations—investigations that, I need hardly say, will not affect you, your person ..."

He went on, "In one pocket of Sandoz's jacket, we found this card." He pulled out of his own pocket a little rectangular ivory-colored card. "On one side, typewritten, there is your name: Cesare Aurispa, President, U.I., and on the other, in handwriting, 'I'll kill you.' A place marker, as can be easily seen ... but the 'I'll kill you'?"

"A threat carried out there and then, you must have concluded. And, plainly, by myself in person." The president laughed: an ironic, indulgent, bitter laugh.

The chief's reserve vanished immediately. He protested with vehemence: "Whatever makes you say such a thing? For goodness' sake I'd never forgive myself for thinking ..."

"Not at all," said the president generously. "You can forgive yourself. It's just that you've got it wrong: and we have seen too many men in your position fall in love with their mistakes, cultivate them like flowers, wear one or two in their lapel. It's normal, quite normal. That's how, sometimes, the most simple things in the world become damnably complicated. Your deductions were totally correct. That card marked my place at the dinner yesterday evening organized by the local cultural society named after Count de Borch; and it was I who wrote that 'I'll kill you.' A little joke between me and Sandoz, as I'll explain. I gave the card to a waiter to take over to poor Sandoz, who was seated on the other side of the table, five or six places along from me. The joke was that we were both pretending to be flirting with Signora De Matis, and since the lady, as had happened at other dinners of the same kind, had been seated beside him ..."

"You were pretending to be flirting, you say." The chief adopted a tone of disbelief, an incautious trick of the trade. The president, in fact, noticed it; and with a touch of disgust: "You can take my word for it; in any case, just look at her."

"I wouldn't dare doubt it," said the chief. But the deputy thought to himself: You did doubt it, you are still doubting it: it's a credit to your profession, to our profession. In spite of his resolution not to speak, he directed a question at the president in the standard police form of a statement or an assertion: "And Mr. Sandoz replied by writing on the place marker in front of him . . ."

The chief looked over disapprovingly; as did the president, who seemed to become aware of his presence only at that instant. "Yes, he scribbled a reply. He was playing the game. He said he accepted the risk, or something of that sort."

"But you haven't kept the card."

"I left it on the table. I might have stuck it back in the little ironwork stand; it was flower-shaped, if I remember correctly."

"Whereas the unfortunate Mr. Sandoz put the one you sent to him in his pocket: absentmindedly, automatically," said the chief, scarcely concealing in the servility of the phrase a touch of incredulity, of suspicion.

"Exactly: absentmindedly, automatically," approved the president.

"What a problem," said the chief.

"Did you come here in the belief that I was the solution?" asked the president: ironic, annoyed, almost enraged.

"No, no, absolutely not. We came because it was necessary to clear up this detail, to get it out of the way at once; so as to be able to pursue other lines of inquiry."

"Do you have any other lines of inquiry?"

"For the moment, none at all."

"For what it is worth—and personally I believe it to be worth very little—I may be able to give you one." He remained silent for some time, leaving the chief in a state of anxiety that to the deputy appeared too clearly expressed to be true: just as the president's face also turned exceedingly expressive, with the promise of what he was about to reveal and, simultaneously, with regret for the puny content of the revelation itself. And indeed: "It is not that it seems to me a line of inquiry with any real foundation; in fact, it seems to me more of a joke: poor Sandoz, too, spoke of it as a joke." (Another joke, thought the deputy; these people spend their lives making jokes.) "No later than yesterday evening, as we were making our way out of the restaurant, he told me he had received a threatening telephone call—perhaps one, perhaps more than one; I can't recall—from a ... let me try and remember from whom, because it couldn't be ... the words coming into my head right at this moment are 'The Boys of Ninety-nine.' That can't be right: The Boys of Ninety-nine were the ones who were called up after Caporetto in 1917: 'the Piave was murmuring,' and all that. Any of those boys still alive would be nearly ninety today; and in any case, it would be a reference to an indecently patriotic event ... no, no, it couldn't be ... let me think ..." They let him think, until they saw his face light up with the relocated memory. "That's it: 'The Boys of Eighty-nine,' I think ... yes, eighty-nine. But not the boys, now that I think of it: the children, perhaps ..."

"The Children of Eighty-nine." The chief savored the words but found there the bitterness of incomprehension. "Eighty-nine, then. The children of the present year—1989."

The deputy, who, observing the outcome of the president's efforts of memory, had thought that it would have been much easier to remember the year '89, since only a very few days had passed since the New Year festivities, than the year '99 for all its associations with the Piave, found himself saying: "More likely 1789. A wonderful idea, that."

Neither the president nor the chief found this intrusion to their liking. "You are always obsessed with history," said the chief. And the president said, "What idea?"

"That notion of '89. Where else does the idea of revolution spring from if not from that year? It does not take much now to admit that, as they used to say of a certain drink, it was the first and remains the best ... Yes, quite wonderful."

"Wonderful is hardly the word I would use." The president gestured as though swatting a troublesome fly.

"Anyway, 1989 or 1789," said the chief, "we will discover which in due course. Indeed, I am confident we will know very soon. What matters here and now, so as not to waste your time, which I know is valuable, is this: we must know exactly what poor Mr. Sandoz confided to you yesterday evening about these Children of Eighty-nine and their threats."

"For goodness' sake, who said anything about confidences? He spoke to me with an offhand nonchalance. He was quite blasé about it. As I said, he was convinced it was a joke."

"But it was nothing of the kind," said the chief, with a fondness for the Children of Eighty-nine that, for all its suddenness, gave every promise of developing into bulldog tenacity.

"I have nothing more to add," said the president, rising to his feet. "Try talking to other friends of poor Sandoz, or to his closest colleagues."

S o," said the deputy, "exit the president."

"You'd prefer to hold him onstage?"

"Not exactly; it's just that I have a certain curiosity."

"Keep it to yourself," said the chief, irritably, brooking no opposition. As if to stress the point, he went on: "I know them, these curiosities of yours: they are so fine as to be practically invisible to the naked eye."

"Another reason for satisfying them."

"Quite the reverse! I can't see them, and neither can any man of down-to-earth common sense; but the people who are the object of these attentions, sooner or later they become aware of them. And then the troubles start, with a vengeance. For the curious."

"I understand you," said the deputy. He was rambling somewhat. Since the pain had long since succeeded in taking a grip, giving him colors, images, and above all thoughts (but not in the nighttime hours, when it seemed to have no bounds but to penetrate every part of the mind and of the universe), he now felt and saw it as a slow wave in its ebb and flow: gray, leaden. But the conversation with the president, arousing him to a state of suspicious attention, had been a diversion, which he was now prolonging in the conversation with the chief. So, as a blandishment to him: "I am sure that you, too, must feel some measure of curiosity."

"Let's make an exception for once: tell me about your curiosity, which you seem to think I share."

"To know exactly what was written on the card Sandoz sent to Aurispa."

"Yes, it may just be that I do have this curiosity: but on a personal, whimsical level that has nothing at all to do with the investigation we are embarking on."

"Do you have it or not?"

"I confess to having it; but any investigation in this direction would hardly be viewed in a kindly light by the president."

"He was so vague, so offhand concerning Sandoz's reply, which—call it a joke if you like—was still the last thing written by a man who was murdered immediately afterward. I would say it was our duty to make inquiries: as a pure formality, nothing out of the ordinary. To tie up this business, in other words."

"All right, I will drop you in front of the restaurant, and I'll send along two men to assist you in your search. But let's be clear about one thing: that card has no bearing on our inquiries."

"You've got a line of inquiry already?"

"I will: within an hour or two."

"Dear God!" invoked the deputy.

The chief read the turmoil in his face but restricted himself to a rancorous silence. Then, when they had arrived at La Nuova Cucina and the deputy was on the point of getting out, he asked, "What exactly fails to convince you?"

"The Children of Eighty-nine. If you let the word out, you know what is going to happen: all the way from Sicily to the Swiss border, they'll turn up by the dozens."

"I won't say a word about them, if the friends and acquaintances of the victim do not oblige me with some confirmation and a few extra details thrown in."

"I have no doubt that you'll receive your confirmation and extra details."

"I have never seen you so optimistic."

"On the contrary, I have never been so pessimistic."

"I beg you"—the words, however, spoken authoritatively—"please do not make my poor head spin."

The deputy made a gesture of compliance. He went off to the café next door to phone the owner of the restaurant to come and open up. While waiting, he ordered coffee.

The morning was glass clear and icy cold: as cold as the stinging pain in the joints of his bones. Nevertheless, these eccentric, peripheral pains had the power to lessen the overwhelming central pain; or at least to give him that illusion.

He drank, one after the other, two cups of strong espresso. They said coffee deadened pain, but these gave him only the lucidity to put up with it. His mind, meanwhile, was occupied with the refuse that would shortly be put before him. Garbage science. A parable, a metaphor: we are now concerned with garbage; searching for it, shaping it, reading it, seeking in it some trace of truth. In refuse. A journalist had once sought political secrets in the refuse of Henry Kissinger, and the American police the secrets of the Sicilian-American Mafia in the refuse of Joe Bonanno. "Garbage never lies" was an accepted precept of sociology. But Bonanno's garbage had lied to police officer Ehmann: CALL TI-TONE WORK AND PAY SCANNATORE. Nothing could be clearer, for Ehmann; if in Italian *scannare* means "to slaughter," a *scannatore* is one whose job it is to slaughter. Had he known of *L'Aria del Continente,* the play by Nino Martoglio based on an idea from Pirandello, he would have been aware of the extent of a Sicilian's inferiority complex regarding his native dialect once he acquires a smattering of Italian. For this reason the Sicilian word *scanaturi* had been Italianized to *scannatore*, in the Bonanno household. The jotting was no more than a note, an aide-mémoire to remind the writer to pay a Sicilian-American joiner, Titone by name, for one of those huge, meticulously planed tables of strong wood on which the women—once in Sicily, now in America—knead the bread, make lasagna, tagliatelle, pizza, or focaccia. *Scanaturi:* "an instrument for kneading dough," in the definition given, in the year 1754, by the Jesuit Michele del Bono. Had Bonanno naively Italianized the word, or had he set out to play a joke, a joke for his own benefit, on Ehmann?

Odd, thought the deputy, that the word "joke" should have made its appearance with such frequency in these last few hours. And it was a joke that he was playing on his chief. He was certain that Sandoz's card would not be found among the refuse of the night before. And in fact, after two hours and more of searching, it was not found. Garbage never lies: in this case, by default. It was a different thought that unnerved him: that man was heading for death in the midst of garbage.

S o as not to give the chief headaches, he listened in silence to the interrogation of the friends and colleagues of poor Sandoz (whom, alive, no one would have considered calling poor, rich as he was in talent, possessions, power, and women; and there was every reason to doubt whether he had in fact been assumed, a few hours earlier, into the heaven of the poor). Some confirmed the broad outlines, others added new details. Yes, poor Sandoz had spoken of phone calls from the Children of Eighty-nine; but as a joke, since, among other things, the last caller had seemed to him to have a child's voice—thin, hesitant, almost babbling. And he had spoken reflectively of the other calls, four or five in all, which, as he recalled, had seemed to have been made by different voices, belonging to people of varying ages. All disguised, obviously; so perhaps it had always been the same person on the telephone, making the first call with an old man's voice and, regressing, the last with the voice of a child. "The next time," Sandoz had told his secretary, "I'll get a call from a toddler." He joked about it and had even told the secretary that he had his suspicions about who was playing jokes of this kind on him. The Children of Eighty-nine: what an odd notion! And everyone, including Sandoz, had thought of 1989; newborn revolutionaries, which explained the falling age of the callers.

"As you can see," said the chief, "your 1789 has bought it."

"Perhaps," said the deputy.

"Far be it from me to deny that your pigheadedness has, occasionally, paid off. But right now, trust me, it would be better to pack it away."

"I don't believe there will be a better time than this. But I have no wish to cause you headaches, or to upset you."

"Go on, upset me."

"All right. I believe that the joke—let's go on calling it a joke—was deliberately calculated to give rise to two successive hypotheses: the first, while Sandoz was still alive, and principally aimed at Sandoz himself, was that we were genuinely dealing with a joke: something innocuous and laughable; the second, once Sandoz had been murdered, that we were dealing with no such thing. For the first hypothesis, 1989, the comedy of people transforming themselves into the babes of some unspecified revolution, worked perfectly. What was it but a word, a mere word? For the second hypothesis, it is the threat, which begins to take concrete form with the murder of Sandoz, of imitating and rounding off the revolution of 1789, of renewing all its pomp and terrors, that works."

"I'm in agreement that the two jokes, as you like to call them, are linked."

"Yes, but there's another point on which we are not, and will not be, in agreement: that without our being aware of it, in the midst of the recent celebrations of the 1789 revolution, there was born a terrorist organization utterly convinced of those principles and now ready and dedicated to breaking the law to restore the part of that revolution which was once defeated; because this has to be the sense of the title Children of Eighty-nine. This association does not exist, but somebody wants to will it into existence, as a shield and a specter for quite different purposes."

"And who, in your view, had this wonderful idea? 'Wonderful' was your word, right from the first; love at first sight, a coup de foudre," said the chief, with near-hysterical irony.

"As to who had the idea, I do not know, and I do not believe we will ever know. But to judge from the effect it will in all probability produce, it is undoubtedly wonderful. Just think: now that the red flag no longer flies high, what revolutionary banner could be unfurled to seduce feeble minds, to attract the bored and the violent who need to dignify their instincts, or to appeal to those with a vocation for sacrifice and lost causes? I could add that your conviction that the Children of Eighty-nine exist in the form they claim proves just how brilliant the original idea was."

The chief turned serious, solemn, and peremptorily decisive: "Listen here: I let you have your way over the rubbish at the restaurant. A waste of your time and of the two men, and God knows how much I could have done with them here . . ." He sighed his habitual long-suffering sigh over the shortage of men and equipment.

"I would not call it wasted time: the card, as I foretold, was not there."

"All the worse, we wasted time in the full knowledge that it would be wasted. Now listen to me: I am no fool; I can see your suspicions and intentions quite clearly, and I know what you are driving at and where you want to bring me. And I am telling you quite bluntly: No. And not only because I have no inclination for suicide but because the line you are following is lifted straight from fiction, from one of those so-called classical detective novels, where the sharp-witted reader can guess, after the first twenty pages, how it is all going to turn out. Let's forget about the novels, shall we? We'll proceed calmly, with deliberation, without any brainstorms, without impulsiveness, and above all without prejudice or preconceived ideas. In any case, the whole affair is about to be handed over to a magistrate: if he turns out to have the same taste in novels as you, you can put your heads together and speculate to your hearts' content, and I'll wash my hands of the entire business. Meanwhile, I would like to point out that in the course of your lucubrations, you have overlooked one hypothesis, which seems to me promising: that someone present at the banquet may have noticed that little game with the cards and may have seen Sandoz slip the 'I'll kill you' into his jacket pocket; and that he may just have decided to take advantage of it."

"A technically correct hypothesis but, I believe, in the overall view of the matter, irrelevant."

"You never know. Check it out. Make the cultural association hand over the guest list and find out who, among the diners seated next to Sandoz and the president, had the opportunity to watch the game. And next, obviously, who among them had any motive for detesting Sandoz. And finally, no brainstorms; not a step without informing me first. All right?"

S andoz numbered an actor among his friends, and a colleague who remembered having seen them photographed together indicated him to the chief as a possible perpetrator of the telephone joke. Since Sandoz had said he knew who was responsible for the joke, who could be more likely than someone with the professional ability? The actor had a certain reputation in the world of cinema and theater, and the chief recalled having heard him imitate a range of voices, from the guttural Catanian accents of Musco to the more polished, melodious tones of Ruggero Ruggeri. Without conviction, being now enamored of the Children of Eighty-nine, he instituted a nationwide search for him. Finally they found him where they could have found him all the time if they had taken the trouble to glance at the pages of the morning newspapers devoted to cinema and theater.

Over the telephone, after listening to a cursory explanation of why he was being sought, the actor admitted that he had known Sandoz (a grudging admission, the only sort ever afforded to police questions), but not with sufficient intimacy to play jokes on him: and such a senseless joke in the bargain! Of itself, this served as the required corroboration for the police and the magistracy, which had taken over the conduct of the investigation, that there was a close connection between the phone calls from the Children of Eighty-nine and the murder. Meanwhile, as invariably occurred when responsibility for an investigation changed hands, the Children of Eighty-nine story leaked out. And obviously, since the year was 1989, almost all the newspapers assumed that the name indicated a newborn, new-style brand of terrorism. However, an anonymous phone call to the biggest-circulation daily taxed the police, magistrates, and journalists with ignorance and shortsightedness and pointed them in the direction of 1789. "We will reestablish the Reign of Terror," said the anonymous informant, adding that the execution of Sandoz—regrettably, not by guillotine—was only a foretaste of what lay ahead. A further call gave the group a more precise title: Children of Eighty-nine, Saint-Just Action Group.

"So you were right," said the chief. What he was paid in wounded pride, he believed he repaid in generosity: the generosity of a superior who gives way to his deputy.

"Yes, but this is not the point. The point is that the Children of Eighty-nine are being born now—of mythomania, of boredom, maybe of a vocation for conspiracy and criminal activity—but they did not exist a moment before the radio, television, and newspapers carried stories about them. The calculation of the people who murdered Sandoz, or who had him murdered, has created them. They calculated that at the very least they would confuse us, and that at best some fool would answer the call and proclaim himself one of the Children of Eighty-nine."

"You've lost me. I cannot follow you in this work of fiction."

"I understand. Anyway, even if you did agree with me, we would still be on our own."

A period of civic mourning and an official state funeral had been decreed for Sandoz, for who would now have had the audacity to lay to rest in a more humble tomb that victim of political criminality, of antidemocratic fanaticism and terrorist madness?

"I'm glad to hear you acknowledge it: there would be no more than two of us, always assuming that your novel had the slightest element of credibility for me."

"Just to continue with the novel ... we are facing a problem, a dilemma: were the Children of Eighty-nine created to murder Sandoz, or was Sandoz murdered to create the Children of Eighty-nine?"

"I'll leave it to you to solve that one. As far as I'm concerned, and as far as this office is concerned, I proceed on the basis of established fact. Sandoz received menacing phone calls from the Children of Eighty-nine; Sandoz was murdered; the Children of Eighty-nine have claimed responsibility. Our job is to find them and bring them, as they say, to justice."

"The Children of Eighty-nine."

"The Children of Eighty-nine, precisely. And look: as regards that dilemma of yours, I could even, in an abstract way, as a game, as a purely literary concern, go along with the first of your two extremes: that the Children of Eighty-nine were born to dispatch Sandoz more conveniently and make our task in getting to the guilty party or parties more difficult, or even downright impossible. As to the second possibility, the one about Sandoz being murdered so as to give birth to the Children of Eighty-nine, I'll leave that one to you. And have fun with it."

"For over half a century, in all branches of the police, we have had to swallow so many toads that I believe we have earned the right to a little fun. Apart from the many I have personally swallowed in nearly thirty years with this division."

"One toad more, one toad less . . . what can I say? If you really see this business shaping up as yet another toad to swallow, get ready to swallow it."

He was disobeying, being disobedient. In a little sitting room in the De Matis house, with the lady herself at his side. She had sat down beside him, perhaps, because curiosity had overcome her to the point that she instinctively imagined that physical proximity would create the best conditions for shared confidences.

"The moment the porter told me that a police officer

wanted to speak to me, I understood: I have no doubt that you want to know about the cards that Sandoz and Aurispa exchanged three evenings ago."

She had an intelligent face and beautiful eyes, which seemed to flicker with an amused, ironic light. Anything but unattractive. Aurispa had said that a glance at her was enough to make anyone aware that the desire to have her at your side could never be more than a game, a fiction, but that only revealed that he had the decidedly unsubtle view of female beauty of a purchaser whose only ambition was not to be shortchanged. She was thin but not displeasingly so; she could be said to be slight, and her movements and gestures were light and almost fluttery.

"I have to say at the outset that I am indeed a police officer, but I came to you in a private capacity and in total secrecy."

"Tell me the truth, do you suspect him?"

"Do we suspect whom?"

"Him, Aurispa." The amused, ironic light seemed to have spread out, adding a splendor to the eyes of indefinable blue, of indefinable violet.

"No, he is not a suspect."

"It would give me enormous pleasure to know that at least the shadow of suspicion had fallen on him."

"Really?"

"Yes, enormous satisfaction. And I still hope it will happen: there are so many murky matters in which he has a hand."

"Why would it give you such satisfaction?"

"I could say to you: for the sake of justice, but it would not be the whole truth. Basically it is because I do not like him, I find him repulsive. He is such a cold man, and he appears to exist only in profile, as though on a coin, on various coins."

"Anything in particular?"

"No, nothing ... or rather something, but something so vague that you cannot put your finger on it. But then I always allow myself to be guided by vague, indefinite impressions, and I am never wrong, believe me. But I see you won't be giving anything away. So let's see how good I am at making out what's behind your questions."

Intelligent, very intelligent, thought the deputy, and the reflection gave him a feeling of near panic. To gain time, to purify the questions of the suspicions that Signora De Matis was prepared to detect in them, he said: "They are not really questions, the things I want to put to you."

"Out with them, then," said Signora De Matis, even more amused.

"I am engaged on an unremarkable, straightforward reconstruction of the last hours of Mr. Sandoz. It is the sort of thing we are obliged to do even in cases, like the present one, when we are convinced beforehand that it serves no useful purpose."

"Unremarkable, straightforward ... serves no useful purpose." The Signora's voice echoed his. She played her part in the game with ironic comprehension and indulgence, but also with barely restrained laughter. "So what is the question?"

"As I said, it is hardly a question at all. I take it you are aware that the two of them were engaged in a ... shall we say romantic game, at your expense. Aurispa regretted not having you at his side and pretended he was in the grips of uncontrollable jealousy because Sandoz twice in as many days had had the good fortune of a place beside you."

"It had occurred more than twice. I could never understand why at those infernal official or society dinners they nearly always put me alongside that Sandoz, who used to bore me to death. Not only that: that little game of theirs, which you call romantic, bored me to distraction, or rather enraged me. It was as if they said to each other: Poor thing, she's so old, so unattractive, that we really should give her at least this satisfaction. I do not need anyone to tell me that I am not pretty, and I am well aware that I am getting on in life, but that does not seem to me a sufficient reason why those two brainless creatures should dedicate a whole evening to letting me know it."

"No, not at all, you mustn't think that," said the deputy, conscious of his own hypocrisy, because he had learned from Aurispa that things stood exactly as she had understood.

"Please don't you start romantic games with me."

"It is not a romantic game. You—forgive me, it is the first time I have met you, and I do not imagine we will have the opportunity to meet again—you are so radiant." The word came to him unbidden, as though he had fallen in love on the instant. The pain pressing in on him more and more sharply, making him aware of the other, the only love now available to him.

" 'Radiant.' Very gracious of you. I will remember that. There are not many joyful things left to one at this point in life. You know I am almost fifty. But let's get back to the question, shall we?"

"Yes. The president sent the card over to Sandoz; written on it were the words—"

" 'I'll kill you.' "

"Did Sandoz write his reply on the same card?"

"No; he stuck Aurispa's card in his pocket, after giving

it to me to read, with the delight, so it seemed to me, of an autograph hunter who has finally managed to secure a much desired specimen. He scribbled out his answer on his own place marker, which was there in front of him, clasped onto a kind of iris, which was too silvery to be genuine silver.''

"And what did he write on his card?''

"The odd thing was that he did not let me read it, and I had not sufficient curiosity to peer over his shoulder while he was writing. He simply bored me, as did that stupid game of theirs.''

"Do you remember who Aurispa was sitting beside? I imagine he would have been seated between two women.''

"Yes, between two women: Signora Zorni and Signora Siragusa. But since Signora Zorni was seated on his right— you know who I mean; pretty enough, even if, to my mind, a bit empty-headed, but with just the right degree of empty-headedness to transform a pretty woman into a ravishingly beautiful one in the eyes of most men—he lavished more attention on her than on the other.''

"You saw the card arrive at its destination?''

"Not exactly: I watched Sandoz look over at Aurispa with great attention, with a sense of anxiety. I had the impression he was studying the impact with much more interest than their futile little game warranted. Then I saw him smile. I turned to look at Aurispa, and he was smiling as well: but both wore a smile that was—how shall I put it?—strained, sour. That exchange of smiles between them made a deep impression on me: that's why, since Sandoz was murdered a few hours later, I asked if you in the police had suspicions regarding Aurispa.''

"No; we don't have any.''

"Then you should. Maybe it goes back to the first

time I heard the word, and maybe it is just childish, but I still associate the police with the idea of polish. You know what I mean: cleanliness. Is there cleanliness in the police?"

"As far as there can be."

"And as far as there can be, there ought to be suspicions regarding Aurispa, but there is very little to be done, isn't that so?"

"Not a great deal."

"If you tell me there is not a great deal to be done, I think it can be deduced that there is nothing to be done. The thing is that you appear to suffer over that."

"I suffer over so many things now."

"I would really love to know why you joined the police."

"From time to time I ask myself the same question, but I have never managed to give myself a precise answer. Sometimes I unearth a dignified, high-minded reply, which soars upward like a tenor's chest notes: more frequently the replies are more humdrum: the necessities of life, chance, laziness . . ."

"You are Sicilian, aren't you?"

"Yes, but from the cold side of Sicily: from a tiny village in the interior, among the mountains, where the snow lies for long periods in the winter. A Sicily that figures in no one's imagination. I have never again in all my life felt such intense cold as I did in that village."

"I remember that cold Sicily as well. Usually we went in summer, but sometimes there were additional trips at Christmas. My mother was Sicilian, and her parents never left that village; they never ever moved from that great house of theirs, which was cool in summer but bitterly cold in the winter months. They died there, and my mother died there too, before them. I never went back. I receive a letter after every All Souls' Day from one of my relatives, telling me about his visit to the graves, about the flowers and candles he brings along to decorate them. It is almost a reproach for me, because, emotionally and sentimentally, the fact that my mother wanted to go back there to die ought to count for something. I am afraid the truth is that even this choice of my mother's, if I think about it, causes me some dismay. It is simply not possible to love a place or a people to that extent, especially when it was a place where you suffered so much and a people with whom you do not have anything at all in common. My mother experienced only pain from her life there, and finally rebelled and fled, and yet she felt a love for it that went beyond the tomb. And do you want to know why the thought of that gives me such a sense of dismay? Because every so often I bewilder myself by feeling an echo of the same love, of the same memory, of the same choice ... but perhaps it is only an expression of that remorse my relative is so anxious to make me feel."

"I don't know if you have read that page of D. H. Lawrence's on Verga's novel *Mastro Don Gesualdo*. At one point he says: 'But Gesualdo is Sicilian, and it is here that the difficulty arises.' "

"The difficulty ... Yes, perhaps that's where my difficulty in living comes from." As if to change the subject, very deliberately: "You read a lot, don't you? I read very little, and now I find more enjoyment in rereading: you discover things that were not there at the first reading—I mean, were not there for me. Do you know what I am rereading? *Dead Souls*: packed full of things that were not there before; and who can tell how many other things I would find if I were to return to it twenty years from now? Enough of books. We were talking about the reasons that impelled you to join the police."

"Perhaps, since crime belongs to us, to get to know it a little better."

"Yes, it's true: crime does belong to us; but there are some people who belong to crime."

Signora Zorni. Unquestionably beautiful, to the point of insipid perfection, and of a garrulousness that accorded with that perfection: head in the clouds, abstracted, afloat in the heavens of a stupidity she knows is both celestial and unfathomable; as do the genuinely intelligent, but they, experiencing that stupidity as a seductive force, openly fear it. She never seemed quite to grasp any question put to her, but the overall sense of the inquiry must somehow have nested in a recess of her beautiful head, since a reply could eventually be put together, even if it entailed picking and choosing the pieces that fitted best from a pile of multicolored stones, like a mosaicist. An operation the deputy carried out as he went along, and we will follow suit; if it is to the detriment of the portrait, it is perhaps to the betterment of the narrative.

Yes, she knew about the half-pitying, half-mocking game the two of them played on Signora De Matis: the president had informed her. She had seen the president write "I'll kill you" and had laughed at the idea, even if, she was anxious to add, she did not herself consider Signora De Matis as plain as many people thought; on the contrary, she was quite handsome, in her own way. And she had read Sandoz's answering card.

"Do you remember it?"

"Of course I do; I am blessed with a good memory as well." That "as well" spoke volumes. "It was two lines of verse."

"Verse?"

"Yes, there were two short sentences, written as lines of poetry; they even rhymed. They seemed to come from a song, and I had a terrible urge to hum them." She began humming them for him, using the tune from a melancholy number in vogue several years earlier: "I have no doubt that you will try: But who'll be victor, you or I?"

The deputy felt a sense of exultation, but only said: "The president read the card aloud, or gave it to you to read?"

"No, he didn't give it to me; I read it while he was reading it himself. Then he slipped it into his pocket."

"Are you quite certain about that—that the president put it in his pocket?"

"Absolutely so." At that moment, a look of concern appeared on her face. "Does he insist that he didn't?"

"Even if that were so, would you continue to be sure that he did?" His words were intended purely to cause her a moment of anxiety, to upset that icy perfection, reminiscent of a newly excavated, totally intact statue.

"He is a gentleman of such irreproachable ways that I would begin to entertain the tiniest doubt."

"You can continue to be certain: the president claimed that he put the thing in his pocket mechanically; only he then, equally mechanically, threw it away."

The signora gave a sigh of relief, the carefully cultivated

image reabsorbing that moment of life. The deputy thought that she did not really deserve to be called stupid, considering that in Italy, by current hazy standards, no one is judged stupid by the majority.

Leaving Signora Zorni's house, he felt numbed. Drawing precise replies from a speech that resembled the Trevi Fountain—cascades, sprays, streams, and torrents of running water—induced in him a feeling of tension, followed by weariness and numbness. His pain, too, was numb, less sharp but more diffuse. Strange how physical pain, even when its source is stable and, unless deteriorating, unalterable can still grow, diminish, change in intensity and quality, according to opportunities and encounters.

He walked under the colonnades in the piazza, his mind occupied with that card, with those lines from the song; with Signora Zorni, young and lovely, her lithe, harmonious body: but how much more beautiful and desirable—in those flashes of desire that momentarily pierced his pain—was Signora De Matis, for all her fifty years.

He relished the colonnades, enjoyed strolling at ease among them. In the island of his birth, there was no city that boasted colonnades such as these. Arches make the heavens more lovely, in the words of the poet. Do colonnades make cities more civil? It was not that he did not love the land where he was born, but all those invariably bitter and tragic events that day after day made the news there caused him a sort of resentment. Not having been back for years, he searched for it, behind mere occurrences, in his memory, in the emotion of something that no longer existed: an illusion, a mystification; he an emigrant, an exile.

There could be no half measures with his disobedience. He had taken a chance with Signora Zorni, and the results would be apparent in due course. While neglecting to recommend that she maintain silence— a recommendation everyone, everywhere, is irresistibly driven to betray—he had nonetheless done everything in his power to convey the impression that his investigations were purely formal and superfluous, a downright nuisance even for the people charged with carrying them out. It was, however, unthinkable that she had such a feeble memory as totally to forget, and that, having not forgotten, she would forgo the pleasure of informing one, two, or more of her friends; and that from one woman to the next, the news would not reach the president's ears, and from the president the chief's, or those of the occupant of a higher, much higher, position. Things stood differently with Signora De Matis: there was no such risk. Between the two of them, there had been the kindling of the spark of fondness, and a certain complicity had been established.

From what he had heard about the exchange of cards, a question formulated itself in his mind, a question he had to put to a person able to provide a definite answer.

Kublai Travel Agency. Proprietor, Dr. Giovanni Rieti: doctor in what having never been satisfactorily established. An acquaintanceship of long standing, perhaps a friendship, at least on the basis of the story of human tenderness that lay behind it. It had begun with their fathers in 1939. The deputy's father was a government official in the Sicilian town where the father of Dr. Rieti, a Jew, had, by chance, been born. Rieti senior, in a state of despair, had come to the town from Rome, anxious to ascertain if in his birth certificate there might be some pretext for not considering him Jewish in the strict sense of the term. There being none, they—civil servants, mayor, priest, municipal guards—made one up. Fascists to a man, each with party membership card in his pocket and badge in his lapel; if the priest had neither card nor badge, he was Fascist in spirit. But all were unanimous that they could not abandon Mr. Rieti, plus his wife and children, to the mercy of a law that was intent on his ruin. So they forged the documents in the duly accepted form, because to them the fact that a man was Jewish meant nothing if he was in danger, if he was in despair. (What a great country Italy was in these matters, and perhaps still is!)

Nothing more was heard of the Rieti family, and even if the deputy retained some recollection of the case as one that had, among the many that occurred in the first ten years of his life, made its mark, he had nonetheless forgotten the name. However, one evening, in the city that had now been his home for some years, he attended a party in the prefect's office, and there he was introduced to a Dr. Rieti, who, on hearing his name, asked if he was Sicilian, if he was from such-and-such town, and if he had a relative who was in local government. It was like a reunion.

They met again, with increasing frequency, until the chief, with great tact and hinting at weighty matters left unsaid, advised him not to let himself be seen too often in the company of Dr. Rieti. Still giving the impression of leaving the bulk of his information unspoken, he let it be understood that he had been tipped off by that service which in other times and in other countries would be called "intelligence"; and though perhaps here and now it did not merit the title, its practitioners nevertheless were aware of certain things and in any case—this was the gist of the chief's talk—"knew one another," this being the ultimate goal to which the intelligence service of every country aspired. Knowing one another, they knew Dr. Rieti, and while it was permissible for them to be in communication with him, it was ill-advised for any other officer of the state to do so, especially a member of the police force.

The deputy had continued to see Dr. Rieti, but with greater caution; he gave up meeting him for an aperitif in a bar or for a meal in a restaurant, since suspicions regarding possible secret activities could arise if he appeared unusually well informed on economic or financial deals, on internal rivalries inside the political parties, on the making and unmaking of alliances, on events in the bishop's palace or in terrorist circles.

On account of his illness and of his work, which consumed more time and became more of a burden as his illness increased in severity, he had not seen Rieti for some two months. Dr. Rieti greeted him with effusive cordiality, expressing his delight at seeing him in such excellent health. "I knew you were not well. Someone from your office told me a couple of evenings ago. But you look all right now. A bit slimmer, certainly, but they tell us nowadays that losing weight does nothing but good."

"You don't sound convinced."

"I admit it. When I see what my friends and relatives have to do to lose weight, and the troubles they put themselves through, it's my view that all these various dietologists and inventors of diets should receive the same treatment as drug pushers. What illness did you have, exactly?"

"Exactly an illness for which I should be receiving cobalt therapy, or something of that sort."

"I had no idea it was anything so serious."

"It's even worse. I am dying," he said, with such serenity that the other felt the words he was about to speak freeze from sheer insincerity. He muttered only "My God," quietly, then after a long silence: "But a course of treatment ..."

"I have no desire to die fortified by the comforts of science, because not only are they as religious as the usual sort but they are even more harrowing. If I should ever feel the need of comfort, I would have recourse to the more ancient rites. In fact, I would be quite glad to feel such a need, but I simply don't." He continued in an offhand tone, almost with delight: "Have you noticed? It is impossible to be bored in this country: we are all Children of Eighty-nine now."

"Indeed, the Children of Eighty-nine." With irony, with malice.

"What do you make of it?"

"I think it is all so much hot air, pure fantasy. And you?"

"So do I."

"I am glad you agree. I read in the papers that your office is taking the whole thing seriously."

"Yes, of course. Do you expect them to miss out on such a splendid invention?"

"That's it exactly. It seems to me something invented around a coffee table, as a game, as a calculation. What is going to become of these poor devils, these poor idiots who want to continue believing in something after Khrushchev, after Mao, after Fidel Castro, and now with Gorbachev? They must be thrown some kind of sop, something that can be tossed back in the oven after two hundred years, something soft and scented with celebrations, rediscoveries, and reassessments: and inside, the same hard stone to break the teeth."

Always the same with Rieti: complete agreement over the evaluation of the facts, over their interpretation and the identification of their origin and purpose. Most frequently speaking of them hazily, by allusion, in parables or in metaphors. It was as if the same circuits, the same logical processes, operated in both their minds: a computer of distrust, of suspicion, of pessimism. Jews, Sicilians: an atavistic affinity in their condition. Of energy. Of defense. Of suffering. A sixteenth-century Tuscan once wrote that the Sicilians are of a dry intelligence. So, too, are the Jews. But war had now descended on them: war by different means, but war nonetheless.

"I would like to ask you, for the first time since we met"—and with these words he revealed his knowledge of the real, secret activity of Dr. Rieti—"a precise question: What was the relationship between Sandoz and Aurispa?"

"They detested each other."

"Why?"

"I don't know what set them off on their mutual detestation, and it is not something it would be easy to establish, because from what I hear, they were school friends. I do know that they both dedicated themselves with a will—all the while maintaining a relationship of seeming friendship— Aurispa to ruining Sandoz's business and Sandoz, with less success, to ruining Aurispa's. The consequence was that Sandoz, who had no intention of settling for second place, decided on a policy of blackmail, but here, too, with negligible results. Obtaining a warrant for Aurispa's arrest, maybe even one that ended after a few months in an acquittal for lack of proof, had become the dream of his life. It never became anything other than a dream."

"What were the grounds for blackmail?"

"I understand that the least ludicrous was based on a large-scale act of corruption and fraud perpetrated by Aurispa against the state, for which Sandoz was in possession of proof, or believed he was. However, I don't believe he would ever have gone to the length of making a statement to the police. There would have been reactions, counter-moves, and he would certainly not have emerged unscathed. Aurispa's only fear would be that Sandoz might have gone completely insane, because as long as he remained in possession of his faculties he would never have dared shake the columns, with the risk of bringing down the temple on his own head as well, their temple, the temple of so many Italians who matter. The other grounds for blackmail were concerned with private matters, and they were at least thirty years out of date. Women, cocaine: what impression did he imagine they were going to make at this stage?"

"What about their business affairs?"

"War, war of every type. There is so much of it in the world ... and so much trade in arms, poisons."

"Do I understand you to be saying that you do not see the hand of Aurispa in the murder of Sandoz? Let me phrase that better: you do not believe that the threats issued by Sandoz would have constituted sufficient reason for wanting him eliminated."

"Exactly."

"Another reason, then."

"You used the correct term: sufficient. Sandoz's threats

did not constitute sufficient reason for Aurispa to want him out of the way, but at a certain point, when other needs became more urgent, in the preparation of some project or other which, when subjected to cool examination, did not necessarily require the elimination of Sandoz. Well, the opportunity presented itself, as the proverb has it, of killing two birds with one stone."

"You mean that the victim could easily have been not Sandoz but someone else, with—what shall we say?—equal qualifications. However, since Sandoz was more of a nuisance than any of the other candidates, the choice fell on him."

"Exactly."

"That is my opinion too. Immediately after listening to Aurispa, I said to my superior, who obviously takes no heed at all of my dilemma: The problem is whether the Children of Eighty-nine were created to kill Sandoz or whether Sandoz was killed to create the Children of Eighty-nine. And I tend to resolve my dilemma in the sense you indicate, that with one stone they have killed two birds: primarily that of creating the Children of Eighty-nine. But why?"

"As to why, I would say that through an ancient premonition, and a not-so-ancient admonition, we know without knowing. In our childhood, we felt, rather than really knew, a power that today might be called total criminality, a power that, paradoxically, could be regarded as wholesome and healthy—always granted that it was crime—compared to the schizophrenic criminality of today. The criminal nature of that power took the form principally of not permitting any other crime apart from the much-vaunted, aesthetically embellished crime committed by itself. There is no need for me to say that I prefer schizophrenia to good health, as I believe you do too. The important thing is that this schizophrenia has to be taken into account if certain otherwise inexplicable phenomena are to be explained. By the same token, it is vital to make allowances for the force of stupidity, of sheer stupidity insinuating itself and prevailing. There is one power, which is visible, identifiable, and numerable, but there is another, which is not numerable, which is without name or without names, and which swims underwater. The visible power is in permanent conflict with the underwater power, especially at the moments when it has the gall to break the surface with vigor, that is to say with violence and bloodshed: but the fact is that it needs to behave that way. I trust you will not object to this piece of homespun philosophy, for where power is concerned, I have no other."

"There are grounds for suspecting, in other words, that there exists a secret constitution, whose first article runs: The security of power is based on the insecurity of the citizens."

"Of all the citizens, in fact. Including those who, spreading insecurity, believe themselves to be safe. This is the stupidity I was referring to."

"Then we are tied up inside a *sotie*. But let us get back to today's goings-on. Even if the newspapers have made no mention of it, you undoubtedly know all about the cards Sandoz and Aurispa exchanged at that banquet as if it were a game. What did you make of that?"

"It seemed to me a fact of some importance, but not one on which it would be possible at this moment to formulate reliable conclusions. A genuinely ambiguous fact, which could be clarified only by ascertaining the role of Aurispa in the whole business. If he was the prime mover, if he was involved at the highest levels, he must have calculated that with that bit of nonsense over the cards, he would, because of the way it occurred, have immediately been ruled out of the inquiries; if his part was secondary, it is possible that he was not kept informed of the timing of the action; in that case, it becomes feasible to believe in the chance nature of that game and in a fortuitous, and even fortunate, coincidence."

"I would go on the hypothesis that he was involved at the highest levels."

"Perhaps, perhaps . . ." said Rieti, but as though speaking out of courtesy. Plainly he knew something more, or believed he did. It was not right to press him on that point, so the deputy said: "One more question, perhaps the most indiscreet I can ask you: In your . . . let's say functions, in the tasks you perform"—the time for allusions was past; it was now the moment of truth for their acquaintanceship, or friendship, as for everything else—"are you more interested in the business affairs pursued by Sandoz until yesterday, or in those of Aurispa?"

"In both, regrettably, although rather more, until yesterday, as you put it, in those of Sandoz"—with an expression in which the disgust for that business was possibly also disgust toward himself.

He returned to headquarters, to find the beehive gone berserk. One of the Children of Eighty-nine had been captured while making a phone call. It turned out to be one of those cases that exist to defy all laws of probability. On the outskirts of the city, a deaf-mute was sitting on a park bench, three or four meters from a phone booth inside which a youth, while talking, kept glancing nervously over his shoulder. For anyone not accustomed to picking up the silent shaping of words on lips, the experience would have been like staring at a fish in an aquarium. The deaf-mute read a dozen times, on the lips of the youth making the call, such words as "Children of Eighty-nine," "revolution," "virtue." The man happened to have in his hand a newspaper carrying reports of the Children of Eighty-nine and in his pocket a scarlet marking pen. Scrawling on the paper, "Children of Eighty-nine," he went off in search of a policeman. He located a member of the local force, who had a pistol suspended from his waist but could hardly have been, in every other way, less suited for the job. He grew faint on merely reading the writing; he pretended not to take the business seriously, to regard it as a joke, to dispatch the deaf-mute with a little slap on the cheek. When the other, with the aid of dramatic and excited gestures, persevered, the policeman gave in and allowed himself to be escorted to the phone booth.

The youth was still inside and still talking: he was summarizing, for the benefit of the switchboard operator of some newspaper, duly trained in techniques of giving enough rope to callers of that kind, a chapter of Mathiez's *French Revolution,* which he had only just read himself. Since, to the best of his recollection, the police had never, irrespective of the length of the call, managed to catch anyone phoning to claim responsibility for terrorist crimes or for kidnappings, he felt, although nervous, safe. The policeman waited behind a magnolia bush until the call was over, crept up silently behind the youth, then leaned heavily on his back so as to leave him in no doubt about the pistol pressed against his kidneys. Fortunately for both their sakes, he had forgotten to release the safety catch. In this condition, closely followed by the deaf-mute, he marched him to the nearest police station; this turned out to be not particularly near, so he was obliged to declare on several occasions to the crowd that began to form—and had become a triumphal procession long before they reached their destination—that the prisoner was an alleged member of the Children of Eighty-nine: never forgetting, as the law requires, the word "alleged," which is, as anyone familiar with current journalistic parlance will be aware, a synonym for established guilt. However, at a certain point, listening to the muttering of the crowd at his back, he found himself breaking out in a cold sweat, in fear that their inclination was to implement swift justice rather than put up with the law's delays, with the risk that things might take an ugly turn for him, constrained as he would be to uphold the law's delays.

As God willed it, they arrived safely at a station house, where all three—policeman, deaf-mute, and Child of Eighty-nine—were loaded into a van and dispatched to headquarters.

The youth was now in the chief's office. Initially he had attempted to deny the content of the phone call, but the deaf-mute was there at hand, adamant in his determination to write out the entire text, even if with occasional gaps. Finally the young man caved in and made an admission, insisting it had been a joke. That was not yet the whole truth, because he had believed that that call would gain him admission to the Children of Eighty-nine, or at least advance his candidacy. Joke or demented act of self-assertion, a glance at him was enough to make clear that he could not have been in any way implicated in the murder of Sandoz. This thought ran through the deputy's mind the moment he eased open the door of the chief's office. The boy was in a state of collapse, while the chief radiated, like a halo around his massive head, the weary satisfaction of the athlete who has breasted the tape first.

The deputy closed the door gingerly behind him, ignoring the frenzied, avid stares of the reporters congregated in the corridor. Among them, preening himself and foaming like a thoroughbred stabled among pit ponies, stood the Great Journalist. With his articles, from which the moralists without morals drank their fill week in, week out, he had acquired a reputation for being relentless and implacable, a reputation that boosted his price among those who felt the need to buy silence and freedom from obtrusive attention.

As the deputy made his way toward his office, the Great Journalist stopped him and requested an interview: "a brief one, very brief," he specified. The deputy made a gesture more of resignation than of assent, while from the surrounding crowd murmurs of protest were raised.

"A private matter," said the Great Journalist, to the accompaniment of a chorus of ironic, incredulous remarks: "You bet," and "Sure enough," and "Right you are."

In the office, where they sat face-to-face—a desk covered with papers, books, and cigarette packets between them— eyeing each other in wordless distrust as though locked in a conflict to determine who could remain silent longest, the Great Journalist reached into his pocket for pencil and notebook.

The deputy raised the index finger of his right hand and waved it in a slow but definitive No.

"An automatic gesture, a professional reflex ... I have only one question to ask, and I do not expect an answer."

"Then why bother?"

"Because neither you nor I are idiots."

"I am very grateful. What is your question?"

"This story of the Children of Eighty-nine: was it you in the police force who invented it, or was it handed to you prepackaged?"

"I will give you your answer: It was not us who invented it."

"So they delivered it ready-made?"

"Could be ... That is my own suspicion, but it is no more than a suspicion."

"Does the chief believe that too?"

"I don't think so, but you'd better ask him."

The Great Journalist now wore a perplexed, mistrustful look. He said: "I did not expect you to reply, and instead you did; I expected you to brush aside my suspicions, and instead you added your own. What's going on?" His mind, as could be seen from his face, was a morass of discarded ideas, corrections, reworkings, and hesitations. "So what's going on?" This time the words were tinged with anxiety.

"Nothing at all, I would say." Then, to insult him: "Have you ever heard of the love of truth?"

"Vaguely." He spoke with disdainful irony, as though cynically noting the insult were the only means of reacting to it: he was looking down on an individual far beneath his notice.

The deputy returned to the attack with an "Indeed, indeed," and added: "Tomorrow, then, I expect to read an article of yours setting out all the suspicions and doubts that I, in my personal capacity, have just confirmed."

The Great Journalist was red with rage. "You know perfectly well that I will never write it."

"How could I know such a thing? I am still full of faith in humankind."

"We are in the same boat." His anger was tempered by a touch of frailty, of weariness.

"Don't you believe it. I have already landed on a desert island."

The conversation had left him drained, but the pain had gone: it cowered like a beast—squat, ferocious, repulsive—lying in ambush in one sole point of his being. The final words of the conversation, however, left him with a yearning for the deserted island, for a spot where, as though huddled over some map, he could give free rein to an ancient dream and an ancient memory: inasmuch as certain things from childhood and adolescence were now ancient to him. *Treasure Island*: a book, someone had said, that was the nearest thing to happiness attainable. He thought: To-night I will reread it. His memory of it was clear, since he had already reread it many times in that old, unlovely edition they had once given him. In the course of his transfers from city to city, from one house to another, he had lost many books, but not this one. Aurora Publishers: yellowing paper, which after all these years seemed to have left the print parched and faded, and on the cover, from the black-and-white film, a scene featuring a feckless and lackluster Jim Hawkins together with Wallace Beery's unforgettable Long

John Silver. The same man had been equally unforgettable as Pancho Villa, so much so that after having seen both films, it was impossible to read either Stevenson's novel or Guzmán's work on the Mexican Revolution without the characters presenting themselves with the physique, the gestures, and the voice of Wallace Beery. He thought of all that the cinema had meant to his generation and wondered if it would have a comparable impact on the new generation, and whether that scaled-down cinema, totally insufferable to him, on television could ever have any impact at all.

He returned to the island, and a new character, Ben Gunn, appeared before him. His mind was so free, so unfettered and capricious, that from Ben Gunn, via a detail he suddenly recalled, he moved on to think about the advertising industry, which threatened to flood the world. Even the producers of Parmesan cheese undoubtedly paid their dues to advertisers, but not a single advertising executive had ever remembered Dr. Livesey's snuffbox. He gleefully imagined the poster or full-page ad that could be made from that scene: Dr. Livesey proffering, to potential buyers, the open snuffbox, with a piece of Parmesan inside, just as he did in the narrative to Ben Gunn, himself a great lover of cheese. "A delicious cheese, produced in Italy," the doctor would be saying, or something of the sort.

Meantime, his eyes were fixed on *The Knight, Death, and the Devil*. Perhaps Ben Gunn, from Stevenson's description of him, had some resemblance to Dürer's Death. The thought prompted him to view Dürer's Death as though reflected by the grotesque. Death's haggard appearance had always unsettled him, with its implication that Death arrived on the scene wearily and slowly at the point when people were already tired of life. Death was weary, his horse was weary, both a far cry from the horses of *The Triumph of Death* or *Guernica*. Death, the hourglass or the menacing serpents notwithstanding, expressed mendacity rather than triumph. "Death is expiated by living." A beggar from whom alms are begged. As for the Devil, he was as weary as the rest, too horribly demonic to be wholly credible. A wild alibi in the lives of men, so much so that there were moves afoot at that very moment to restore to him all his lost vigor: theological assault therapies, philosophical reanimation techniques, parapsychological and metapsychic practices. But the Devil was tired enough to be content to leave it all to man, who could manage everything better. And the Knight: where was he bound, armed from head to toe, so unshakable in purpose, dragging behind him that weary figure of the Devil and so haughtily refusing Death charity? Would he ever struggle up to the walled citadel on high, the citadel of the supreme truth, of the supreme lie?

Christ? Savonarola? No, no; far from it. Perhaps what Dürer had placed inside that armor was the real death, the real devil: and it was life that, with that armor and those weapons, believed itself secure.

Wrapped up in these thoughts, themselves affected by a strain of incandescent delirium, he had almost dozed off. The chief, who came bursting into his office, found him in that state and said: "You really are unwell." Since he had become aware that the deputy was failing and in pain, the chief no longer sent for him when he had to talk to him: a kindness the deputy appreciated, but not without an element of annoyance.

"Not as much as I would like to be," replied the deputy, shaking himself awake, and feeling his pain reawaken too.

"What are you saying?" the chief replied, pretending to

be scandalized, but having understood perfectly well that the point the other wished to reach in feeling unwell was the point where he would feel no pain at all. Still, he was too blissfully happy to be sidetracked by anyone else's problems: "Have you heard? What do you think?"

"Undoubtedly," said the deputy, with measured and gleeful malice, "he deserves some punishment for what he's been up to: a charge, as well as the obvious one of self-calumny, of giving misleading information, of conduct likely to provoke a breach of the peace."

"What do you mean?" pronounced this time not formally but as a cry from the soul.

"I mean what I have meant from the very beginning: If we go along with this game of the Children of Eighty-nine, if we give a hand in creating them, this story will have no end; there'll be victims one after the other, and I do not just mean in the form of the corpses of murder victims; I mean people like the one you have in your clutches right now."

"What do you mean?" once more, but this time heartfelt and almost imploring. "What we have in our hands is a vital link in the chain, and you want us to toss it away as if it were worthless."

"You're quite right: a link in a chain, but it is a chain of stupidity and human suffering, a chain of a quite different sort from what you have in mind. Be patient, listen to me for a moment. This boy will continue to deny today, maybe even tomorrow, for a whole week, let's say for a month; but the day will come when he will confess to being a member of a subversive, revolutionary association called the Children of Eighty-nine. He will declare himself ready . . . no, desperate to collaborate and, with our assistance, will provide the names of one, two, three accomplices, fellow members. I wonder if he'll choose from those of his acquaintances he likes most or least; that's a psychological mechanism that would repay study, don't you think? In any case, we'll soon have further links to our chain. By this time—you don't need much imagination to picture it—the police will be out and about, talking to professors, janitors, barmen, disco owners, managers of take-out restaurants. There they are, busily interrogating, with the aim of getting as many names as possible of the people this young man saw regularly. In the unlikely event of his obstinately refusing to talk, of his refusing to name names, we would have no problem in picking one or two names at random from the list that will emerge from these inquiries."

"You really are unwell," he said in a concerned, persuasive tone. "Take a holiday; a couple of months off. You're due it. I'll see to it right away, if you like."

"Thank you. I'll think it over."

Morphine is wonderful: it is essential to take it when you cannot stand any more," a medical friend had advised him, handing over a little packet. The effects of a morphine dose were wonderful, more so when they succeeded an intolerable level of pain. The stronger the storm, the greater the peace. "Peace After the Storm," "Saturday in the Village," "The Solitary Sparrow," "Infinity": Giacomo Leopardi, that poet happy in his unhappiness ... What great and profound sentiments, expressed with utter simplicity and even with banal images, had he revealed and stamped indelibly on the memory of that generation of Italians who could now be called aging: in their far-off school years and thereafter. Did they still read him nowadays in school? Maybe so, but there was certainly no child who knew his poems by heart. *Par coeur,* as the French teacher would put it, distributing the poems of Victor Hugo, almost invariably Victor Hugo. He could call them to mind even now:

> Devant la blanche ferme ou parfois vers midi
> Un veillard vient s'asseoir sur le seuil attiédi ...

> Oh! combien de marins, combien de capitaines
> Qui sont partis joyeux pour des courses lontaines
> Dans ce morne horizon se sont évanouis ...

And he had them even more *par coeur* now: the sheer beauty of the expression, which he translated "in the heart, from the heart, and for the heart." He discovered himself sentimental to the point of tears. But the doctor, with that sibylline, contradictory phrase, had only intended to warn him against dependency.

But what was the point at which a person just could not stand any more? He pushed it further and further into the future, like some finishing line in a contest between the will and pain. And not out of any fear of dependency, but from a sense of dignity, in which the mere fact of his having been for the greater part of his life an upholder of the law, and of its proscriptions and prohibitions, played a part. He was well aware of what morphine was in a pharmacopoeia, in a hospital, in a doctor's bag, or at the bedside of someone who had arrived at the point of being unable to take any more.

Still, he could not quite bring himself to view it in the sun-
light of permitted things, removed from the shadow of transgression and crime in which years of practice had accustomed
him to consider it. The law. A law, he thought, however in-
iquitous, is still a form of reason; to obtain the objective of
extreme, definitive iniquity, the very people who willed and
framed the law must themselves distort it and do it violence.
Fascism was, among other things, this: a constant evasion of
its own laws. So, too, was Stalin's communism, even more so.

And the death penalty? But the death penalty has nothing to do with the law: it is an act of self-consecration to crime,
of the consecration of crime. A community will always, by a
majority, proclaim the need for the death penalty, precisely
because it is a consecration. The sacred, whatever it had to
do with the sacred ... The dark pit of being, of existence.

Morphine, then. And a curious thought, prompted by
curiosity, occurred to him: he wondered if in the year in
which Tolstoy set the death of Ivan Ilyich, the use of morphine for that purpose was already known. Was it 1885, 1886?
It was reasonable to assume it was known, but was there any
reference to it in the story? He thought not, and drew a kind
of comfort from that reflection. Tolstoy was motivated by
perhaps the same considerations as his own in refusing his
character morphine. Thinking over that story, he began to
search inside himself for comparisons. Death as a quiddity,
a quantum that coursed in the blood among bones, muscles,
and glands, until it found the niche, cradle, or tiny cavity in
which to explode. A minuscule explosion, a point of fire, an
ember initially flickering, then of constant, penetrating pain:
and it grew and it grew until, having reached the point where
the body no longer seemed able to contain it, it overflowed
into everything around. Only the mind, with its tiny, momen-

tary victories, was its enemy, but there were moments, interminably long moments, when pain fell on every single thing,
darkening and deforming everything. It fell on every pleasure
that remained within reach—on love itself, on well-loved
pages, on happy memories. Because it took possession of the
past too, as though it had always been present, as though
there had never been a time when it was not there, when the
body was healthy, young, and given over to joy, in joy. Something resembling a satanic inversion of inflation was under
way: those tiny reserves of joy that had been put aside successfully in the course of a life were being malevolently de-
voured by that pain. On the other hand, perhaps everything
in the world took place under the sign of inflation; every day
the currency of life was losing its value: all life was a kind of
empty monetary euphoria bereft of purchasing power. The
gold standard—of emotions, of thought—had been pillaged:
the things of real value had now an unaffordable, if not wholly
unknown, price.

Without having really decided, he was embarked on a
search to check what was left of his personal reserves. He was
walking along the banks of the river, stopping every so often
to look at the muddy water, to watch life and time flow by.

He arrived at her house worn out: only one flight of
stairs, of old stairs with low, smooth steps, but for him every
ascent was now an exertion. Strangely, though, the exertion
chased away the pain. He decided he must discuss it with a
doctor; for all he knew, there existed an exertion therapy;
these days they discover so many, grow tired of them, redis-
cover them, only to grow tired of them all over again. The
fact is that just as nature with precious few elements at her
disposal is capable of forging an infinity of different faces,
so it is, obscurely, with the intestines. What can a doctor

know about all that? Even when there is the will to communicate to him that little which each of us feels—of the heart, of the lungs, of the stomach, of the bones—a doctor has no option but to refer it all to abstractions, to universals: even when everything is reported to him with the greatest of precision, like Proust in the dentist's waiting room, describing his toothache to Roditi, giving Roditi the consolation of discovering his own to be identical.

He rang the doorbell. Carillon notes in the distance: something that always upset him, but more so now than ever. As usual, she came to the door a few minutes later, in the dressing gown that, he was fully aware, she had slipped on that very minute. *Mais n'te promenes donc pas toute nue ...* Never walk about completely naked. He remembered, many years previously, in a small theater in Rome (in Via Santo Stefano del Cacco, alongside his office and that of Inspector Ingravallo, familiarly known as Don Ciccio Ingravallo, because such was the truth of the pages of Gadda's novel that he had the impression of having bumped into him in those offices rather than on the printed page), having seen Franca Rame walk about the stage, certainly not naked but clad in a nightdress that was anything but transparent: because in those days, transparent attire, let alone nudity, could provide one of his colleagues with the justification for girding himself in the tricolor sash and having the curtain brought down in any theater. No longer: today clothes are removed without a second thought, in the theater as in reality; and to think that in his childhood, taking off one's clothes was considered the height of madness. "He stripped himself bare naked": reason enough, if anyone appeared in that state, for the straitjacket, the doctor's office, the asylum.

At home she walked about completely naked, to the

delight, no doubt, as in Feydeau's farce, of the people in the building opposite, but causing him moments of searing jealousy. Inside himself, now, he laughed at it, and a sketch featuring the De Rege brothers (the theater again) flashed into his mind. One of them came on limping, with his head bandaged, his arm in a cast, blaming it all, it seemed, on "jealousy." The dialogue between the two went back and forth on the subject of the wife's jealousy, until it became clear, in the course of the conversation, that those injuries were the effect not of an emotional spasm but of a fall from a *gelosia*, that is, a shutter. It may even be that the *gelosia* had been dreamed up to ward off the tormented emotion of the same name, but the two had nothing at all in common now. It seemed that the emotion had been, in recent years, abolished, although, possibly, it was now making a comeback, but stripped of the overtones of tragedy: more redolent of ascetic preoccupations.

In the midst of these thoughts, which hardly deserved the name of thought, fleeting and pell-mell as they were, her amazement and momentary hesitation before recognizing him caused him to see himself as though reflected in a mirror. The image, irrationally, irritated him profoundly, as though she had gone into one of her once adorable little huffs. It lasted, like his regret for having returned to visit her at all, the merest moment.

"At long last," she said. "Where are you coming from? What have you been doing all these months?"

"I was in Switzerland: didn't you get my letter—"

"Postcard," she corrected him, angrily.

"That's right, a postcard ... and this last couple of days in the office, I've been snowed under with work."

"The Children of Eighty-nine?"

"The Children of Eighty-nine, among other things."

"And this business about Switzerland?"

"A medical checkup. Very grueling."

"And what came of it?"

"All clear."

He could see from her eyes that she did not believe in that medical all-clear, but she had the shrewdness, the delicacy, the love, perhaps, not to insist. She began to talk ramblingly about other things, but only about what had been happening to her during the period when they had not seen each other. She uttered no reproaches over his absence or his silence.

He stared at her, guessing at that familiar body underneath the flimsy clothing, the body he had loved and desired for years, never more than when she became conscious of her youth passing and her body fading. She had felt herself menaced and offended, as though by an injustice or a criminal assault. At the same time there grew in him a feeling of tenderness, which nourished and sharpened his desire. Desire and tenderness: all serene after the passion of the early years, when their meetings were filled with problems and occasioned misunderstandings and resentments, from which pain and despair rose up like hurricanes. However, once the problems were ended, the passion was spent. Gone were the obsessions and agonies that she perhaps enjoyed but that he lived like one of those fevers in which the rise and fall of temperature, of delirium and lucidity, mark the passage of days and hours. They always met with joy—the joy of their bodies, the only sort of which they could be mutually convinced. There was no need to ask more. They traveled together, at times undertaking journeys of unplanned character and duration, although ever less frequently of late. Everything withdrew, everything was now far off. There remained in him that feeling of tenderness, now almost transformed into pity. Odd how in him now, every feeling that had been love or dislike was changed to pity. And even odder was how memory transfigured those far-off sufferings and despairs into beauty. Everything lied, memory included.

"What about these Children of Eighty-nine?"

"Somebody felt they were necessary." Dürer's devil from the print came to mind. "There has to be a devil before there can be holy water."

Y ou seem more at peace," said the chief.

"Oh, as to peace ... as regards what is happening inside here, I would rather say that I have reached a state of indifference. Forgive me if I speak to you this way, with the sincerity of two equals: you are my direct superior and—"

"Don't say that. I have always treated you as a friend, and I am aware of what is going on inside you, of your pain. And as a friend, I want to put a clear, direct question to you: What do you want? From me, from us, from everybody involved in tackling this case."

"Not a thing. At this point, nothing at all. I see quite clearly that things can only go in the direction they are going, and that it is impossible not just to turn back but even to stop."

"Tell me the truth: you wanted a warrant for Aurispa's arrest." The fact that he now called him Aurispa and no longer the president was a sign that he felt, equally ardently, the same futile desire—to see a warrant issued.

"Look: anytime, in other places—thank God not in this one any longer—anytime I have had to execute warrants, I always felt like one of those sinister characters who, in the Stations of the Cross in country villages, crept up to take Christ prisoner. No matter how vile the person to be arrested, my state of mind was always the same. Yes, it was necessary to execute the warrant; often, if by no means always, it was right; but I could never manage to get over that sensation."

"It's a feeling that does you credit. But in our job . . . forgive my asking this, but why didn't you become a lawyer instead of a policeman?"

"Perhaps because I deluded myself that you could best be a lawyer by being a policeman . . . just take that as a joke. It isn't true. People lie constantly, we do nothing but lie—to ourselves more than to anybody else. Anyway, no, I wasn't looking for a warrant for Aurispa's arrest, but I did want us to concentrate a little more on him, on his life and interests. And more than anything else, I would have preferred us to pack that putative Child of Eighty-nine off home. Where is he now, by the way? In isolation, I presume, in a cell two meters by three."

"What do you expect?"

"Between friends, if you will allow me . . . in all sincerity, do you really believe that boy has any part in some terrorist group that made its debut with the murder of Sandoz?"

"I wouldn't take an oath on it, but in the normal run of things—"

"In the abnormal run of things," the deputy corrected

him. To bring this useless discussion to an end, he went on: "I took your advice. I handed in a request for a leave of absence. For two months. I think that will be sufficient."

"Sufficient for what?" asked the chief, all ready with words of comfort and encouragement.

"To get my health back. What else?"

He returned to his office, opened the drawers of his desk, and took out some letters, a packet of cigarettes, and Gide's pocket edition of Montaigne, which he knew almost by heart. He left other cigarettes and other books. He stopped in front of the Dürer, uncertain whether to take it or leave it. He decided to leave it, indulging, with some relish, a fantasy over what would become of it. He imagined his successors regarding it as part of the furnishing of that office, like the map of the city and the portrait of the President of the Republic. Then someone would become aware of its status as *res nullius,* would carry it triumphantly home or, possibly, to a flea market, where a dealer would discover it and the whole itinerary by which things end up at nearly chic auction sales would be under way all over again. At least in that way it would come to the attention of lovers of such things, or to one lover, someone like him, perhaps: an extemporized, incompetent lover.

He strolled around the city, relishing a sense of freedom that he did not remember experiencing before. Life retained all its beauty, but only for those who were still worthy of it. He felt himself to be not unworthy, indeed to be almost among the select. It was time to cry out: "God hath given you one face, and you make yourselves another": not in the spirit of Hamlet to women, with their cosmetics, face creams, or nail polishes, but to all who merited the tag "unworthy," to the whole worthless mass, who multiplied day by day and filled the earth. He burned with the wish to bellow to the world that this was its new essence—that it had shown itself unworthy of life. But had not the world, the human world, always obscurely aspired to be unworthy of life? An ingenious and ferocious enemy of life, of itself, while at the same time the inventor of so many benevolent forces—law, rules of play, proportions, symmetries, fictions, good manners ... "The ingenious enemy of myself," the dramatist Vittorio Alfieri had said of himself, of himself the man; but equally the ingenious friend, at least until yesterday. As usual, however, when he arrived at the misery of today and the despair of tomorrow, he wondered whether in his deploring the indignity into which the world was sinking there was not an element of rancor at being about to die and of envy toward those who would remain. Perhaps it was so, even in the midst of the all-embracing pity he felt for those who would remain: so much so that at certain moments, embittered, he found himself repeating to himself, like the emcees of variety shows in his younger days, "Have a wonderful time, ladies and gentlemen": like a scoffing farewell. Nonetheless, in the awareness that there would be no "wonderful time," there was, however perversely, a hint of pity.

He was walking now through the park. The children, yes, the children: so graceful, so much better fed than in the past (the frail and hungry childhood of those who were now elderly), perhaps more intelligent and undoubtedly, overall, better informed. Yet he had for them an enormous compassion and apprehension. Will they still be here in 1999, in 2009, or in 2019, and what would this succession of decades bring them? Immersed in these thoughts, he realized he had reached, as it were, the threshold of prayer, which he glimpsed as a deserted, desolate garden.

He stopped to follow their games, to eavesdrop on what they were saying to each other. They were still capable of joy, of imagination, but lying in wait for them was a school without joy and without imagination, the television, the computer, the car from home to school and from school to home, and food that was rich but as tasteless as blotting paper. Never again, committed to memory, the multiplication tables, the poems ... "The maiden from the country came ... ," or "All trembling on the threshold ... ," or even "The cypresses which at Bolgheri ... ," torments of other times. Memory was to be abolished, all memory, and accordingly those exercises that aimed at making it flexible, subtle, or retentive.

In the small towns, children could still enjoy the same freedom as before, but in the cities, everything, by necessity and science, was like an assembly-line hen farm. Some were intent on having them born as monsters, perhaps prodigious monsters, for a monstrous world. "What we are doing," a famous physician had once told him, "is all flowers and roses compared to the things biologists are up to." He was somewhat confused by the expression "flowers and roses," as though the rose, by virtue of literature, had been separated from the genre "flower." The roses I failed to pluck, he thought to himself. But it was not true: it is not true that life is made up of missed opportunities. No regrets.

A dog, an Alsatian with a good-natured, worn-out appearance, had approached a carriage in which a fair-haired baby was peacefully asleep. The girl who was supposedly looking after the child was engaged in a conversation with a soldier. On an impulse he went over and positioned himself between the dog and the baby. The girl stopped talking to the soldier, threw him a reassuring smile, and, gazing affectionately at the dog, said it was an old, friendly thing that would never harm a living soul. He continued on his way and, noticing how many dogs were roaming around the park, attempted to count them. So many dogs, perhaps even more than the multitudes of children. What if the slaves were to count themselves? Seneca once asked. Supposing the dogs were to count themselves? There had one day appeared among his routine cases the horror of a child savaged by a Great Dane. The family pet: no doubt old, and friendly, never having harmed a living soul, just like the girl's Alsatian. Looking around at the many children running through the park and at the countless dogs that seemed to be running alongside them or watching over them as they played, he recalled that case from long ago as an apocalyptic vision. He could feel it on his face like an unclean, clinging spiderweb of images. He lifted his hand to wipe it off, warning himself to die better. The dogs were still there, too many of them; they had nothing in common with those of his childhood. His father had been an avid hunter, and kept small dogs, a pack of squat Sicilian mongrels: always playful, tails wagging, filled with a love of the countryside rather than of the hunt. These dogs, on the other hand, were enormous, doleful creatures, their minds seemingly set on thick, dark woods or impenetrable stone quarries. Or Nazi concentration camps. In any case, for anyone who gave it any thought, it was clear there were too many of them everywhere. And too many cats. And mice. What if they were to count themselves?

That obsession fading, he passed from one thought to the next and began to recall the dogs of his childhood—their names, the prowess of some, the laziness of others—in the very way his father had talked about them in conversation with fellow hunters. A thought that had never previously occurred to him now suddenly flashed into his mind: not one of them had died at home. None of them had been seen dying or found dead in their bedding of straw and old blankets. At a certain stage in life, or at a certain stage in the progress of their bronchitis, it had been noted that they had no further taste for food or play, and they simply disappeared. The shame of themselves dead. As in Montaigne. And the fact, asserted almost as the Kantian imperative, as an illustration of that imperative, that one of mankind's highest intelligences, in his wish that death should come to him, preferably in solitude, but at least far away from those who had been close to him in life, had by meditation and reasoning attained what the dogs instinctively felt, seemed to him sublime. This train of thought, mediated by the great shadow of Montaigne, succeeded in reconciling him with the dogs.

After one of his more peaceful nights, with pain awakening him at the end of dreams in which something or someone seemed to be continually beating him on the side, on the shoulder, or on the neck, he passed the following morning with his newspapers, magazines, and books. The Great Journalist had written an article in which he bitterly accused the police and security services of having fostered the reemergence of the cancer of terrorism, and of having realized what had happened only when they were confronted with the corpse of poor Sandoz in the morgue. The Catholic journal *The Pilgrim* published a lengthy article dealing with the wickedness of the Eighty-nine and of these its blessed offspring of today. They were not exactly called blessed in the article, but since they were engaged in killing, a certain measure of understanding and indulgence, in anticipation of final forgiveness, had to be afforded them.

The pain appeared to be dimmed and to have taken on the semblance of a milky, off-white substance. He finished rereading *Treasure Island,* which still resembled happiness. He was on the point of replacing it on his bookshelf, when the woman who came every morning to tidy up what little there was to tidy up arrived. She had not expected to find him at home and asked if he was not well or if he had decided to take a break.

"A break, a short break."

"Good for you," she said. There had been, that morning, a murder, something really big. It was not hard to imagine how busy the police would be.

He asked about the murder as he rushed over to switch on the radio. The woman said that the victim was a friend of the man who had been killed the week before, but she could not remember his name.

There was not, in all the hubbub of music and chatter that the radio dispensed, a single voice giving any news. He switched it off.

To make up for the radio silence on the murder, the woman did her best to remember. "It was the name of a town in southern Italy."

"Rieti?"

"Yes, that's it. Rieti." The woman brightened at the recollection. She thought to herself: These people know everything that is going to happen before it does. She, too, though not from southern Italy, and proud of her northern origins, was harsh in her judgments of the police.

A friend of the man who had been killed a week previously, the name of a town in southern Italy: the name Rieti had immediately occurred to him. Now, more than pain, stronger than pain, a feeling of defeat overcame him. He felt as though entangled in one of those detective stories where the author, without warning, applies and misapplies toward the reader a meretricious duplicity that never even manages to be clever. Except that in this case, the duplicity was a mistake, his mistake. Had it possibly also been Rieti's mistake? Or had Rieti hidden that part of the truth in which he was most directly interested?

He spent hours turning it over in his mind, as though engaged in an endless game of patience in which something always went awry: one card that refused to be fitted into place, one space into which the awkward card could not be placed.

He left his house as night, mixed with fog, was falling. He headed, without having decided on it—like a donkey for the stables, he thought, when he noticed what he was doing—for the office.

He heard the shots, or so it seemed to him, an incommensurable time before feeling himself hit. Falling, he thought: You fall as a precaution and as a convention. He believed he could rise to his feet but found himself unable to. He raised himself on an elbow. Life was draining out of him, effortlessly, in a flow: the pain was no more. The hell with morphine, he thought. Everything was clear now: Rieti had been murdered because he had spoken to him. At what point had they started following him?

His elbow no longer had the strength to support him, and he fell back. He saw the lovely, immobile face of Signora Zorni light up with malice. He watched it fade away, at the end of the time whose threshold he was even now crossing, into the headlines of the following day's papers: CHILDREN OF EIGHTY-NINE STRIKE AGAIN. COLD-BLOODED MURDER OF INVESTIGATING OFFICER. He thought: What confusion! But it was now, eternally and ineffably, the thought of the mind into which his own had dissolved.

A
STRAIGHTFORWARD
TALE

TRANSLATED FROM THE ITALIAN BY

JOSEPH FARRELL

Yet again my purpose is to examine scrupu-
lously the possibilities even now afforded to
justice.

Friedrich Dürrenmatt

Justice

The phone call came at 9:37 on the evening of March 18, a Saturday, the eve of the refulgent, rambunctious festivities the city dedicated to Saint Joseph the Carpenter. In the Carpenter's honor, bonfires consumed unwanted pieces of furniture in the working-class areas of the city, as though in pledge to those few carpenters still in business that there would be, for them, no shortage of work. Throughout the city, offices were even more deserted than was normal at that hour. Even if the windows in the police station were still ablaze, the late-evening and all-night illumination was no more than a tacitly agreed sop to give the citizenry the impression that their security was the constant concern of the people employed within.

The switchboard operator noted the hour and the name of the person making the call: Giorgio Roccella. He had a cultured, calm, persuasive voice. Like all cranks, thought the operator. Signor Roccella asked to speak to the chief superintendent, no less: sheer madness, especially at that hour, and on that evening of all evenings.

The operator made an effort to adopt the same tone but managed only a jeering imitation, made all the more obvious by the brusqueness of his words: "The chief superintendent is never in the station at this hour." The brusqueness reflected the attitude current in the office on the subject of the chief superintendent's frequent absences. "I'll put you on to the inspector," he added, delighted to be riling the inspector, who would undoubtedly be on his way out at that very moment.

The inspector was indeed getting into his overcoat. The brigadier, whose desk was at right angles to the inspector's, picked up the phone. He listened, rummaging about on the desk for pencil and paper, and as he wrote, he replied yes, they would be there as soon as possible, just as soon as humanly possible, but his words indicated that possibility and swiftness did not necessarily coincide.

"Who was that?" asked the inspector.

"Somebody who says he has to show us immediately a thing he has found in his house."

"A body?" joked the inspector.

"No, his exact words were 'a thing.' "

"A thing ... and does this somebody have a name?"

The brigadier picked up the notepad on which he had scribbled a name and address: "Giorgio Roccella, in Cotugno, four kilometers from where the road to Monterosso forks to the right; that makes fifteen from here."

The inspector turned back from the door to the brigadier's desk, picked up the notepad, peered at it as though convinced he would uncover something more than the brigadier had read out. He said: "Can't be."

"What can't be?" asked the brigadier.

"This Roccella," said the inspector. "He's a diplomat,

a consul or ambassador somewhere or other. He hasn't been here for years. He closed up his house in the city and rented out his cottage in the country. It's on a hilltop, more like a minifortress."

"The old farmhouse," said the brigadier. "I've passed it dozens of times."

"Inside the compound—which is what makes it look like a farm house—there's a beautiful little villa ... or a least, there used to be. A big family, the Roccellas, but the only one left is this consul or ambassador or whatever he is. I didn't even know he was still alive. It's so long since he's been around."

"If you like," said the brigadier, "I'll go and have a look."

"No need; I'm sure it's only a hoax. Tomorrow, if you've the time and the inclination, drop by and check that everything is all right. As far as I'm concerned, whatever happens, don't come looking for me tomorrow. I'll be celebrating Saint Joseph's with some friends at their place in the country."

The following day, the brigadier set off for Cotugno, and both he and the two officers accompanying him were in high spirits, people on a day's outing. From what the inspector had said, they were sure that the place was uninhabited and that the call the evening before was no more than a hoax.

A stream, which had once run at the foot of the hill, was now no more than a pebbly riverbed, lined with stones white as bone, but the hill leading up to the ruined farmhouse was covered with green foliage. Their plan was to carry out a swift search of the house and then, in a more festive mood, to start gathering asparagus and chicory. All three, like the good peasants they were, prided themselves on their skill in identifying the best wild herbs.

They got inside the enclosure, which was made up not of ordinary walls, as seemed from the road below, but of outbuildings. The doors were secured by shining locks, and the buildings were grouped in a circle around the little villa. The villa was indeed a jewel, even if it now showed signs of decay and dilapidation. All the shutters were closed except for one, which allowed them to peer inside. The bright light of that March morning afforded them at first only a confused glimpse of the interior. Gradually they managed to make things out, and as all three, shielding their eyes from the sun with their hands, repeated the exercise, it became clear that a man, his back toward them, lay slumped over the desk where he had been sitting.

The brigadier took the decision to break the glass, open the window, and enter the room: the man might have been taken ill, and possibly they were in time to offer assistance. But the man was dead, and not from any stroke or heart attack; on the head, which rested on the desk top, a clot of blackish blood had formed between the lower jaw and the temple.

The brigadier shouted to the two officers, who had climbed over the windowsill after him: "Don't touch a thing!" To avoid touching the phone, which was on the desk, he ordered one of the officers to return to the police station, make a report, and dispatch a doctor, a photographer, and those two or three officers with scientific expertise. Unwarranted privileges, in the brigadier's view, for he had yet to see a single case where their contribution had been helpful rather than the reverse.

Having issued these orders, the brigadier, repeating to the officer who had stayed with him not to touch anything, began his inspection. He was deeply conscious of the written report that it would be his duty, in due course, to file, and this task invariably weighed heavily on him, for his schooling and his limited reading had done little to instill in him much confidence in his use of the language. But curiously, the fact of being compelled to write about the things he had seen, and the worry and near panic involved, gave his mind such a capacity for choice, for selectivity, for identifying the essential detail, that what eventually emerged in written form was invariably penetrating and judicious. Perhaps it is so for all writers from the south of Italy, and from Sicily in particular—high school, university, and wide reading notwithstanding.

The immediate impression was that the man had committed suicide. The pistol was on the floor, to the right of the chair on which he was seated: an old weapon, German, dating from the 1915–16 war, the sort of thing survivors would bring home with them as souvenirs. But one detail canceled out that first impression in the brigadier's mind: the right hand of the dead man, which ought to have been hanging limply over the fallen pistol, was instead resting on the top of the desk, holding steady a sheet of paper on which was written: "I have found." The full stop after the word "found" burned into the darkness like a flashbulb, lighting up, swiftly and fleetingly, the murder scene that lay behind

the imperfectly constructed suicide scene. The man had begun writing "I have found" in the same way he had informed the police that he had found something he had not
expected to: Unsure whether the police would arrive, and
perhaps growing afraid in the silence and solitude, he was
about to write down what he had found, when a knock came
at the door. The police, he thought, and instead it was the
murderer. Perhaps the person introduced himself as a policeman: the man brought him in, sat down again at his desk,
and began to tell him about his discovery. The pistol might
have been lying on the desk; probably, in his growing fear,
he had gone to retrieve it from some old hiding place where
he remembered leaving it (the brigadier did not believe that
a killer would have such an ancient piece of weaponry in his
possession). Seeing the gun lying there on the desk, the murderer possibly asked about it, checked that it was still in
working order, before suddenly pointing it at the man's head
and firing. At this point, he had the idea of adding a full
stop after "I have found." "I have found that life is not
worth living," or "I have found the ultimate and only truth";
"I have found, I have found . . ." everything and nothing. It
did not make sense. From the murderer's point of view, however, that full stop was not wholly a mistake. In support of
the suicide hypothesis that would undoubtedly be ad-
vanced—the brigadier had absolutely no doubt on that
score—all kinds of existential and philosophical significance
would be adduced from that full stop, especially if the personality of the deceased offered the slightest pretext. On the
desk there was a bunch of keys, an old pewter inkwell, and
a photograph, evidently taken in the garden some fifty years
previously, of a large, happy party of people. Perhaps it had
been taken there, outside the window, when there would have

been rows of trees creating their own harmony and shade, while now there was nothing but the untended barrenness of weeds and scrub.

Beside the sheet of paper with "I have found" lay a fountain pen with the cap neatly screwed on. A fine flourish, this, by the murderer (the brigadier was becoming more convinced by the second that he was engaged in a murder inquiry), to convey the impression that with the full stop the man had put a final stop to his own existence.

The room was furnished all around the bookshelves, almost all empty of books. The few works that remained included bound copies of a year's legal reviews, some agronomy manuals, and random bundles of a magazine entitled *Nature and Art*. Some volumes, which must have been very old, lay in a pile, and on their spines the brigadier read *Calepinus*. He had always believed that a calepin was a pocket-sized booklet, like a notebook or a handbook, and it struck him as odd that a word more appropriate for miniatures should be applied to great tomes weighing at least ten kilos each. Scruples over not leaving fingerprints, although he had precious little faith in them, made him check his curiosity and leave the volumes unopened. The same scruples caused him, as he wandered around the house followed by the officer, not to touch furniture or handles, and to enter only by doors already open.

The house was much bigger than would have seemed possible from the outside. There was an enormous dining room, with a large oak table and four dressers of the same wood, and inside he found dishes, soup tureens, glasses, and coffeepots, as well as old toys, papers, and linen. There were three bedrooms, two with mattresses and pillows stacked on the springs, but the third appeared to have been slept in the previous night; there could have been yet others behind the doors that the brigadier decided not to open. The house had been abandoned and stripped of all furniture, books, paintings, and ceramics—there were clear marks where objects had been removed—but it did not have the air of being uninhabited. Cigarette butts filled the ashtrays, and the dregs of wine stained the bottoms of the glasses, all five of them, that had been carried into the kitchen, no doubt to be rinsed. The kitchen, complete with wooden fireplace, oven, and decorative Valencian tiles on the walls, was spacious; even if they were now turning green with sulfate, the copper pots and pans hanging on the walls conferred, in the uncertain light, a certain splendor on the scene. From the kitchen a low door opened onto a narrow, dark staircase, which ascended toward some unseen area.

The brigadier groped around for a stair light to enable him to see his way. Unable to find any switch except the one for the lamps over the fireplace, he took the risk of climbing the stairs in the dark. After five or six steps, still fumbling forward, he began to strike matches, and had used up several before reaching a kind of attic at the head of the stairs. It was as wide as the dining room but was so low-ceilinged that a person of normal height would find it difficult to avoid bumping his head. It was filled with couches, armchairs, broken seats, strongboxes, damaged picture frames, and dusty drapes. Around ten gilded bust reliquaries of saints stood around in a circle, but one larger bust, with a silver chest, a black cape, and bulldog features, attracted his attention. The gilded busts each carried the name of the saint they represented on their Baroque pedestals, but the brigadier lacked sufficient familiarity with saints to recognize, in the larger and darker bust, the figure of Saint Ignatius.

The brigadier lit his last match and hurried downstairs. "A stuffy loft packed with saints," he explained to the officer waiting for him at the foot of the stairs. He felt as though spiderwebs, dust, and mildew had fallen on his head. He jumped over the windowsill back into the cool, bright morning, back into the sun and the grass glistening with frost.

With the officer, who remained the regulation two paces behind him, the brigadier made a tour of the exterior of the house. Among the weeds and undergrowth, there was a clearing, which had plainly been used by cars and possibly trucks to turn around. "There's been a fair bit of traffic here," said the brigadier. Then, pointing them out to the officer, "What do you make of these chains?" he asked. They were used to secure the doors of the barns or stables that circled the house like a fort in a Western.

"They're new," said the officer.

"Good for you," said the brigadier.

A little more than two hours later, all those who were supposed to arrive did: the chief superintendent, the procurator of the republic, the doctor, the chief superintendent's tame journalist, and a squad of officers, including, standing on their dignity, those of the scientific unit. There were in all six or seven cars, which, even when they had come to a halt, continued to roar, screech, and blare their horns, just as they had done when exiting from the city center, arousing thereby the curiosity not only of the citizens but also of the rival police force, the carabinieri, and in so doing achieving the very result the chief superintendent had ardently desired to postpone as long as possible. The consequence was that half an hour later, the colonel of the carabinieri, scowling, furious, and desperate to engage—with all due respect—the chief superintendent in a quarrel, arrived on the scene. The locked doors had been opened with the keys that had been found lying on the desk, the taking of fingerprints was, somewhat haphazardly, under way, and the body had already been photographed from every conceivable angle. With barely repressed fury, the colonel said: "You might at least have kept us informed."

"I beg pardon," said the chief superintendent, "but it all happened so quickly . . . a matter of minutes."

"Of course, of course," said the colonel ironically.

The gun was lifted by a pencil inserted in the trigger guard, delicately placed on a black cloth, and equally delicately wrapped up. "The fingerprints, quickly, don't waste time," said the chief superintendent. The dead man's had already been taken. "A worthless chore," he intoned, "but it has to be done."

"Why worthless?" asked the colonel.

"Suicide," said the chief superintendent solemnly. The words had the effect of persuading the colonel of the opposing view.

"Excuse me, sir," interrupted the brigadier.

"Anything you have to say can wait for your report. Meantime . . ." But he had no idea, meantime, of what to say or do other than repeat: "Suicide, an evident case of suicide."

The brigadier tried again: "Chief Superintendent . . ."

He wanted to tell him about the phone call the previous evening, about the period after "I have found," but the chief superintendent cut him off. "We require the report," he said, indicating himself and the procurator of the republic. Glancing at his watch, he added, "Early in the afternoon." Addressing the procurator and the colonel: "A straightforward case; no need to make too much of it. Should be all tied up in no time. Off you go, and write it up right away."

Instead, quite automatically, the colonel saw it shaping up as a very complicated business, as something that would not be tied up in no time. The unbridgeable disparity of viewpoint between the two institutions—the carabinieri and the police—came to the surface immediately, instinctively, as was invariably the case, independently of the individuals who represented them. A long history of rivalry separated them, and any citizen who became entangled with it inevitably ended up as grist for the mill.

The brigadier said: "Yes, sir," and went out to get into the patrol car that had brought him there, only to find it had gone off. Since the chief superintendent had upset him, and since he was almost entirely bereft of what is normally called esprit de corps—in other words, of the propensity to regard the body to which one belongs as the greater part of the whole, to consider it infallible or, in the event of its showing itself fallible, untouchable, and as always in the right even when it was wrong—a quite outlandish idea occurred to him.

His counterpart, the carabinieri brigadier, was seated at the wheel of the colonel's car. Knowing him fairly well, although not to the point of sharing confidences with him, our brigadier went over and sat beside him. He poured out to him all he knew about the case, detailing the various suspicions he harbored. He even pointed out the shiny new chains on the doors of the outbuildings, and, that task completed, set off in a more cheerful frame of mind for the office, where he devoted over two hours to setting down in writing the things he had explained to his fellow officer in five minutes.

In this way, on the way back into the city, the carabinieri colonel learned from his brigadier all he needed to make the case more complex than the chief superintendent wished.

A lthough it was Sunday and the feast of Saint Joseph, data on personal history and family property, together with a host of other more or less confidential pieces of information, flowed into both police and carabinieri headquarters; the same data, or almost, from the same sources and the same informers. Had they been able to work harmoniously together, one party or the other would have been spared time and effort that could have been more profitably expended elsewhere; but now we are yearning for something as impossible as collaboration between a builder and a dynamiter—and let it be clearly understood that neither role is being assigned to either of the two sides in question.

Identity of the victim: Giorgio Roccella, born in Monterosso on January 14, 1923, a retired diplomat. He had been Italian consul in various European cities before being sent to Edinburgh, where, having separated from his wife, he now resided with his twenty-year-old son. For the past fifteen years he had not set foot in Italy, returning only to die in tragic circumstances on March 18, 1989. Even if he took little care of it, he was the only member of the family to retain some fragment of what had been a vast and varied estate: all that remained was a semi-derelict house in town and the villa with its small surrounding plot. He had arrived in town that very day, March 18; having lunched at Tre Candele restaurant on spaghetti in cuttlefish sauce and octopus with salad, he called a taxi to take him to the villa. He had, according to the taxi driver, made sure that his keys opened the doors before allowing him to go, but he gave him orders to return the following day at eleven o'clock. "I am prone to insomnia," he explained, "and will work through the night." The next morning at eleven, the taxi driver, seeing the bustle of police and carabinieri, had turned back without going up to the villa. Perhaps the man was a dangerous criminal. Why go looking for trouble?

The chief superintendent, already more than sufficiently irritated by the brigadier's report, which hinted at murder, found in the discovery that the man had separated from his wife (or, preferably, his wife from him) grounds for reinforcing his belief in the suicide hypothesis. He did wonder why he had gone to the trouble of first calling the police, but the question did not cause him any anxiety. He wanted, he replied, to kill himself under the very eyes of the police force, and so ensure maximum impact and originality for his gesture. The brigadier, studying the official forms more attentively, pointed out to the chief superintendent that the separation had occurred some twelve years previously. Whatever heartbreak it might have occasioned, it was hard to imagine it coming to a peak of despair twelve years after the event. The chief superintendent did, however, reach his own peak of irritation with the brigadier there and then. "How dare you address such remarks to a superior officer?" he said. "Go at once and find the inspector, wherever he is."

The inspector, precisely as he had promised on Saturday, remained incommunicado until Monday morning. At eight o'clock on the dot, complete with hat, overcoat, and heavy gloves, wrapped about with a scarf that covered even his mouth, he made his entry into the office. He removed these articles of clothing one by one, shivering continually as he did so. "It's just about as cold inside as out. If there were any birds in here, they'd drop dead with the cold."

He had learned about the weekend's events from the radio and the newspapers. Scanning without comment the outline report prepared by the brigadier, he hurried out to confer with the chief superintendent.

On his return, he gave every impression of being at daggers drawn with the brigadier. "Enough of your clever tales, eh?" But the clever tales were already in the air. Two hours later, Professor Carmelo Franzo, an old friend of the victim, was seated in the office, giving them further sustenance. He told how on Saturday, March 18, Giorgio Roccella had arrived out of the blue at his house. Explanation of that surprise journey: he had remembered that in a chest that must have been left in the attic of the villa there were bundles of old letters—one packet from Garibaldi to his great-grandfather, another from Pirandello to his grandfather (they had attended high school at the same time). Acting on an impulse, he had decided to pick them up and do some work on them. He asked Franzo to accompany him to the villa in the afternoon, but the professor, that very afternoon, had a regular, prearranged dialysis session: to miss the appointment would have meant days of painful immobility. Otherwise he might have been delighted to go back to the villa after all those years and give a hand in the search. After agreeing to meet the following day, Sunday, they parted, but on Sunday afternoon the news of his friend's death came over the radio.

However, the professor had further, vitally important, information to add. On Saturday evening, a phone call had come from his friend. He was phoning from the villa, and his first words were: "I had no idea they'd put a phone in." Then he said that while searching for the letters, he had found—the very words—he had found the famous painting. "Which painting?" the professor had asked him. "The one that disappeared a couple of years ago—don't you remember?" The professor was not clear which one he was referring to, but advised him to call the police.

"What a complicated story," said the inspector, with a mixture of concern and disbelief. "The telephone, the picture: two things Signor Roccella had just found a moment before talking to you." And in an even more incredulous tone to the professor: "And you believed all this?"

"I believed him all my life; why should I have changed just the other day?"

Meanwhile, the brigadier picked up the telephone directory, flicked through a couple of pages, cast his eye down the columns, and read aloud: " 'Roccella, Giorgio, Monterosso, Cotugno, 342260' . . . it's in the phone book."

"Much obliged," said the inspector acidly. "It isn't the fact that it's there which interests me; I am intrigued by the fact that he was unaware of it."

"Perhaps we could . . . ," the brigadier began.

"You could; and you will attend to it at once. Go to the office of the telephone company, get all the details of the application, the date of installation, bills paid—better still, make them give you photocopies of the lot."

Turning to the professor, he went on: "Can we go back to the famous picture: disappears, turns up at your friend's, and presumably disappears once more. You gave me the impression that you had some notion of the painting your friend was talking about."

"You haven't?" the professor stonewalled.

"No idea," said the inspector. "I have no interest in painting. God knows how many missing paintings there are in Italy. I have a friend in Rome who specializes in that kind of thing. We could get in touch with him. But in the meantime, tell me which painting you think we are talking about."

"I am no specialist in stolen works of art," said the professor.

"But you have an opinion."

"The same one you ought to have."

"God almighty, it's always the same, even with professors."

"Even with police inspectors," the professor replied sourly.

The inspector restrained himself. Had it been anyone

else, he would probably have had him locked up, but Professor Franzo was known and respected by the whole city. Generations of pupils had fond, grateful memories of him. So: "Kindly repeat, as accurately as possible, what your friend said to you in person and on the telephone."

The professor, nervously, so nervously as almost to spell out every syllable, repeated all that had been said.

"You're sure you are not omitting anything?" said the inspector, getting his own back.

"I have an excellent memory, and am not in the habit of omitting things."

"Good, good," said the inspector, "but just bear in mind that within a short time you will have to repeat everything, word for word, before the judge."

The professor smiled, half pityingly and half sneeringly, but the chief superintendent, who had been a student of the professor's, came in at that moment and put an end to the skirmishing.

"Professor! You here?"

"And with an intresting tale to tell," said the inspector.

The return of the brigadier disturbed the fragile peace. "I've got the request; made three years ago, but with a forged signature. The carabinieri are already onto it."

"Damnation!" screamed the chief superintendent, addressing himself to the carabinieri.

Now that the professor's evidence had undermined the suicide theory, the police chief superintendent, who had originally accepted it, and the carabinieri colonel, who had instantly rejected it, found themselves under pressure from their superiors to get together, clear the air, exchange information, hypotheses, and suspicions. They met, so to speak, with clenched teeth, but could not contrive to be entirely vague and inconclusive.

Reconstruction of the event: Signor Roccella, moved by a whim, returned unexpectedly after many years to search for the letters from Pirandello and Garibaldi; he turned up at his friend's house; he dined at the restaurant; he took from his town house, or already had in his possession, the keys of the villa; he traveled out by taxi. There, having ascertained that the keys still worked, he let the taxi driver go and began his search. But what had taken place from that moment on? He had plainly found a telephone installed, but judging by the professor's report, he did not appear unduly surprised by this discovery. This implied that he had some idea of who was responsible for the installation. On the other hand, the discovery of that painting in the loft, where he had gone to look for the letters, had evidently left him stunned, perhaps even terrified—which explained the telephone calls to his friend and to the police. Since the police did not come immediately, he had begun to write: "I have found ..." But no doubt in a state of fear, he had gone to look for his old Mauser. And in all probability, it was just at that moment that he heard a knock at the door. At last, the police. He went to open up; instead it was his murderer.

Points for further inquiry: Had the telephone indeed been installed without his knowledge? Was his return indeed dictated by his desire to repossess the letters from Garibaldi and Pirandello? Had he indeed seen *that* picture, or was it simply some old family painting, which he had completely forgotten about and which had turned up as he was rummaging about in the loft?

A further, more meticulous search of the villa was called for, but just as they were making up their minds to order it, an event occurred that created intense activity and confusion.

A local train, normally packed at that hour—two o'clock in the afternoon—with students, had been stopped at the signals just outside Monterosso. They waited for the signal to change, but half an hour went by and nothing happened.

The railway line ran alongside the main road, and students and railwaymen swarmed onto the highway, liberally cursing the stationmaster at Monterosso, who had plainly either forgotten to clear the line or fallen asleep.

There were very few cars on the road at that hour, and only one stopped to ask what was the matter with the train. A Volvo. The engineer asked the motorist to do him a favor: Would he be good enough to drop in at the Monterosso station and wake up the stationmaster? The Volvo made its way to the station; they watched it park and then drive off, disappearing from sight. Evidently it had rejoined the main road by a different side road.

After a while, since the signals remained red, the engineer and a group of passengers made their way on foot to the station, a distance of some five hundred meters. They discovered to their horror that the stationmaster and his assistant were indeed asleep, but from their sleep there would be no awakening. They had been murdered.

Impartially, both police and carabinieri were summoned to the scene. Both, instantaneously, gave all their energies to a search for the Volvo man. Their energies were not likely to be stretched, considering that there could not have been more than thirty Volvos in the entire province. The same calculation was made by the Volvo man himself when he learned from the radio that the police were hunting for him. Having no doubt that it could only be a matter of time before they caught up with him, he went to the police station reluctantly and apprehensively but, as was recorded in the opening words of the official statement, voluntarily.

Name and surname, place and date of birth, residence, profession, previous dealings with the police.

"Not even for a traffic offense," the man said. However, his declaration of profession—representative of a pharmaceutical company—gave the inspector the immeasurable delight of being able to adopt a tough tone for the interrogation.

"Do you own a Volvo?"

"Of course."

"Don't say 'of course' when you are replying to my questions. Your Volvo is very expensive."

The man nodded his head.

"Would you include, among the drugs you sell, things like heroin, cocaine, opium?"

"Listen," said the man, holding back anger and fear, "I came here of my own free will, with the sole purpose of telling you what I saw yesterday afternoon."

"Go on then," said the inspector, in a tone of disbelief.

"I went to the station, exactly as the engineer had requested me to do. I knocked at the window of the stationmaster's office, and he came to the door."

"Who?"

"The stationmaster, I suppose."

"So you don't know him."

"No. I've already told you what the engineer asked me to tell him. I hardly glanced inside the office: there were two other men, and they were rolling up a carpet. I went on my way."

"But by a different road," remarked the inspector, "and since no one saw you going back down . . . Anyway, they were rolling up this carpet."

"The painting," the brigadier let slip.

The inspector turned a look of anger on him.

"Much obliged, but I would have come to that conclusion without your aid."

"Pardon me," said the brigadier. "Who am I to imagine . . ." Then, ingenuously, with a confused stutter, he added: "You've been to university."

The remark, which sounded sarcastic to the inspector, drove him into a rage against the Volvo owner. "I am sorry, but we will have to keep you in custody. We have further inquiries to make."

B rigadier Antonio Lagandara was born in a country village so near the city as nowadays to be considered part of it. While he was in his final year of a course in economics and business, his father—a farmhand who had risen to become a highly esteemed and much sought after tree pruner—died in a fall from the top of a cherry tree, which he was stripping of dead branches. Antonio had taken his diploma, but neither having nor finding employment, he joined the police force. Five years later, he received his first promotion. He found the job stimulating and decided to make a career of it. He enrolled at law school, attended lectures as and when he could, and studied hard. A degree in law was the supreme ambition, the ultimate dream of his life. The remark that the inspector had taken amiss was made in all innocence. It plainly still rankled in him when the brigadier returned from escorting the Volvo owner—whose howls of protest echoed through the building—down to the cells. "Been to university, eh? I can't work out in my mind whether you're really a moron or whether you're just pretending to be. University! In a country where cinema ushers, waiters, and even trash collectors must have degrees."

"I am very sorry," said the brigadier sincerely but peevishly.

"Forget it. I've got an appointment with the chief superintendent. Bring along the Volvo man in a quarter of an hour."

The carabinieri colonel was already in the chief superintendent's office, and the inspector brought them up to date on what had happened. When the Volvo man was brought in by the brigadier, the chief superintendent came straight to the point: "So you saw three men in the stationmaster's office rolling up a carpet. Was there a body inside?"

"A body? No, definitely not."

"How wide was the carpet?"

"Couldn't really say ... perhaps a meter and a half."

"How can you be so sure it was a carpet?" asked the colonel.

"I never said I was sure of anything. It looked like a carpet to me."

"Describe it."

"They were rolling up the carpet so that the underside was on top—a rough, unworked, canvaslike material."

"But the underside of a carpet is not like that at all. Is it possible that it was a painting they were rolling up?"

"It is possible, yes."

"Let's move on. There were, you were saying, three men in all."

"That's right, three."

The chief superintendent handed him two photographs: "Here's two of them; recognize them?"

They were attempting to lay a trap for him. The man cursed them inwardly. "How could I recognize them? I don't believe I've ever seen these two in my life before."

"Know who they are? The stationmaster and his assistant. The people who were murdered."

"But they're not the ones I saw!"

"Didn't you tell us you saw and spoke to the stationmaster?"

"All right, then, it was somebody I took to be the stationmaster."

"I am sorry," said the chief superintendent, "but I have no option but to hold you in detention for a further period."

The wretch began anew his howls of protest.

C hief superintendent, colonel, and investigating magistrate met to establish how the inquiries were going. The magistrate assumed an air of deep thought and then said: "Do you know what I think? However unplanned the whole thing may seem, the Volvo man forced his way into the stationmaster's office, saw the painting, was completely bowled over by it, shot the two men dead, and made off with it."

The chief superintendent and the colonel exchanged glances of perplexed and ironic disbelief.

"You know these instinctive feelings you get about certain characters. I've had one about this Volvo man from the very first, and I very rarely get it wrong with these intuitions of mine. Keep him locked up for me." Since he had to talk to Professor Franzo, the magistrate showed them to the door.

On the way out, the chief superintendent muttered: "Dear God!" and the colonel. "Terrifying!"

The magistrate was already on his feet to welcome his old teacher. "I can't tell you how glad I am to see you after all these years!"

"All these years, and they're beginning to show," agreed the professor.

"What do you mean? You haven't changed a bit."

"That's more than I can say for you," said the professor, with his customary bluntness.

"This damn work ... But why are you being so formal with me?"

"I always was."

"But even now?"

"I prefer it that way."

"You do remember me?"

"Of course I do."

"Can I ask you one thing, before we pass on to other matters? Whenever I had an essay to do, you always gave me three out of ten, because I used to copy. But one day you gave me five. Why?"

"Because you had chosen a more intelligent author to copy from."

The magistrate burst out laughing. "Italian: it was never my best subject. However, as you can see, it was no great drawback. Here I am today, procurator of the republic."

"Italian is not Italian: it is training in reasoning," said the professor. "With less Italian, you might have risen higher."

The remark was wounding. The magistrate turned pale and made his interrogation all the tougher.

The victim's son arrived from Edinburgh, and his wife from Stuttgart, on the same day. The meeting between mother and son was, even for the investigators who had to be present, an unpleasant affair. The wife, quite clearly, had come to see how much of the inheritance she could grab for herself; the son was there in part to prevent her from doing so, but more especially to find out why his father had been killed, and by whom.

The meeting took place in an office in the police station. They did not exchange any form of greeting. The son's first words were: "You can go back to Stuttgart. There's nothing for you here."

"That's your opinion."

"It's not a matter of opinion. It's all laid down in the papers my father filed in the registry some years ago."

"I am not sure whether those papers are worth much. Anyway, they can be challenged. Look, let's sort things out between us. Why don't we sell up and get out?"

"I'm not selling. I might even live here. I came back and stayed a long time, many years ago. My grandparents were still alive then. I remember it very well. We had a lovely time. Yes, perhaps I will stay on. I used to have long conversations with my father about coming back and settling here."

"With your father!" the woman repeated sarcastically.

"Are you trying to say that he was not my father? Look,

there is no choosing mothers, or I certainly would never have chosen you—and by the same token, you would never have chosen me as a son. But you can choose your father, and I chose Giorgio. I loved him, and I mourn his death. He was my father. You attribute far too much importance to the mere fact of having been to bed with another man, or with other men."

The delicately manicured and expensively ringed hand of the mother flashed against the son's cheek. The boy turned his back on her and stared intently at the rows of books, as though they held some deep interest for him. Tears filled his eyes.

The chief superintendent interrupted. "This is none of our business. I want to know from you, Signora, if you have grounds for suspicion regarding the murder of your husband."

She shrugged her shoulders. "He was Sicilian," she said, "and the Sicilians have been killing each other for years. You tell me why."

"What insight!" said the son ironically, returning to his seat on the other side of the desk from the chief superintendent.

"What about you? What's your opinion? What do you know?" the chief superintendent asked him.

"As to why he was killed, nothing. I was hoping to find out from you, sooner or later. For the rest ..." He told them about his father's decision to return and unearth the Garibaldi and Pirandello letters, of his own regret at not being able to accompany him, of the telephone call assuring him that the journey had gone well. Nothing else.

"Tell me something about your properties here. Were they completely abandoned?"

"Yes and no. Every so often my father would write to

someone or other—a priest, I think—to ask about the general state of things."

"Had the priest been put in charge of maintenance?"

"Not exactly, as far as I know."

"Did your father send him any money?"

"I don't think so."

"Did he reply to your father's letters?"

"Yes; he always said that everything was in good order, even though no one was living there."

"Did this priest have the keys of both the town house and the villa?"

"I don't know."

"Do you remember his name?"

"Cricco, I think. Father Cricco. But I can't be sure."

F ather Cricco—a striking man, tall and stern in his clerical attire—insisted that he had never had the keys in his possession. At the most, he had peered into the town house and the country villa from outside, and his reports were limited to issuing assurances that they were still standing, without prominent cracks or irreparable damage.

The inspector, all deference and finely turned compliments, conducted the interrogation, while the brigadier wrote out what was said. The first words were: "You are one of the few priests who still dress as priests, and I personally find this greatly encouraging, even if I am at a loss to explain why."

"I am a old-fashioned priest, and you are an old-fashioned Catholic. And both of us are much the better for it, if I may say so."

"As a priest, as an intelligent man, as a friend of the dead man, what is your opinion of this case?"

"In spite of the elaborate fiction that is being constructed around this business, I have to confess that I cannot get the likelihood of suicide out of my mind. Giorgio did not have peace of heart."

"Indeed: that wife of his, that son who was not his son . . ."

"I understand that the police scientific unit—"

"That's right; they found more than one fingerprint belonging to the deceased on the gun, but at the very point where his hand should have gripped it most tightly if he was to shoot himself, the prints seemed to have been rubbed out, as though the gun had been held by a gloved hand. But I, with the greatest respect for the lab men, have little faith in this finding."

The brigadier, who could not rid himself of the vice of butting in, said: "I have practically no faith in them either, but it is hard to imagine a man getting out a gun and then, on the very point of committing suicide, putting on a glove and shooting himself, still leaving himself the time to take the glove off and hide it away. Quite a vaudeville turn, eh?"

"Enjoying ourselves, are we? You carry on enjoying yourself," said the inspector sourly.

The police and judicial authorities decided that a further search of the villa was necessary and decreed that the presence of mother and son, as well as of Professor Franzo, was indispensable. The inspector, the brigadier, and a group of policemen went along. Father Cricco declined his invitation: he was a highly emotional man, and in any case, his presence would serve no purpose.

The brigadier was dispatched to collect the professor from his house. They made the brief journey on their own, to the great delight of the brigadier, who was always intoxicated by the prospect of talk with people who enjoyed a reputation for intelligence and culture. As it happened, the professor spoke exclusively of his aches and pains, producing a phrase that the brigadier savored but, in the full energy of his thirty years, could not accept, to the effect that at a certain point in life, rather than hope being the last to die, dying is the last hope.

The professor knew the place well, having spent many hours of his childhood and youth there in the company of his friend. As soon as he was inside the compound, he pointed to the barns and said: They were once the stables. The brigadier was taken aback to discover that the doors were wide open and the chains had been removed. He assumed it must have been the carabinieri and mentioned as much to the inspector. Later, back in the city, they phoned the carabinieri, but they knew nothing about the matter.

Nervously the brigadier examined the barns one by one. A smell of something indefinable, perhaps burnt sugar, soaked eucalyptus leaves, or alcohol, hung in the air. He said to the inspector: "Do you smell that?"

"Smell what?"

"Is there not a strange smell in the air?"

"I can't smell a thing. I've got a bit of a cold."

"We should get some expert, a chemist or something, to come along; maybe we'd be better with those dogs the customs people use."

"There's no dog like you, from customs or not," said the inspector. "However, just to keep you happy, we'll bring in the experts and the dogs."

The others were waiting in front of the door of the villa. The inspector handed the keys to the brigadier, saying: "You open up and show us around. I've never been here before."

They all swarmed in: the officers in a frenzy of excitement, as though expecting to catch a burglar red-handed; the son gazing around with eyes that glistened with emotion; and the woman ice cold, seemingly bored.

On the ground floor there was nothing new for the officers, nothing they had not seen before. They made their way up to the first floor and trooped into the kitchen. The trapdoor that led to the attic was lying open, revealing only darkness. They all stopped, until the inspector pushed forward and climbed nimbly and surefootedly up the wooden ladder. When he reached the top, the attic and the people at the foot of the stair were suddenly flooded by a bright light.

The brigadier, moving gingerly among the various objects piled pell-mell on the floor, scrutinized the walls with evident care.

"What are you looking for?" asked the inspector.

"The switch."

"Of course. You never managed to locate it. There's no problem. It's here, behind the bust of Saint Ignatius."

"But you can't see it," said the brigadier.

"Intuition," said the inspector. He risked a joke: "You're not going to tell me I found it because I've been to university." His eyes, however, glazed over, as though in apprehension.

"I didn't say a word," said the brigadier darkly.

On the chest, an outlined area, free of the thick layer of dust that had settled everywhere else, indicated that something had lain there for a considerable time. The rolled-up canvas, thought the brigadier, and said so. Poor Roccella had obviously seen it even before opening the chest to look for the letters. They were inside in two neat bundles, one containing those from Pirandello and the other those from Garibaldi. The professor had even seen them, years before. He turned the pages of Pirandello's correspondence, pausing over the occasional arresting phrase. At eighteen, Pirandello was already thinking the thoughts that would still appear in his writing when he was well into his sixties.

On the return journey, the professor said to the brigadier: "I would be glad of the chance to read those letters of Pirandello's at greater leisure."

"There should be no problem in getting hold of them," said the brigadier, but his mind was elsewhere, and his mood was dark, unsettled, edgy. He felt the need to confide in someone, to give vent to his concerns. Along the road, he stopped the engine and broke into hysterical tears. "We have been together for three years, in the same office."

"I understand," said the professor. "The light switch."

"The light switch ... He said he had never been in that house before. You heard him yourself. I went through a whole box of matches searching for that switch; the rest of them spent ages groping about the room with their flashlights, looking for it, and yet he found it right away, first time."

"An unbelievable mistake on his part," said the professor.

"How could he have made it? What happened to him at that moment?"

"Perhaps the phenomenon of instant personality split: at that very moment he became the policeman hunting for himself." Enigmatically, as though talking to himself, he added: "Pirandello."

"I want to tell you about every single thing, starting from the light switch. I am putting it all together with mathematical precision."

"Mathematical." The professor smiled. "But there is always some lurking doubt."

"That is why I am asking your help."

"What little I can do ... Why not come up to my house. We'll be more peaceful."

They spoke for hours, coming to the conclusion that as far as the gang was concerned, the canvas was an ill-advised venture, a marginal activity, almost a piece of whimsy. The place was being used for quite different purposes, and that was why the unfortunate Roccella, turning up unexpectedly, had to be murdered.

As they stood at the door, saying good night, the professor asked: "Do you intend ... ?"

"I really do not know," answered the brigadier, unnerved and distraught. "I just do not know."

T he following morning, the inspector arrived at the office at the usual time, in his customary high, almost euphoric, spirits. He removed his hat, his gloves, his overcoat, his bright but elegant scarf; he stuck the gloves in the pockets of his coat and hung everything in his personal closet. The gloves. While the inspector, as every other morning, was trembling with the cold, saying that the birds would fall dead from the sky, the brigadier was already behind his desk, trembling for a different reason. The gloves, of course, the gloves.

"Hard at work already," said the inspector, by way of greeting.

"It's hardly work. I'm just reading the morning papers."

"Anything interesting?"

"Interesting, no; no more than usual."

Behind that exchange of banal and unremarkable pleasantries there lay an unease, a coldness, a feeling of fear and anxiety.

The switch. The gloves. The brigadier neither knew, nor would have appreciated, a famous series of engravings by Max Klinger with the appropriate title *A Glove,* but in his mind the inspector's glove flew, soared, and puffed itself out as a glove had once done in the imagination of Max Klinger.

They sat at their desks, at right angles, the inspector pretending to be immersed in the documents in front of him, the brigadier in the perusal of the newspapers.

Several times the brigadier was on the point of rising to his feet and going to the chief superintendent to make a full report, but he was held back by the thought that the chief superintendent would regard all he had to say as lacking substance. The inspector—as the brigadier immediately noticed—had other and more directly murderous thoughts on his mind.

After a certain time, the inspector got up and went over to a little cupboard, took out a bottle of lubricating oil, a woolen cloth, and a pipe cleaner. He said: "It must be years since I gave my gun a good cleaning."

He removed it from the holster on his belt, placed it carefully on the table, opened the barrel, and let the bullets fall onto the tabletop.

The brigadier understood immediately. On the newspaper, which he held open in front of his face and continued to pretend to read, the inspector saw the words dissolve, melt, and merge into one huge headline, which he believed he could read on the following day's front page: POLICE INSPECTOR KILLS JUNIOR OFFICER IN TRAGIC ACCIDENT.

He said: "I always clean my own ... are you a good shot?"

"Excellent," said the inspector.

The brigadier, to give due warning and keep faith with his own conscience, went on: "To be a good shot, it's not enough to score a bull's-eye. You need swiftness of hand, skill."

"I know." No, you don't, thought the brigadier, you don't know at all. Or at least, you don't know the way I do.

Every morning, he meticulously placed his own pistol in the top right-hand drawer of the desk, and now he leaned over and opened it slowly, quietly, with his right hand, while with the left he kept the paper upright in front of him. His fingers had suddenly acquired a greater nimbleness, his hands seemed in some way to have multiplied, and each of his senses was keenly alert. Every part of his being quivered like a fine, tightly drawn cord, while the atavistic instinct of the peasant to be distrustful, suspicious, vigilant, to expect the worst and not be surprised by it when it came, had been reawakened in him to the point of paroxysm.

The inspector finished cleaning his pistol, reloaded it, gripped it firmly in his hand, taking mock aim at the calendar, the light bulb, the door handle, but at the moment when, with unexpected speed, he swung around, pointed it at the brigadier, and fired, the brigadier had already thrown himself and his chair to the floor, had pulled from behind the newspaper in his left hand the pistol he had removed from the drawer, had fired a shot at the inspector's heart. Now he was watching him crumple on top of the papers spread in front of him, staining them with blood.

"He was a good shot," said the brigadier, gazing at the bullet hole on the wall behind his desk, "but I did warn him." He sounded for a moment as though he had won a prize, but immediately afterward he burst into tears and his teeth began chattering uncontrollably.

W here have we got to?" said the chief superintendent. "Can we recapitulate and decide what we're doing? I mean, recapitulate and let the procurator decide what he's doing. The journalists will be banging at the door in no time."

They were in the procurator's office. The carabinieri colonel was there too, with the brigadier standing in front of them like an accused in the high court dock.

"Where are we, then? According to the brigadier's account—an account, I may say, not without corroborative detail and elements to which, I am obliged to admit, I failed to attach due weight—according to this account, the material facts are those which I will now briefly set out. On the evening of the eighteenth, a telephone call from Signor Roccella was logged in the police station. He requested someone to go to his house in order to see a certain object. The brigadier replied that someone would go at the earliest opportunity. He then communicated the content of the call to the inspector, offering to go himself. The inspector claims not to believe in the return of Signor Roccella after so many years. He considers the matter a hoax. He tells the brigadier to drop by at the locus the following morning and goes off, having announced that for the whole of the following day, being the Feast of Saint Joseph, he will be out of circulation, as indeed proved to be the case. It takes no great effort to suspect that he used the time to alert his accomplices to the unforeseen return of Signor Roccella, and takes even less effort to suspect that he went there in person, had himself admitted in his capacity as police inspector, sat at Roccella's side at the desk where the latter had begun to write about the canvas he had just found, and then, at the right moment, since the pistol on the desktop presented an unhoped-for opportunity, took the gun in his gloved hand and shot Roccella in the head. He then added a full stop after 'I have found,' and having closed the door, which had a spring lock, behind him, he went out. I have to say, in self-criticism, that the full stop after 'I have found,' which the brigadier indicated to me as incongruous, did not at the time make any impact on me. I regarded Roccella as on the verge of insanity and believed that he had come to see suicide as the solution. I further believed that he passionately desired to kill himself under the very eyes of the police. However, the following day the body would unfailingly have been discovered. Hence the need for the speedy evacuation. At dead of night, the whole gang was summoned to the spot. The painting and other implements of clandestine work were transported elsewhere."

"Where?" asked the magistrate.

"In the opinion of the brigadier, which I fully share, to the Monterosso station. The stationmaster and his assistant were members of the gang, even if fringe members, involved in distribution or drug pushing. Doubtless, on seeing that quantity of compromising material being delivered, the pair of them took fright. They must have made protests, threats. As a result, they were killed. They were already dead when the Volvo man made his appearance at the station. This explains his sudden flight. The Volvo man did not see the stationmaster and his assistant; he saw their killers: this has been established by showing him photographs of the murdered men. He denied having seen them. Subsequently there was the episode of the light switch, which made a deep impression—not only, I may say, on the brigadier."

"What an idiot!" said the magistrate. It was the only panegyric the inspector would receive. He went on: "On the other hand, my dear Colonel, my dear Chief Superintendent, this is not quite enough. Suppose we were to reverse the whole story and consider that the brigadier might be lying. What if he were responsible for the deeds of which he is now accusing the inspector?"

Chief superintendent and colonel exchanged knowing looks that expressed the "Dear God!" and "Terrifying!" that a few days previously they had been able to exchange in words.

"It is out of the question," they both said at the same time. The chief superintendent invited the brigadier to step outside a moment: "Go into the waiting room. We'll call you back in five minutes."

It was more than an hour before they summoned him back.

"An accident," said the magistrate.

"An accident," said the chief superintendent.

"An accident," said the colonel.

And the following day, in the morning papers: FATAL ACCIDENT—BRIGADIER CLEANING GUN SHOOTS INSPECTOR.

W hile they were preparing the room in the police station in which to lay out the inspector's body—it had been decided that he would be buried with full honors—the Volvo man was released from prison. He was brought to the station to go through the bureaucratic procedures that would grant him, finally, his liberty.

Having completed the formalities, he was making his way out of the station, flushed and nervously giggling, when he ran into Father Cricco, resplendent in surplice, biretta, and stole, who was arriving to perform the last rites on the corpse.

Father Cricco stopped him with a gesture. He said: "Don't I know you? Aren't you one of my parishioners?"

"Parishioner! Me! I don't belong to anyone's parish," said the man, and went on his way, deliriously happy.

He discovered a parking ticket on the windshield of his Volvo, but such was his state of mind that he merely laughed it off.

He was singing as he left the city, but all of a sudden he drew up sharply. His mood grew darker, his anxiety returned in full force. That priest, he said to himself. That priest ... I would have recognized him immediately if it hadn't been for the clerical garb. That was the stationmaster, or at least the one I took for the stationmaster.

For a moment, he was about to turn back to the police station, but he changed his mind on the instant: What are you thinking about? Going back there to get yourself into an even bigger mess?

He continued on his journey home, singing at the top of his voice.

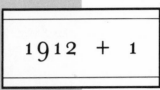

$$1912 \; + \; 1$$

TRANSLATED FROM THE ITALIAN BY

SACHA RABINOVITCH

—Shall we go?

—Let's go.

—Shall we go back?

—Let's go back.

ALDO PALAZZESCHI
La Passeggiata

At least once—and perhaps throughout the year 1913—D'Annunzio wrote the date "1912 + 1." This was in a copy of one of his books and could have been dictated by his own superstition or by that of the dedicatee or by both. For in northern Italy, 13 is considered to be an unlucky number, like 17 in the south—a discrepancy that still persists today but which at the time was so ingrained that southerners had turned the figure 13 into a mascot, a sort of talisman. I still remember the gold pendants engraved with the number dangling from a waistcoat pocket on the majestic paunch of every wealthy landowner. But D'Annunzio, opting for the north insofar as he was a native of the Abruzzi who had triumphantly crossed the border, may have wanted to rush through 1913 blindfolded, as it were. Yet 1913, despite the ill wind still blowing for him in Italy, the debts he couldn't pay, which forced him into exile in Arcachon, was his lucky year—or rather one that could be included among those equally and increasingly lucky years that led right up to the advent of fascism.

In that year exile itself was gilded with a success that in France and the world at large attained its peak. A success that had been growing for ten years or so but flared up then as he was acclaimed to all intents and purposes as a French writer translated into Italian. Already, eight years before, at a performance of *La Gioconda* at the Oeuvre, it was Léon Blum who led the prolonged applause. During the intermission a bitter exchange took place between Blum and Jules Renard. "You seem to be angry," said Blum. To which Renard retorted: "Yes. Because of your enthusiasm." And I believe that my early distaste for D'Annunzio and my actual impatience when I read him may be related to Renard's reply. Far more unbearable than D'Annunzio is the D'Annunzio cult (now esoteric) and unbearable the "D'Annunziani": even those who have never read him, will never read him, and know just enough about him—about his life, his fascism—to believe they are remote from him. But it must be said for the sake of the truth that the Socialist Blum's enthusiasm at the Oeuvre in that distant 1905 can also be seen as a sign—and many were to follow—of the unpredictable inconsistencies within socialism, within the various socialisms and among Socialists.

It isn't hard to imagine Blum's enthusiasm for this French D'Annunzio and for D'Annunzio's French. And I dwell on Blum to give substance to the idea of D'Annunzio's fame in those years, in that year. For as a Socialist in Italy, one could be against the war in Libya only at the cost of feeling guilty, excluded from the feat where, above the waving flags and bersaglieri plumes, the resounding brass bands, and the magnificence of all the patriotic, revivalist tinsel, one heard "Le canzoni della gesta d'oltremare," which D'Annunzio sent from Arcachon to the *Corriere della Sera*. Generals and admirals, soldiers and sailors fallen on the Libyan shores, provided material for the poet's song, and the poet provided the "chosen people" of Italy with his songs. Pascoli, the gentle Pascoli, had contributed his own encouraging fare-well: "The great proletariat has moved" toward the "fourth shore," toward Libya, toward Tripoli. And maybe there was some confusion between Tripoli in Libya and Tripoli in Sy-ria—a confusion that was due to the fact that until then the name Tripoli was engraved in the memory of every Italian because of the moving love story that another poet, who didn't survive to sing the overseas exploits, had recounted in lines that, for all those of my generation, are still unforget-table. (One of which, evoked by the tale I am about to tell, persistently surfaces: "Contessa, what then is life?") It is the story of the Provençal troubadour Jaufré Rudel's undying love for Melisande, countess of Tripoli. Tripoli in Syria. Whence perhaps the song, almost a hymn or march, that accompanied the national anthem and in which Tripoli is referred to as the "fair land of love." Love in a land that is no longer out of reach and of which D'Annunzio relished the flavors, sniffed the perfumes, glimpsed the sands and palm trees, dawns and sunsets: Book IV of his *Laudi*, "Merope"— ten songs (one to Helen of France, duchess of Aosta, whose *Viaggi in Africa* was to be published by Treves the following year—Thursday October 16, to be precise).

"Fair France," "A golden face like Fiordaliso," trips to Africa (even to transport the dead to their "maternal tombs" and the wounded to the Palermo hospital)—everything was grist to the mill for D'Annunzio, luxuriously exiled amid women and greyhounds in Arcachon. He sang and sang: "The fierce breath, the drenched cheeks, the endless toil with heads bent, wrists between the spokes of the wheel, shoulders weighed down by the packs, the order to shoot, taking aim, the first shots into the enemy ranks, the bared soil, the hoarse cries from parched throats as company after company is destroyed, the desperate thirst for danger, oh, Ameglio, and the cold iron ..." (All this is of course in verse, but I am writing it in prose to convey—since prose is ruthless—how really senseless and atrocious it is.) And in Palermo, where General Ameglio (appointed Governor of Cyrenaica after the war was over and guerrilla warfare had begun) was born, the "cold iron" sung by the poet materialized in the form of an ostentatious and festive gift: a double-edged sword whose gold and silver hilt was decorated with battle scenes, female figures, and emblems by the local sculptor Mario Rutelli (sculptor of the nymphs on the Esedra fountain). The overelaborate hilt bore the inscription: "To Giovanni Ameglio from his native town. Palermo MCMXIII."

The guerrilla warfare in Cyrenaica was stimulating. Military tribunals were in constant action judging rebels—every one of them doomed to the firing squad. Intermittent reports reached Italy: sketches, photographs. I wonder with what feelings the Italian public responded to the photograph I have before me now, which portrays the execution of an Arab in the desert. The firing squad lined up in two rows, the captain about to give the order to shoot, and the commanding officer at a considerable distance from the squad, lost in the undulations of the dunes. Dated August 1913. 1912 + 1.

On October 26, 1913, the Parliament of the Realm is elected by vote—for the first time by universal, or almost universal, suffrage. From 3,200,000 votes in the previous election, the number reaches 8,550,000. A gigantic leap. And who can tell (the usual qualms) if it's a leap in the dark?

By and large, the press and the traditionalists can't understand why the crafty Giolitti* should ever have wanted universal suffrage. It's surely a lapse, a blunder.

Election day passes peacefully enough on the whole. The odd stabbing, the odd beating up, a few gunshots. In Parma, Filippo Corridoni—an agitated political agitator and trade unionist—is arrested. Italians of my generation, however, will recall him, from the days when fascism reigned supreme in the classroom, as a man of order—quiet and tidy in appearance, with a starched collar and tie. His birthplace, Pausula in the province of Macerata, would later take his name.

But Giolitti was right. Fears that the 5,300,000 new voters might opt for a Socialist Parliament were unfounded. From 58 the Socialist deputies rise to 78. The left, or nominal left, as a whole has 165 votes. Whereas the majority, behind the aging Giolitti, who complains of being tired and of needing

*Giovanni Giolitti (1842–1928), five times prime minister of Italy, including the period March 1911–March 1914.—Ed.

a rest, has 348. Only Bologna can boast of an "unhoped for" Socialist triumph. In the *Carlino,* Bergeret (Marroni) takes comfort in the fact that: "Experience has shown that when a monarchy requires ministers competent in maintaining order—the kind who are willing to let the police fire at the mob—it always finds them if it seeks them among the lawyers who entered Parliament under the revolutionary banner. In ten years' time ..." A prediction that aims well beyond the stipulated time limit but which was, in fact, to be punctually fulfilled.

But what was happening in Italy to disprove those disconsolate forecasts of an overwhelming Socialist success resulting from universal suffrage? This is what was happening: Relying on the natural and individual wisdom of the Italian people—nicely epitomized in the saying (still in favor today) that the devil you know, however terrible, is always preferable to the devil you don't—a provincial nobleman, a legal criminologist whose favorite pastimes were agriculture and hunting and who was also a private (and active) attendant upon His Holiness, having been put in charge of a Catholic Electoral Union, had devised a pact based on seven articles, which would ensure the totality of Catholic votes to those traditionalists who accepted it. Apparently 330 parliamentary candidates signed it, and at least 228 of these were elected—a reasonable percentage! This was the Gentiloni Pact—from Count Vincenzo Ottorino Gentiloni, born in Filotrano in the district of Ancona in 1865. Thus in 1913, at the age of forty-eight, he was, to judge by his portraits, still a pleasure-loving man in his prime. However, he would survive by only three years the overwhelming success of his pact.

Before this success Count Gentiloni was unknown, his name no more than that of a pact. But as soon as the electoral result became public, everybody began to ask who the crafty and mysterious author of this pact might be. And first of all, what was his Christian name, the "gentle readers" of the *Illustrazione Italiana* wanted to know? And if the "gentle readers" were intrigued, what must the whole population's reaction have been! After hurried inquiries, the *Illustrazione* was able to reply that Gentiloni was called Ottorino—ignoring or suppressing his first name in its eagerness to impart that Ottorino was "short" for Ottone, that Ottone was Bismarck's name, and that Gentiloni, in this recent electoral event, had been "a sort of Bismarck," in miniature, of course, and in minor matters, but of comparable skill. Vincenzo Ottorino— this recalls Antonio Baldini's joke about Aleardo Aleardi, who had been christened not Aleardo but Gaetano: "The opinions of a true Aleardo couched in true Gaetano terms, and the opinions of a true Gaetano in Aleardo terms." Thus Count Gentiloni, at a given point, behaves like a Vincenzo and deigns to be interviewed by the press. The same *Illustrazione* deplores the fact: "The spell of the mystery is broken—the charm has been dispelled." But since I prefer the name Vin- cenzo to Ottorino, I find that when he behaves like a Vin- cenzo and reveals what there was to reveal, Gentiloni puts the final touch to his enterprise. He had not, as the Italians liked to believe, created a more secret, genuine, and powerful Freemasonry—he had created that Roman Catholic policy which partially, and precisely only partially, would later be called a party: the People's party of Don Luigi Sturzo; the Christian Democratic party of De Gasperi, Fanfani, and Moro.* I say partially because the rest would merge and

---

*Don Luigi Sturzo (1871–1959), Sicilian priest and leader of the *popolari*, a Catholic party somewhat inclined to the left. Alcide De Gasperi (1881–1954), Chris-

dissolve into the general policy of political non-saying and non-action—leaving only the odd scrap or crumb of reticence.

While the Gentiloni Pact triumphed, Cardinal Mariano Rampolla del Tindaro died in Rome. As secretary of state to Leo XIII, he would normally have been his successor. But when, at the first ballot of the conclave after Leo's death in 1903, he had twenty-nine votes, the cardinal archbishop of Vienna was obliged to announce the Austrian emperor's veto. This could have been ignored—indeed, at the second ballot Rampolla obtained thirty votes. But it was a short-lived revolt. Cardinal Sarto was finally elected as Pius X. Perhaps more than the imperial veto (which condemned Rampolla's long-standing friendship with France), what influenced the conclave was his inflexibility, his staunch defense of the *"Non expedit."* (Panzini, *Dizionario Moderno:* "A Latin phrase signifying *it is not expedient,* not necessary, therefore forbidden. *Non expedit* is the Apostolic Chancery's proper ritual formula when nothing requested is to be granted. In political terms, this *Non expedit* signified until the present day the prohibition imposed in Italy on all good Roman Catholics against participation in political elections, since such participation implied the recognition of the events which led to the abolition of Papal temporal power.")

This was the beginning of that long period—which still prevails and in all probability will outlive us—of transactions, reconciliations, and agreements, accompanied by a more or less clamorous publicity. The Gentiloni Pact. The Lateran Pact. Article VII of the Lateran Pact voted by the Republican

tian Democrat prime minister 1945-53. Amintore Fanfani (1908-), secretary of the Christian Democrat party, prime minister 1960-63. Aldo Moro (1916-78), prime minister 1963-68, president of the National Council of Christian Democrats when he was assassinated by the Red Brigades.—Ed.

Assembly. The National Union or Coalition, on whose altar Moro was recently sacrificed.

And I recall as a sort of "cautionary tale" the one occasion on which I saw and heard Giorgio La Pira.* At Messina during the great Antonello exhibition, thirty years ago. Pira described, not to me but to his old friends Vann'Antò and Pugliatti, whom I had joined, the parliamentary City Council in Florence and what it sought to achieve and occasionally did achieve. An agreement. "We must agree," he kept repeating. "We must all agree." He made constant gestures with his little hands as though to shape it materially, this agreement—a soft, malleable substance. It made me giddy. So I withdrew as from a window open on the void and contemplated Antonello's paintings. Which didn't seem to agree. Luminous and cold as diamonds, every single one of them—and the portraits stared down skeptically, ironically.

T he text of the Gentiloni Pact is brief and informal and unemphatic—subdued and modest. Only when referring to divorce does it become decisive and intransigent: "Total opposition to divorce." A pact *to which anybody could subscribe.* Even the most rabid petitioners for divorce couldn't fail to admit that the Italians were not yet

*Giorgio La Pira (1904–), Catholic mayor of Florence, who tried to create a dialogue with the Communists after World War II.—Ed.

"ripe for divorce"—with the approval of a good proportion of the "unripe." This matter of the Italian's "unripeness" for certain liberties, even for liberty itself, is an amusing if irksome opinion, which, from the summits where it is propounded, descends to find ample acknowledgment at the base. In the train, on the bus, at gatherings and in waiting rooms, every conversation on liberties and liberty is rounded off with the wistful remark that "we aren't yet ripe for it." At least we are ripe enough to know that we are "unripe"—which may lead to decay.

Among the seven articles of the Gentiloni Pact, what emerges from the general vagueness as at all significant is: "opposition to any bill against religious instruction and which tends in any way to disturb the nation's religious stability"; "that no proviso be made to hinder or discredit the institution of private education"; "to provide legal facilities and efficient practical guarantees to entitle fathers to obtain serious religious instruction for their children in state schools"; "to withstand any attempt to undermine the unity of the family— and therefore total opposition to divorce." A program keenly upheld later by the Fascist government and the Lateran Pact, not to mention the ample support it obtained subsequently from the governments of the reestablished democracy.

Thus, foremost in the thoughts of Count Gentiloni and the Catholic Electoral Union, foremost among their preoccupations, was the family, the unity of the family. And at this point—two weeks after the elections and while the papers were still busy calculating the gains and losses of the parties, the majority's stability and that of the opposition; still writing biographies of successful candidates and waving a perfunctory goodbye to unsuccessful ones; especially busy praising Count Gentiloni's foresight and the toughness and positiveness of his policy (even while wishing that he were less explicit, more reticent and mysterious)—there emerged somewhat clamorously in San Remo an affair that could be seen as characteristic of the Gentiloni Pact, in all that it implied and all that it concealed, in all that concurs to make me see it today as ambiguous and typical, typically ambiguous, ambiguously typical.

On November 8, 1913, Contessa Maria Tiepolo, wife of Captain Carlo Ferruccio Oggioni, shoots her husband's orderly, the bersagliere Quintilio Polimanti.

Signora Maria Oggioni, née Tiepolo. But in the papers she figures as Contessa Tiepolo. At first she is said to be a descendant of "the famous painter Tiepolo." Later, however, the doges take over: "the family of the Venetian Doge." Longanesi remarks fifty years later that: "There isn't a Communist who, sitting beside a duke, doesn't feel a thrill of joy." Fancy what thrills of joy must have been experienced when writing and speaking about Contessa Tiepolo rather than Signora Oggioni! With the added thrill of knowing that, with a single shot, the contessa had put an end to a bersagliere's life! A bersagliere, native of Monsampietro Morico in Piceno, who gets his own share of promotion from the press: from the "carpenter" he had been until his national service, he becomes an "ebanista" (cabinetmaker). According to Tommaseo's Dictionary: "An 'ebanista' should work only in ebony, but in some parts of Italy a cabinetmaker who makes refined objects even out of ordinary wood is called an 'ebanista.' " I myself, since early youth an assiduous frequenter of carpenters' establishments, where I would have liked to learn the trade, have never seen in them a single piece of ebony; thus I had assumed that of all the carpenters of the town, the one known as "ebanista" (in honor of his superior skill) must have earned this title through trials and tests carried out on a piece of ebony—a wood that served, I knew, in the fabrication of certain expensive walking sticks. But Quintilio Polimanti had earned his title through his death. "Ebanista." However, he was mainly known as the plaintiff. Or the bersagliere, and the orderly, which was more fitting and seemed to identify him more aptly than his name, which was rather hard to remember and Savinian *avant la lettre.** Quintilio Polimanti. And he had a brother called Paride—Paris—and an uncle called Priamo—Priam.

The fact that he had been enrolled as a bersagliere proves that he was sturdy and agile, broad-chested and deep-lunged, a capable and untiring runner. A bersagliere, except when off duty, must always run. And "sweep all before him." On command, General Alessandro Lamarmora created the corps for rapid disposition and sweeping action. And maybe that bunch of iridescent feathers cascading from their hats was also his idea. And not cock's feathers for nothing, but to add that touch of Italian cockiness.

Local reporters having been launched on the tracks of Polimanti and family, the papers informed readers the following day that his father and uncle still lived in Monsampietro Morico, where they owned a "cigarette store"—that is, they were tobacconists—whereas Quintilio, together with his brother Paride, a tailor, had moved to Fermo; that Quintilio was better known as a cyclist than as an "ebanista"; that he was a pleasant, fun-loving youth; and that all those who knew him were surprised to hear that he had settled for the "humble duties of a batman."

---

*Alberto Savinio (1891–1952), major exponent of surrealist taste and theory in Italy; painter, musicologist, and writer.—Ed.

A batman. Or, more romantically, an orderly. Foscolo plays with the term: "Give orders to your orderly..." And De Amicis in *Vita militare* relates his own experiences with two orderlies, one of them upright, reserved, and humble, the other senseless and irresponsible. He describes the latter as "an eccentric." But he was, in fact, a fool—and one doesn't see why he put up with him, since he gave him nothing but trouble, without any affection to make up for it.

But for an exact definition we must turn to Alberto Guglielmotti's *Vocabolario marino e militare* (some passages of which have been skillfully—truly skillfully—put into verse by D'Annunzio): "*A naval or military orderly* was until recently one of those soldiers or sailors who had been exempted from normal duties and was employed solely in the personal service of some officer." Which makes it abundantly clear why Quintilio Polimanti chose to assume this perhaps humble role, one that nonetheless exempted him from the exhausting duties of the parade ground—very exhausting indeed for a bersagliere. Those of Polimanti's fellow citizens who were surprised by his role as batman had perhaps never done their national service; or their memories of it, linked to their happy youth, were invested with its flattering hues. After a couple of days' drill, the young peasant or craftsman who has, as they say, joined up, will—if he has any sense and no special vocation for endless marches under rain or sun with a twenty-kilo pack on his back and the constant risk of being confined to barracks on bread and water for the slightest mistake—eagerly apply for the post of batman. Among the men I used to hear long ago reminiscing around the threshing floor or in their shops about their years in the army or at war, the shrewdest were those who had found a certain degree of safety by acting as batmen. Some would recall the foibles and eccentricities of the officers they waited upon—or those of their wives and children; but with indulgence and affection, like the orderly in De Amicis (not the eccentric one). And more than the officer, it was the wife, the children, who figured in these reminiscences, these anecdotes—which were always entertaining and sometimes, when the wife was involved, worthy of Boccaccio.

"Better a pig than a soldier" was a current saying—referring mainly to the rations, that nauseating bean and pasta soup in those nauseating mess tins. (Since each soldier had to wash his own, this consisted in holding them under the cold-water tap for a second or so; and they were passed on to the following intake of conscripts without ever being properly cleansed.) But a batman, on the other hand, returned to the barracks only at night; he was exempted from mess and reveille timetables. And he could delude himself—nor was it always a delusion—that he was leading a family life amid family feelings and concerns. He did the daily shopping, on his own or with the lady of the house, took the kids to school and went to fetch them back, and polished the silver; if he happened to be a tailor by trade, he was given clothes to mend or to alter; if a carpenter or a mechanic, there was the garden or the henhouse—a frequent appendage in those days.

National service was much longer than it is today. But Polimanti was about to be discharged—a matter of days. And this is perhaps what precipitated the tragedy, whatever its motive may have been—whether the legitimate defense of her honor, as the contessa and her supporters maintained, or, according to the majority, a means of putting an end to a risky relationship, or indeed some other, more sinister and complex motive.

The contessa had declared from the start that "the orderly had tried to come into her bedroom and rape her and that she, seizing the gun, had shot and killed him." *Il Messaggero* of November 9 states: "This seems to be the correct version" and heads the article: "To Protect Her Honor." However, it adds that the lady is "very beautiful" and that Polimanti was "a tall, handsome youth with curly golden hair." Details that cast upon that "seems" various shades of diffidence or doubt—or turn it into something quite different. In Italy, to say that between a beautiful woman and a handsome man who have lived for months under the same roof, often alone, nothing has occurred involving their emotions and instincts is simply a contradiction in terms. And indeed, a few days later the same paper notes that public opinion is not satisfied with the version that had seemed correct and that many people see in the incident—and in certain facts concerning the contessa, which the paper refrains from reporting—evidence of love or a love affair between the contessa and the orderly, which, for reasons as yet unknown, came to this tragic conclusion. "The truth will emerge only at the judicial inquiry." In the meantime, friends and relatives reveal that the contessa had been suffering from epileptic fits for about three years and that, in fact, a few days before the incident she experienced a violent one.

However, while Polimanti's remains were still in the bersagliere barracks' mortuary, pending the arrival of his parents for the funeral, the contessa had named, as lawyer for the defense, Orazio Raimondi, a Socialist recently elected as deputy for the constituency of Oneglia, who had already had occasion to speak at great length in Parliament. Rather than avail himself of the Socialist party's insignificant progress to defeat his "moderate" opponent, the Onorevole Marsaglia, Raimondi based his electoral campaign on the memory, still vivid in Oneglia, of his grandfather Onorevole Biancheri, who had been president of the Chamber of Deputies. Thus Contessa Tiepolo was indeed in good hands: Raimondi was a militant Socialist with a liberal background. And he was, according to parliamentary reports, gifted with a fluent and resounding rhetoric. If eight months later the papers speak of him as an "ex-Socialist representative," this implies that he had left the party but doubtless asserting that he held to its policy—a case not dissimilar to many we have witnessed in the last forty years. More than any other, the Socialist party is subject to dissensions and defections—due to the assumption (or presumption) that one is more Socialist than the party tolerates at the moment. But more often than not, the defector who states that he is more Socialist than his party is in fact less so—or perhaps even no longer a Socialist at all.

After barely more than a week, the Tiepolo affair ceases to make the headlines. Other topics have taken over: the tango, newly arrived from Paris; *Parsifal* produced at La Scala with an intermission that allows the public ample time to dine (a subject of controversy between those who find this novelty very pleasing, for a change, and those who criticize it in the name of Italian traditionalism); and there is the reappearance in Florence of Leonardo's *Mona Lisa* or *Gioconda*, stolen from the Louvre two years earlier. It had vanished inexplicably, mysteriously; its recovery is somewhat trivial. The thief turns out to have been an Italian workman who wanted to restore it to his country—not without any advantage to himself. General disappointment: the public had imagined some picaresque hero, and all they have is a housepainter already known to the police for some minor theft or infraction. Thus it became an excuse for blaming the French police force: they knew the Italian housepainter was one of the workmen who had gone into the Louvre on the day of the robbery and had even questioned him, but they hadn't bothered to compare his fingerprints with those left on the empty frame of Leonardo's masterpiece, nor to search the room he occupied, where it had lain under his bed for two years, depriving innumerable viewers of the Gioconda smile. A smile that José Ortega y Gasset would try to desecrate and "His Master's Voice" to trivialize, selecting the figure of the Gioconda to decorate their boxes of gramophone needles; not to mention the Futurists' childish and admittedly rather silly idea of adorning that smile with a great drooping mustache. But perhaps it was his vision or re-vision of the *Mona Lisa* in Florence that inspired Aldous Huxley's far wittier joke in the tale called "The Gioconda Smile," which, to me, is an inevitable, if perhaps fortuitous, reminder of Contessa Tiepolo. Was the contessa's smile like Mona Lisa's?

But even the *Mona Lisa*—whose restitution to France signals a revival of Latin fraternity and, given the remarks on the occasion both in France and in Italy, reminds us that the Triple Alliance between Italy, Austria, and Germany isn't perhaps quite as harmonious and happy as the Marquis of San Giuliano would have us believe—even the *Mona Lisa* is obliterated by the tango craze. Thus Marinetti, an opponent of the tango since the previous year, when it was launched in Paris, publishes a "Futurist circular letter": "Down with the tango and *Parsifal.*" *Parsifal* as well: "a cooperative factory of sadness and despair." But who would dare say such a thing to present-day *Parsifal* enthusiasts?

D'Annunzio, it is said, called Marinetti a fool with odd sparks of imbecility. And one could say that the letter against the tango and *Parsifal* is sparkling—but in this day and age it might be seen as a spark of brilliance, of genius. Oh, these trailblazers! At least five thousand misprints have been found to date (since 1922) in Joyce's *Ulysses.* But Professor Richard Ellman, editor of the final corrected edition, observes reassuringly that "since the book was reputed to be incomprehensible, the misprints passed unnoticed. When readers found a passage obscure, they thought the fault was Joyce's." I haven't the original text before me, but can Professor Ellman really have said "fault"? Whose fault? Neither Joyce's nor the typographer's. And if fault there was, *felix culpa.* Happy, lucky fault. Most happy, most lucky.

On April 29, 1914, the contessa's trial opens at the Oneglia superior court. Many more people would have attended than the courtroom can accommodate. But for the most part they must be content with seeing the contessa arrive in a closed carriage and go inside, veiled, flanked by two carabinieri. Not until she is seated in the courtroom does she remove her veil. She is a beautiful woman and must appear extremely lovely, with her pale, delicate face, light chestnut, almost golden hair, bright, clear eyes, and profound gaze. The spectators are struck but not moved. Nearly everybody has come to confirm what they knew already: that the law is not the same for everyone, that justice is unjust. When Polimanti's mother arrives, crying: "Where is my son?" then and only then does a tremor of emotion flow through the crowd and reach the accused, who fumbles in her handbag for a handkerchief and smelling salts. These, which have now disappeared from a lady's accessories, were then an indispensable item. Contained in tiny cut-glass or silver phials, they were a mixture of pungent salts, which were supposed to have revivifying properties when sniffed. But perhaps at a given point—or so I seem to recall— smelling salts were no more than sulfurated ether, a combination of ether (the poet's ether) and sulfur: in other words, the purest heaven mixed with the earth's infernal vein. When heaven and hell existed.

The morning is spent over a first motion on the part of the plaintiff's lawyers, Rossi and De Bello. They request that a specialist answer for the accused's soundness of mind and judgment, in order to forestall any doubts on the subject that the jury might raise. They had assumed that by anticipating the defense in asking for a psychiatric assessment, they would unsettle them. But Raimondi dispels any such hope: he is not opposed to the request; he has no objection to it; but he considers that such an assessment is irrelevant, whatever its outcome—his strategy will be to plead legitimate defense. The prosecution withdraws its request, apparently defeated in this first motion. But in fact they had probably thus unwittingly obtained an insight into their opponents' strategy for the defense.

In the afternoon, the contessa relates in slow, even tones and a strong Venetian accent the events of that fatal day: "That morning I wasn't feeling too well because I'd spent a practically sleepless night. At about ten o'clock I heard the bell and went to open the door. It was the orderly who attends to the stairs, not Polimanti, who was out taking the children to school. I saw him later as I was going to the kitchen. He came toward me and tried to kiss me, saying that he loved me. I repulsed him and withdrew to my room, locking the door, but he knocked on the door and begged me to let him in. I didn't answer and went back to bed. But shortly after, I decided that it was time to put an end to this state of affairs; it would be a mistake to stay there, and I decided to pack my bags and go away at once. Later the orderly came and knocked on the door again, asking for instructions concerning the meal he had to cook. Thinking he wouldn't try to renew his attack, I opened the door and found myself thus face-to-face with Polimanti, who, clasping me in his arms, said: 'You must be mine, you must be mine, I've been wanting it for too long!' I resisted him for some time, struggling with all my might. When I felt he was beginning to give up, I seized the opportunity to break free from his embrace and managed to get him out of the room. Then I grabbed the revolver from a drawer of the chest and aimed at Polimanti, who was still talking to me. I said: 'If you don't go away I'll shoot.' But he, instead of being impressed, came toward me with open arms as though to embrace me, saying: 'I'm not afraid.' So I fired, and the boy, struck in the face, from which I saw blood gushing, fell to the ground." "Thus Signora Oggioni Tiepolo concludes her account somewhat coldly, having overcome the agitation to which she had first appeared to be prey," states the report. The reporter should have been more subtle and sensitive in describing the passage from agitation to coldness. He seems to have noticed it only because the opposite would have been more natural, her agitation increasing to the point of tears—as is customary. Indeed, he himself is so upset that he unconsciously distances himself from the accused, dissociates himself from her: "Signora Oggioni Tiepolo."

There are many questions this brief account might have suggested to the public prosecutor and the prosecution lawyers. But they are persuaded that others they already have in store will be more emphatic and convincing—circumstantial evidence to prove that a guilty relationship existed between the contessa and the orderly and that the crime was almost certainly premeditated. Nor can they wait to reveal this evidence and confront the accused with it. Thus the story of the locket immediately emerges, together with its mysterious disappearance. It was a double-faced locket encircled in gold; one of those lockets that today are only seen dangling from a chain on the breast of some widow or bereaved mother but that betrothed couples used to wear at the time and that contained each other's portraits: the girls wore them exposed, the men (especially if the relationship was clandestine) wore them tucked inside the collar of their shirts as a hidden (sometimes purloined) amulet. Polimanti's double locket contained a picture of the contessa on one side and a lock of hair on the other.

The contessa admitted that she was aware of the locket's existence. Polimanti had shown it to her only the night before, taking it not from under his shirt but from his trouser pocket. The contessa had been amazed: "How do you happen to have my portrait?" How indeed? That's what the prosecution lawyers, the public prosecutor, the president, the jury, the courtroom audience, and the readers of the daily papers would dearly have liked to know. And quite frankly, me too. It wasn't easy to obtain a young woman's photograph without her knowledge in those days and in what was then a particularly reserved social group. To be in possession of it implied either betrothal or close kinship. And even in the case of kinship, it implied a more or less final separation: a man would wear it or receive it as a souvenir when oceans were about to intervene (and the word America rings like a death knell). Polimanti could have stolen it, of course; but harder to account for was the lock of hair. It was the custom then for women to wear their hair long and done up in a bun. This was an added charm, if one is to judge by the way old men when I was young would praise and lament the plaiting and knotting of those tresses in a bun. An unparalleled symbol of modesty and reserve. And of sensuality. Thus in Cordova, in the gallery that contains the works of Julio Romeo de Torres, a painter probably only remembered in Italy in relation to Vittorio Pica, I came upon a really delightful painting: a homage to long hair, to the bun; the young woman's face, which one senses is beautiful, is turned away, while she raises in one hand like an offering a ruddy apple. The title is *Viva il pelo*. And in the year it was painted, 1928, this was an obvious reference to the distressing craze for cropped locks, for the shaved nape, for what was known as bobbed hair, I believe.

Thus that lock of hair could only have been cut off and given by the contessa herself. But she clings to an explanation nobody takes seriously: it was a lock of her son's hair, which was the same color as her own. Could an unrequited lover's fetishism achieve this kind of transfer? All this seems beyond credibility to people who are acquainted with the transports of love, with passion, with its homeopathy and allopathy, with the masochism and fetishism to which it is prone, not, as today, through psychological reports but by personal experience or direct observation. But whether or not one admits that a guilty relationship had existed between the contessa and the orderly, one thing is certain: the orderly had been prey to a violent infatuation with all its attendant symptoms and rites.

The contessa acknowledged that she had been more friendly and familiar with the orderly than was seemly for an officer's wife with his orderly, for a mistress with her servant—for he was after all (though this may no longer be the case in the Army of the Republic) no more than a servant. She had certainly been rash—a rashness that even involved her writing to him during their brief separations: "Think of me"; "I think of you with lively affection"; "I kiss you." But the accused justifies such expressions by the fact that, following Polimanti's instructions, letters and cards were addressed to Dina Polimanti; thus it seemed to her that insofar as they were sent to a woman (the orderly's sister, whom she didn't know), they should contain some such expressions. A justification that could serve in the case of the kisses; but there seems no reason why Polimanti's sister should think of the contessa or be thought of by her. Moreover, Polimanti received at approximately similar dates missives addressed to him directly, where, says the reporter, the contessa is more "correct"—that is, more in keeping with the forms and formalities that should be observed in a relationship between a mistress and her servant, even when it involves the natural affection that arises between a good mistress and a good orderly (see De Amicis). But on this point, which must have been harshly contested by the public prosecutor and the prosecution, the report is somewhat obscure. Thus the perceptive reader is left to draw his own conclusions, relate appearances to reality, and observe how the tricks of appearance lend weight to reality.

Although a long and bloody war was to intervene, with its avid and frenetic aftermath of intellectual and political excesses of various sorts, already in the Oneglia courtroom there is a whiff of *Lady Chatterley's Lover*—which in 1928, to avoid British and Italian censorship, was to be published privately (in English) in Florence. And incidentally, the bersagliere Polimanti would have been far more persuasive as an incarnation (the word is apt) of that instinctive and happy sexuality with which Lawrence tries to counter intellectual adulterations, sophistications, and theories than the game-keeper Mellors, who emerges as highly tainted with intellectuality. As a matter of fact, D'Annunzio was already going, as it were, Mellors's way—though this only emerges later, from his letters. But that's enough to detract from some of Lawrence's innovative glamour.

There is something of D'Annunzio (of his letters published to date, in a limited private edition) in the draft of a letter found among Polimanti's belongings. According to the reticent reports, there is mention here of "rapturous moments." It is addressed to the woman who shared these raptures but without naming her. The contessa firmly denies that the missing name might be hers and suggests that of a Signora Letizia, with whom, she says, the orderly had an unplatonic affair. But she is unable to give any further details concerning this lady. A fact, if we are to admit her existence, which suggests that the contessa was aware of her only through the rather tactless and immodest confidences of Polimanti himself; and points, at any rate, to an "unseemly familiarity" between the accused and the victim—as the judges, lawyers, and reporters would say. For the lengths to which these gentlemen would go to avoid calling a spade a spade is quite remarkable. Thus women are never women but "the fair sex": "Was Polimanti partial to the fair sex?" asks the public prosecutor. And the contessa replies: "I noticed that he wooed many girls." But the identity of the one he calls "gentle creature" in the draft doesn't emerge.

On the second day of the hearing, the reporter lets himself be carried away: "Observing the accused from the press bench, her face turned toward the public prosecutor, one would say that she has two souls, two distinct personalities, according to whether one sees her in profile or full face. When she is seen at an angle, one notices only the modulated mellifluous singsong of her Venetian accent; and to this impression her immaculate profile and translucent complexion bring an additional sweetness. One would take her then for a madonna, worthy of being painted by one of those artists who left in Venice such admirable documents of their immortal talent. But when, at one of the prosecutor's artful objections, she turns her lovely face, after an almost imperceptible moment of reflection, and from this immaculate visage her gray, ardent eyes flash like lightning as her replies emerge, pondered and direct, one realizes that this woman's soul is not as simple as it might first seem. And more especially one realizes that a youth of twenty, healthy, amiable, and given to transports of passion as was Polimanti, constrained to share her life from morning to night, take orders from her, be at her beck and call, see her in her dressing gown, in her bathing costume, or when she takes her meals at home or walks under the palms and orange trees of San Remo, admired by all the passersby, while the breeze flutters her veil and her fair locks around her lovely visage, that such a youth must have been irresistibly compelled to disregard all conventions and to confess to his mistress that he loved her." Moreover, "to sweep all before one" was the bersagliere motto. And how could he refrain from doing just that when he saw her "take her meals at home"?

But apart from eating at home—a slightly peculiar and unexpected feature of erotic stimulation (unless, as in Casanova, it's a matter of savoring oysters or, more prosaically, as in other writers, biting into an apple)—the reporter's sudden flight of fancy has something very reminiscent of D'Annunzio in its style and tone, of D'Annunzio when he wanders from the "thing seen"—always as vision and revelation—to literary and artistic references, to images and analogies, and finally casts over all things the most sensuous of lights. A kind of net, especially prominent in his diaries and memoirs. But the reporter reproduces it with a less accurate and sumptuous pen (since D'Annunzio knew how to be accurate when he was not merely sumptuous). But D'Annunzio was undoubtedly in the air, or so it seems to me, more than any other writer in Italy has ever been.

However, the reporter's initial flight promptly founders on the harsh revelations and counterattacks by the prosecution and the public prosecutor. And the fair copy of that letter whose draft had been discussed the previous day—when its addressee had remained problematic and the contessa had suggested a certain Signora Letizia with whom, she said, Polimanti had had an affair—now turns up among the folders of the judicial inquiry (whose folds were undoubtedly ample), unequivocally addressed to the contessa: "Dear Maria"—with, it appears, the "rapturous moments" of the draft now deleted but with a proliferation of amorous terms and of the kisses that this missive is charged with transmitting, like a letter in a famous poem by Salvatore De Giacomo, a poet to whom in those days Italians with Polimanti's cultural background were largely indebted for their style and clichés: a sort of poor man's *De l'amour*. For De Giacomo was also in the air. But in a less elevated atmospheric stratum. It will be some time (but not much) before we realize that he is one of the greatest love poets Italy has ever produced, possessed of such subtlety and charm that one truly reads his works as imitations of or variations on Stendhal.

The emergence of this letter is ironically qualified by the defense as "miraculous." A hint at some unspecified suspicion—perhaps of its belated and opportune addition to the papers concerning the affair. A hint that provokes from the prosecution a significant retort: "Don't grumble," says Rossi, turning to the defense lawyers, "since never before have we seen, as in this affair, judicial authority submit to military authority." To which only the accused reacts, exclaiming: "That's too much!" But the president's failure to react may be a sign that the arrow had hit its target. Obviously it wasn't in vain that General Capri, commanding officer of the Genova Brigade, had hastened to San Remo on the day of the crime. And what the prosecution especially deplores is that the military authority's statement that nothing concerning the case had been found among Polimanti's belongings was immediately accepted. What about the draft of the letter? Was that among the things Polimanti was carrying in his pockets? As to the letter and postcards the contessa had written to the orderly, these had obviously been handed over by his relatives. But here we may note the particular affection and popularity the army enjoyed at the time. In the wake of the disastrous 1896 campaign in Ethiopia, some glory had at least been restored by the "overseas exploits," commemorated and amplified by the press and in songs and poems. How could anyone dare to tarnish this army's reputation by questioning the integrity of one of its officers—especially if he happened to be a military attaché? Never mind if a bersagliere has fallen victim to an overwhelming passion—we all know what the bersaglieri are like: that in all things, even in their passions, they go straight to the goal. But that a captain's wife should have requited such a passion was out of the question—even the suspicion of such an eventuality must be eradicated. For what no one seemed to realize was that in the eyes of the public, the image of Polimanti, whose overwhelming passion had overwhelmed the captain's wife, carried more weight with regard to the army's reputation, and to that of the bersagliere regiment in particular, than did the reputation of the captain with his honor unimpaired.

Nothing causes more uncertainty, sows more doubts, and creates greater havoc in a criminal case than expert opinion. "It is a well-known fact that expert opinion is especially invoked so that a case may be judged authoritatively." But it is also a well-known fact that in a trial, in matters requiring expert advice, the authority of one expert's opinion can always be invalidated by the authority of another expert's opposite opinion. When, during a trial, the expert called in by the judge, the one called in by the defense, and the one called in by the prosecution, all enjoying equal authority and reputation, happen to hold conflicting opinions, either the judges must accept the expert opinion that tallies most with their own, which objectively is as good as the other two (since the very fact that there are various answers precludes absolute truth), or they will have to forget them all and rely purely and simply on their own interpretation of human nature and of the law.

In the Tiepolo case, there was only one expert at first: the ballistics expert. But because he kept contradicting himself and because of his vagueness, there might well have been at least two experts with conflicting opinions. The main query concerned the distance at which the shot had been fired. After discussing the matter at great length, he finally reached the conclusion—rather as a concession to all concerned—that the distance was between twenty-five and thirty centimeters. At any rate, not point-blank. Now, since this confirmed the contessa's statement, it seemed to be a point in the defense's favor. If one tries to imagine the scene, however, it becomes obvious that to shoot a man in the face from a distance of twenty-five to thirty centimeters when he stands in front of you with open arms requires a calmness and collectedness more consistent with intentionality than to shoot him point-blank during a struggle. And the crucial question—had she ever used a firearm before?—was never put to the accused. Obviously her husband, who kept the gun in a drawer (oddly enough in the children's room), must have known that she was able to handle it and to remove the safety catch, since he told her she could use it if the need arose. A further controversial question was that of the safety catch. In her first deposition the accused had said that she had released the safety catch before pressing the trigger, but during the trial she emended this statement, saying she didn't know anything about the safety catch and had simply pulled the trigger. The expert was of a different opinion: the safety catch must have been engaged. He asserted this on the grounds that since the revolver had eight bullets, one of which was already missing before the fatal shot, the safety catch must have been engaged and had thus to be loosed. Not knowing what type of gun it was and, even if I knew, having no desire to set myself up as an expert, I'm quite happy to take his word for it.

The fact that the accused had admitted releasing the safety catch in her first deposition and now denied it (but perhaps even more, the defense lawyer's suggestion that judicial authority was overruled by military authority) seems to have inspired the public prosecutor with a ruthless punctiliousness that exhausts the accused and exasperates Raimondi. Was it true that the contessa would have liked Polimanti to remain in San Remo after he had been discharged and had promised to find him a job? The contessa "haughtily" denies this. Why, if not to avoid being witness to the scandalous goings-on, had the faithful housemaid left the Oggionis'? This is not a question but an assertion. And either from lassitude, indignation, or distress, the contessa doesn't even try to contradict it. Or, continues the public prosecutor, had the housemaid been dismissed because she had been surprised one night spying through the keyhole on the contessa and Polimanti? But here the public prosecutor begins to flounder, showing that he has no evidence and is basing his accusations on the gossip that was in circulation on the subject of the housemaid's departure from the Oggionis'. And to the second question—heartened perhaps by the obvious tentativeness of the charge—the contessa replies curtly that there was nothing to spy on, nothing to see through the keyhole. But from now on, as we shall see, keyholes will play an important part in the case: one of those somewhat comic features that consistently deflate tragic reality. But the questions continue. Had the contessa read in *La Nuova Antologia*, No. 7, November 1, 1913, the play *La donna senza pace?* A question previously put to her during the judicial inquiry. No. She hadn't read it. And so on and so forth.

It was thanks to an anonymous letter that the play published in *La Nuova Antologia* figured in the trial. Although anonymous letters, unless they refer to specific evidence, are not accepted in a trial, judges always tend to rely on them. And so it was in the Tiepolo case, when a letter signed "A Southerner" suggested that the judge seek in this drama the contessa's motive for killing the orderly. The heroine in this play murders her lover because he refuses to give back the letters she has written him. And the anonymous "southerner" suspects—or rather is convinced—that the Sam Remo tragedy should be explained in similar terms. A "southerner"? What next? Aren't we all southerners—especially at our worst? And not only do the judges take this suggestion seriously, but the contessa's letters are in fact, if not the sole motive of the tragedy, at least a significant factor in the case, since the contessa herself admits that she dreaded her husband's seeing her letters and postcards, "for I knew that I'd been thoughtless and I was afraid of forfeiting the total trust I had deserved from my husband during our twelve years of married life."

Thus, by charging the contessa with premeditation, it

seems that, on the second day of the trial, the prosecution was wavering between the tragedy "by an English author"— that is, the refusal to give back the letters—and the contessa's jealousy on hearing that "the orderly had a mistress and had made her pregnant." That the contessa had heard this, says the public prosecutor, "there is evidence." It will later emerge, however, that there is in fact no evidence at all. Nonetheless, according to the prosecution, it is clear that the contessa is trying to deny during the proceedings what she had admitted at the judicial inquiry. Like Maria Tarnowska in a famous case dating from some years back. A comparison made by the public prosecutor, which infuriates Raimondi. Especially because Tarnowska had been sentenced to eight years' detention, when he was doing his utmost to obtain the contessa's acquittal.

On the third day, after a final attempt to challenge the accused's account of her actions and Polimanti's just before the fatal shot (the contessa recapitulates: Polimanti takes her in his arms, kisses her, she struggles, even scratching his face, manages to free herself, runs to fetch the gun from the drawer, confronts him with it, and he, with open arms, laughs and says he's not afraid; then the shot that goes off as though by itself), the witnesses are called.

First Dr. Giuliani, a resident in the same building, who

had certified Polimanti's death and had noticed the scratches on his face, which the doctors who carried out the autopsy failed to observe. Then comes a Signora Bosio, in whose flat the contessa had taken refuge after the incident. But since this lady's deposition is identical to that which her husband, a captain in the same regiment as Oggioni and Polimanti, will repeat in greater detail and more restrained tones, I won't quote it here.

Captain Bosio declares: "About twenty days before the incident, one night at about two, Signora Oggioni rang at my door to beg me to come to her assistance in her flat, from which Polimanti stubbornly refused to depart, having even tried to break into her bedroom. I hurried down and asked the soldier to account for his unseemly behavior. He said he didn't dare go back to headquarters because he was absent without leave. Finally he left, and I told the lady: 'You should not on any account keep this orderly in your service.' And to tell the truth, the lady had forestalled me, telling Polimanti as he left not to come back the next morning. But the next morning at seven a.m. Polimanti was at my door. He said: 'Madam has forgiven me and begs you to do likewise. Madam asks you to come down.' I complied, and when I came down to the Oggionis' flat, Signora Oggioni said that Polimanti had humbly apologized and insistently implored her. 'He wept,' she said, 'and he solemnly swore to mend his ways; and I ask you to forgive him, Captain, as I, too, am inclined to do.' I naturally chided Polimanti once again rather harshly. He said: 'You must understand, Captain, that I'd had a drop too much. Besides, I'll tell you frankly, I'd made a mistake.' Words which I took to mean: I'd hoped the lady was easier to persuade; but she's not what I thought she was." Here Perry Mason, had he happened to be prosecuting, would have intervened and requested that this sentence be deleted, insofar as it was a personal impression and inference of the witness—who, according to American procedure, must only refer to facts that have occurred before his eyes and within earshot. And I can't resist the temptation to digress at this point to wonder how many trials in Italy today would not dissolve into thin air and how many offenders would not go free if such methods were applied here. For present-day trials in Italy would collapse like so many card castles if they were deprived of witnesses' inferences and of "rumors" reported by people who are neither implicated nor witnesses in the trial. Since any good citizen is quite incapable of choosing between the wish to see a wealthy, impudent rogue punished and the equally imperative desire that every sentence should be founded on a wider, more reliable and unimpeachable judicial procedure, he would die, like Buridan's ass, of civic starvation: just as in Jean Buridan of Bethune's scholastic sophism, which Dante sums up admirably in the terzina: "Between two dishes, equidistant from him / And equally attractive, a man would starve / Of his own free will, before he ate one of them," which opens the fourth canto of the *Paradiso*.

Thus, according to the practice (if not the rule) that in Italian criminal courts a witness may indulge in reporting subjective impressions, opinions, and judgments concerning events and persons, things he has heard from other people, and even anonymous general gossip (indeed, is often encouraged to do so by judges and lawyers), this particular witness's interpretation of Polimanti's words passed unchecked. And Captain Bosio went on: "Some days later, ten or perhaps fifteen days before the tragedy, going downstairs with my wife, I saw Signora Oggioni at her door, dismissing Polimanti with these words: 'Out of my house! Don't show your face here ever again! You'll settle matters with the captain.' Polimanti left, and Signora Oggioni, when questioned, told me that he had been rude to her and to her son. But I learned the following day that he had been readmitted to their service. A few days later, I was at the barracks when my housemaid arrived out of breath to tell me someone had been killed in the Oggioni flat. I notified Captain Oggioni as tactfully as possible, and we left the barracks together. He got on his bicycle, and I ran toward the house. I hurried up to my flat, where I found Signora Oggioni, in a state of agitation I can't begin to describe, who said: 'I shot him to defend my honor.' I was immediately joined by Captain Oggioni. Signora Oggioni fell into his arms, crying: 'Ferruccio, my Ferruccio—it was so as not to be anyone else's!' "

Although Captain Bosio obviously favors the accused, we feel that he is perplexed by the lady's persistent leniency toward Polimanti. How did she not realize that the captain's advice "not on any account" to keep the orderly in her service was the fairest and wisest thing to do? A perplexity undoubtedly shared by those who, seventy years later, read through the documents of the case.

However, there is just one point in Captain Bosio's deposition that needs clarification. When he says "one night at about two," he would, in those days, have been understood by everyone to mean two hours after Avemaria and not, as now, two hours after midnight. Then—and indeed until well beyond my childhood—the day was not divided civically, as it were, by clock-tower chimes but ecclesiastically, by the ringing of church bells: Salveregina, Noon, Vespers, Avemaria, and the Second Hour of the night. And between Salveregina and Noon, the bells pealed at regular intervals to call the faithful to one mass after another. A timetable that had more significance for the womenfolk than for the men, who were generally at work. A *temps perdu* today. Yet those bells still divide the *recherche* of all men my age.

Thus it wasn't darkest night but early evening when Signora Oggioni went upstairs to ask Captain Bosio to help her get rid of Polimanti. And the reason for her appealing to her husband's colleague and neighbor was that Captain Oggioni was away at maneuvers at the time. An absence of which Polimanti took advantage to try and initiate—or, if we prefer, resurrect—an intrigue with Signora Oggioni.

The Oggionis had two children, a boy of nine and a girl of eight. But at the time of the tragedy another child was expected; which accounts for Signora Oggioni's more or less constant indisposition, her troubled and somewhat deranged state. Questioned by the president, Signora Bosio declares: "She told me she was unhappy about it, and I told her that even this late arrival should be welcomed joyfully and that I myself had had a child after a gap of nearly ten years." Although there are many reasons why a woman should feel depressed at the thought of another pregnancy after so many years, the lawyers for the prosecution see only one: that it is a "child of sin," as contemporary films and soap operas would have said. And thus there were rumors that the miscarriage she had in prison was no accident. Raimondi, the attorney for the defense, was indignant.

But so far as one can see, he was the only one—apart, of course, from the contessa. Everybody agreed, however diverse opinions were on other matters in the affair (except for one fact: that the contessa had certainly had an affair with the orderly and slept with him at least on one occasion), that everything hinged on this pregnancy. Indeed, the news exploded like a bombshell when reported in the press (though it was no news for those who attended the trial), and a vast excited mob tried to break into the already overcrowded law court, regardless of bruises and fractured limbs sustained in the process.

Among the depositions of the Oggionis' friends and relations were those of housemaids, servants according to their employers but "ancillaries" according to the local poet Guido Gozzano: "I sing the praise of ancillary love," he says. What he means, of course, is not love but lovemaking—a simple, expeditious refreshment like drinking a glass of cold water in hot weather; something that involves no sentimental complications. In fact, housemaids play quite a prominent part in Italian literature. Gozzano mentions one who brings him messages from her mistress and how one day when the message is that the lady can't come to a rendezvous the poet loses no time in making up for it: "I'm stirred by her fresh laughter, by the slow / waiting in vain, her sharp remarks, the hour / the scent of something from Boccaccio ... / She likes to mock, to struggle, to implore, / she even brings her mistress into play: 'How shameful it would be for her! My poor, / poor mistress! ...' And she gives herself to me." But she's by no means the only one. There's the maid in his own house, an eighteen-year-old "fresh as a plum." In fact, the poet was a womanizer. Like Polimanti.

Felicina Cordone, the Bosios' maid, has this to say: "When I met Polimanti on the stairs, he often kissed me." And Angelina Gardelli, the maid who had left the Oggionis' service, puts an end to all the envious, spiteful conjectures, stating: "I left because Polimanti wouldn't leave me alone. He was always fondling and kissing me." And she adds that the bersagliere boasted of kissing every woman he met. But according to her, this didn't include Signora Oggioni. Although the orderly made no bones about being in love with the contessa, nor even about his love being reciprocated. One day he bet Gardelli ten lire that he would go into Signora Oggioni's bedroom that very night, but he later retracted the wager, saying he didn't trust the maid's discretion. In Gardelli's opinion, however, he retracted it because that evening the captain returned from maneuvers. But in fact it was nothing but bluff and bragging. Didn't she complain to her mistress about all that fondling and kissing? Gardelli said yes, she complained, but the orderly's only response to Signora Oggioni's rebukes was to sulk. He took offense, became grumpy and gloomy. And Signora Oggioni, instead of sending him away, not only forgave him for fondling and kissing Angelina but even tolerated the bad temper her justified reprimands provoked. So much so that by keeping him in her service she lost a devoted housemaid, who, besides being pleasant, was also very pretty—"fresh as a plum," indeed—a fact that may have displeased her mistress. At least that's what most of those who followed the trial suspected maliciously, and that the maid's departure must have been a balm to Signora Oggioni's jealousy.

But although the contessa's jealousy may have figured prominently in the public's malicious thoughts and served to provide a tentative passing shot from the prosecution, it was Polimanti's jealousy with regard to the contessa that was mainly discussed. It was referred to by a witness to whom the orderly had mentioned—as one bersagliere to another—not only the contessa's incredible beauty when her charms were revealed, unadorned by the "silks and cottons, crepe georgettes, satins, chiffons, and voiles" in which all could admire her, but furthermore that he was not alone in enjoying such marvels, since, through the keyhole, he had himself spied on unequivocal evidence of intimacy between the lady and a certain Vagliasindi, an agriculturist. Consequently, the tribunal having decided to make an investigation in the Oggioni house to reconstruct the "mechanism" of the crime, a member of the jury asked that a check be made on the keyholes to ascertain whether indeed they could have served to frame the scenes Polimanti described to his friend. A suggestion to which no one objected. Thus in the course of the investigations here they all are, judges, jury, lawyers, and reporters, peeping through one keyhole after another: that of the bedroom afforded only a mutilated, inconclusive view, while from the drawing-room keyhole, vision was unobstructed. Since Polimanti had said he'd spied on the contessa and the agriculturist through both keyholes, Raimondi requested that the evidence be entered as inconclusive. To which the prosecution objected. The evidence couldn't be entered in the minutes since it hadn't been witnessed by an expert. An objection that seems utterly idiotic. But if it is really based on the penal code, it has to be admitted that a code that requires the deposition of an expert so that the view from a keyhole may be entered in the minutes was (or is) quite phenomenally idiotic. An expert in "voyeurism" through keyholes? Is it possible that an expert in such a private vice should exist? Yet the tribunal (who knows how and by what means?) was able to find and summon such an expert. On the sofa, the public prosecutor duly embraces the clerk while, through the keyhole, the expert observes, witnesses, and certifies.

The accused—ever thinner and more lovely—is engulfed in a whirlpool of witnesses. There are personal friends and family friends of the Oggionis and the Tiepolos, as well as Polimanti's friends and relations; there are those who had misguidedly told someone what they had seen, what they knew or thought they knew, and had thus found themselves in the witness box, reluctant and resentful. The accused is moved on seeing old friends and on hearing what they have to say about her. She is cool and attentive when those for the prosecution testify. She smiles and even laughs, joining in the general hilarity, when listening to the depositions of the unwilling and the simpleminded.

By and large, the witnesses can be divided into three groups: There are friends and acquaintances, who all assert their unchanging esteem for the family and for Signora Oggioni in particular. Never, they say, have they had the slightest suspicion that the Oggionis' leniency toward Polimanti, excessive though it might be, was anything other than leniency, that is, kindheartedness. The second group, the opposition, consists of Polimanti's friends and relations come from Piceno, who testify to the orderly's innocent, respectful, modest nature and tend to suggest, on the contrary, or even to assert that the contessa's behavior made him totally lose control and that when she began to fear for her reputation, she deliberately murdered him. Prominent among these are Polimanti's brother Paride, the tailor from Fermo, and a certain Strinchini, a fellow countryman recently discharged from the bersagliere regiment, where he had been Polimanti's confidant. The third group includes housemaids, working women, and people who had met Polimanti more or less frequently and heard his boasts and complaints. These had nothing against the accused but on the other hand made no secret of their resentment of the victim, for the simple reason that, having known him, they are compelled to bear witness: a duty that is never willingly undertaken by Italians either in the north or in the south but that tends to become less and less popular—or even rather shameful—the farther south one goes.

Of housemaids, the orderly had handled (the term is apt) quite a few. All of them refer to his "handy" ways, but they are unanimous in saying that they rebuffed him at once or made it a condition of any further encounters that he keep his hands to himself—a condition probably readily accepted but most certainly not respected. According to the evidence that emerged, Polimanti's hands were all over San Remo, fondling maidens and matrons, the plain and the pretty alike. And it's most likely those very hands that two female neighbors, much given to observing the Oggioni kitchen window, noticed one day fondling a female bust—but whose bust it was is in doubt, owing to the position of the blinds, which precluded a complete view of the scene. Nonetheless, one senses that these ladies are persuaded it was Signora Oggioni's rather than her maid's, since they add that she was far too often in the kitchen, chatting and joking with the orderly in a familiar, almost provocative manner. A familiarity unseemly in itself, they imply without actually saying so. And with equal reticence, a certain officer expresses some disapproval of the fact that when Signora Oggioni went to the seaside, the orderly would wander about the beach in a bathrobe—something that was strictly forbidden to all his fellow soldiers. That he then had free access to the cabin where the contessa dressed and undressed, and had even seen her unclothed more than once, was a rumor many witnesses had heard—some from Polimanti himself. For he talked freely about his passion to all his acquaintances and readily exhibited the locket, saying to some, who were less intimate, that the picture was that of a lawyer's wife, but to others that it was the captain's wife. However, even among these last he made some distinction: there were those to whom he confessed his love and his intention to try and have an affair with her; while others were told that his feelings were requited to the extent that this insatiable woman was reducing him to exhaustion and near collapse.

As has been said, he confided in his countryman and comrade Strinchini in great detail. Strinchini describes the scene of seduction in his friend's own words: One day the contessa comes to talk to Polimanti very scantily clad, and he, dazzled by this vision, utterly bewitched, is unable to take in anything she says. When the contessa asks him why he is staring at her like that, all he can reply is that she is beautiful, beautiful. To which she responds with what is more a caress than a slap. At this point he takes her in his arms and kisses her with frenzied passion. Locked together, they collapse into an armchair. The plausibility of this account greatly perturbs the defense lawyers, who do all they can to discredit the witness, referring to his questionable reputation and insinuating that two of his sisters lead a "gay life"—an expression on a par with "easy women," since just as the life referred to was not in the least gay, so there was not much ease for the women who led it. There ensues an argument between the lawyers and an attempted assault by Strinchini on Professor Conti, a far shrewder advocate for the contessa than Raimondi.

In this merry-go-round of depositions, this endless sequence of conflicting evidence, Strinchini's—perhaps because of its impact on the defense lawyers—remains engraved in the minds of those who follow the trial and lends a certain plausibility to other depositions of a similar nature, however implausible these may be. Thus, for instance, that of Paride Polimanti, who had also been an orderly in the Oggioni household, which relates an example of the contessa's rather thoughtless behavior that he interprets as blatant provocation—a provocation, however, that proved fruitless since he happened to be a stronger and more principled person than his unlucky brother. And this term "unlucky" recurs frequently in the depositions of other relations, implying that the orderly was unlucky enough to have come up against a bloodthirsty woman, and having thus "more weighty" implications, "more damaging to moral decorum," than when one says "an unlucky fellow."

In fact, the most sensible picture of Polimanti is that evoked by a café owner (there were no bars and barmen then): "He was a likable lad but a bit of a fool." Also he talked a lot of nonsense, to which the wise café owner paid no heed. And having said this, he slipped away, leaving a scrap of valuable information behind him. Nor do I think it out of place to add my personal opinion, drawn not only from a general impression of the case but from certain facts printed in the papers, which is that the contessa was a bit of a fool too—at least as foolish as a pretty woman usually is and enough to enhance her good looks in most men's eyes.

The problem of the contessa's miscarriage—considered by the prosecution as no accident, whereas the defense indignantly rejected the mere suspicion of such an eventuality—could hardly be solved otherwise than by gynecological expertise. Since an expert had been required for a keyhole, it wasn't likely one could be dispensed with in a matter involving scientific knowledge. It must be said, however, that the accused and her lawyers were asking for it when they unwisely declared that this miscarriage was a consequence of the struggle with the orderly. In view of the fact that it occurred nearly a month after the tragedy and that no mention had been made at the time of her arrest of any signs or symptoms of abuse, this seemed highly improbable. Whence the need for expert advice, which the prosecution hoped would prove she had unlawfully attempted to get rid of "the fruit of her sins." Obviously there was no evidence of this or of the contrary. All was as uncertain as ever after a hearing behind closed doors, where even the most scabrous details of the case were discussed: details that nowadays would seem perfectly innocent (if innocence still existed).

Incidentally, Police Inspector Silvestri disclosed a significant detail concerning this struggle between the contessa and the orderly. Although he himself had no doubts at all as to the legitimacy of the shooting, for some unknown reason—perhaps simply because he was unaware of the significance of what he was disclosing—he stated as proof of the veracity of his opinion that none of the residents in the building had heard shouts or sounds of violence from the Oggioni flat prior to the shot, which everybody heard. This disclosure, which should have been taken up by the prosecution, was engulfed in the quagmire of evidence—a quagmire of ever-increasing depth, tedious and suffocating.

Witnesses succeeded each other in the box to repeat more or less the same things: Polimanti's confidences, his obsessive fondlings, the witness's regard for Signora Oggioni, the fact that nothing had ever been heard about her that might impair her reputation. One hundred and forty witnesses: some of them heard more than once, such as Angelina Gardelli, summoned back to confirm that she had never taken the liberty of peeping through keyholes, and again to testify to the trimming of the lady's hair. Yes, she did trim it, as the contessa had recalled at a given point to account for the lock in Polimanti's possession. But an anonymous letter reaches the prosecution lawyers from a lady who explains: "I am a woman too, and so I am in the habit of trimming my hair so that it will grow thicker. But I can assure you that this doesn't consist in cutting off whole locks. Trimming consists in snipping off the tips. So I can't believe a lover could be reduced to collecting each clipping and tying them up with a ribbon." This is just one of the numberless anonymous letters that rain down upon the judges, public prosecutor, lawyers for the defense and the prosecution—except that these last have every advantage in making them public, since such communications approve, request, and urge the utmost severity. But judges and lawyers for the defense receive their share of letters, all dictated by the same feelings; they are pleas that the judges be unrelenting and reproaches to the lawyers. All from women who see the contessa's acquittal as a threat to the stability of the family, the society, and the nation. A woman who signs herself "Oliva" writes in the name of all Italian schoolteachers: "We who know how much care is required first from mothers and then from us to form men worthy of serving our country, we passionately and sincerely deplore the death inflicted on the soldier Polimanti by the vile and wretched hand of a woman who, after ..." The newspaper refrains from printing the rest, so that it is left to the reader to imagine the obscene descriptions of what had occurred "before" between the lady and the soldier. Such descriptions were surely stored away in the schoolmistress's mind, while only the most chaste expressions were permitted to flow from her pen. And who knows what unfathomable secret passions—erotic and patriotic—motivated the 570 anonymous letters received by the prosecution, the 350 received by the defense, the 120 received by the President and the 69 received by the public prosecutor? Not to mention the countless letters received by members of the jury and representatives of the press, who didn't report them.

The hostility of the women who sent letters to those involved in the trial can be summed up in this prediction of doom: They'll acquit her, you'll acquit her, because she's beautiful! For the desire, the hope to see justice done consists precisely in the contrary: she must be condemned because she is beautiful. Family and fatherland (a fatherland that has proceeded from victory to victory in Libya before proceeding from execution to execution), for which the contessa's acquittal spells ruin, are only pretexts: the true motive is the contessa's beauty. There is besides—more notably among the common people and the men rather than the women—a certain degree of hostility toward the accused owing to class consciousness; eroded by long experience and, for the more politically minded, attenuated by the fact that the defense lawyer is a Socialist.

"The power of beauty!" exclaims Gioacchino Belli in horror when, describing in a sonnet how among newborn kittens we preserve the pretty ones and destroy the others, he exposes in all its starkness a fact we generally accept without alarm or revulsion, for revulsion (goose pimples, hair standing on end) is a consequence of alarm; and we experience it reading the last lines of Belli's sonnet. But beauty ... female beauty, Stendhal declares, is a promise of bliss, whether for us or for others. However the note Toulet added in the margin many years later is very sensible: "No one has ever told us whether such promises are kept."

S andwiched between the deposition of Antonio Sciacca—an ex-bersagliere come from Marsala to testify on the subject of Polimanti's habitual confidences, with the additional detail of the "mess" he'd got himself into through the contessa's pregnancy, which she wouldn't be able to account for to her husband—and that of Clarissa Pasquale, housemaid to the contessa's mother, come from Casal Monferrato to describe Polmanti's advances, which she had energetically repulsed (very plausibly, in view of her size), Professor Pompeo Molmenti's deposition stands out with distinctive prominence. A scholar of the history of Venice and in particular of its eighteenth-century licentiousness, and its most famous exponent, Molmenti, through his extensive research and the austerity of his life, had earned the title of senator. Precisely in that year, he was to publish the *Epistolari veneziani del secolo VIII,* a weighty and still very useful study, while among his other works there was a first edition of the *Carteggi casanoviani,* published as early as 1910, of which a more extensive edition would appear between 1916 and 1919. Indeed, he was probably compiling it when he journeyed from Venice to Oneglia to testify in the trial.

James Rives Childs, United States ambassador and one of the most tireless and perhaps the most authoritative of Casanova scholars (interest in Casanova seems to thrive particularly among diplomats, facilitated perhaps by their perpetual displacements from one capital to another, their leisurely existence and easy access to documents), places Molmenti among those eminent scholars who have distinguished themselves not only by discovering revealing documents but furthermore by spreading Casanova's fame in Italy, where over half a century was to elapse before a first edition of his *Memorie* would be published. But worse even than this delay was the fact that only the more spicy fragments, which in fact are the most mechanical and repetitive, were presented to a vast and more or less uncultured public. And we cannot help assuming that Polimanti was among these and was probably inspired by that distant model, whom he roughly resembled in his insatiable appetite, self-confidence, uninhibited and bold advances—and in his marked partiality for housemaids.

Thus Professor Molmenti: one of those characters from the world of scholarship and culture who interest me inordinately, who fascinate me. Characters who dedicate the best part of their lives to following in the footsteps of, tracking down, as it were, characters who are their polar opposites. And the term "following in the footsteps" brings to my mind the man who is the most notable example of such an activity: the Roman Catholic and almost totally Jansenist Pietro Paolo Trompeo, an austere, home-loving, always well-spoken man who, having set out in early youth to follow in the footsteps of the atheist, libertine Stendhal throughout romantic Italy, pursued him during his whole life, even elsewhere and in different contexts, with a passion and a sensitivity I could almost describe as unequaled. And indeed, his first book bears the title *Nell'Italia romantica sulle orme di Stendhal.*

But in his evidence Professor Senator Molmenti does not of course allow the slightest, the most fleeting hint of Casanovian gloss to transpire. He dwells on three points in favor of the defense: the symptoms of a "delicate" constitution manifested by the contessa in moments of stress, such as the funeral of Senator Tiepolo when, so he had heard, she fainted; the family's distinguished background, closely related as it is to those who gave birth to a doge and a queen; and the excessive sense of honor that had led the contessa's own grandfather to bankruptcy in order to pay a relative's debts. Thus, concludes the senator, the name of Tiepolo and the word "honor" are practically synonymous. And hard luck for Polimanti, appears to be the substance of this deposition, if he hadn't noticed the contessa's "delicate" constitution and if he knew nothing about synonyms.

From newspaper accounts of the flat in San Remo after the inspection of the premises, deserted since the day of the tragedy, dusty, sinister (a neighbor goes so far as to call it ill-starred: a tax collector had tripped on that very landing and dropped dead; the orderly of an officer who occupied the flat before the Oggionis had committed suicide after being reprimanded by his captain, an incident that may have inspired Polimanti when he threatened to kill himself if he couldn't get Signora Oggioni into bed with him), from these accounts the figure of Captain Oggioni gradually emerges and comes to the forefront of public interest. And the long sequence of testimonies from colleagues and superiors helps to build up this image. None of these witnesses has anything to say against this obviously upright and respectable man, although all express the same perplexity as Captain Bosio concerning his attitude to Polimanti. They can't understand why he kept the orderly, since they had all, at one time or another, urged him to dismiss him. And this advice had been given not only privately but also collectively and officially. For the captain's colleagues had actually got together to discuss the Polimanti case and had reported to him their unanimous opinion that the orderly should no longer remain in his service. A fact that gives the lie to the evidence of certain officers, who said they had never heard any gossip regarding Polimanti's presence in the Oggioni household.

To the colleagues who urged him to get rid of Polimanti, Captain Oggioni replied he was afraid that if the soldier returned to the regiment, he would end up under arrest on account of his intractable, eccentric, and violent nature. But this seemed to be a very good reason to avoid having him around the house. Besides, how could a professional officer in an army where discipline attained sadistic proportions and was seen as an unrivaled means of character building wish to deprive of such discipline a man who, more than most, seemed to need it?

The reporter who attended the inspection of the premises and depicted the flat in such gloomy terms wrote: "The children are no longer there, having gone to their maternal grandmother. And the master of the house is far away." Where far away? Very far, no doubt, from his wife, whom he perhaps no longer trusted; or at any rate whom he felt obliged no longer to trust, since others did not trust her. (And caught in a similar trap, Pirandello, too, had been perplexed, anguished, alarmed.) And the captain's absence from the scene of the trial, previously unnoticed—or not noted—acquired from that moment a somewhat disdainful, almost censorious significance as regards his wife. And the moderation of the press in its barely referring to this is truly commendable; nowadays such a murmur would have turned into an uproar, a thunderstorm—as in *Barbiere di Siviglia*, when the account of the scandal starts off to the accompaniment of the flute and ends up on the bass drum. And however far away the captain was, he would have been tracked down, unearthed, importuned, compelled to answer questions, to satisfy the interviewers—that is, to make matters worse for the accused. And even if he had expressed his trust and his love for his spouse, some of his resentment and his suspicion could not have failed to emerge and provide grounds for gossip. Although as we grow older we naturally tend to regret the past, there was nonetheless really some good in it.

Obviously a similar moderation doesn't restrain the public prosecutor's or the prosecuting lawyer's concluding speeches in the trial. Defense Lawyer Conti wisely refers only fleetingly to the captain's "intense sufferings"—an expression that, apart from the rhetoric to which more even than today lawyers were prone, not to say constrained, was undoubtedly consistent with Oggioni's feelings. But the prosecution relentlessly involve him in the affair, accusing him of having failed in his duties as husband and father: on the one hand in the "consideration" he shows for his wife, the contessa; on the other for having kept in his service, notwithstanding his friends' repeated warnings, the enterprising orderly. "Wretched Polimanti—by no means "a wretch," since he was simply an innocent lad of twenty—to have chanced upon Captain Oggioni's patronage!" says Rossi for the prosecution. As to the captain's "consideration" for his wife, this should be understood either as abstinence or precaution in sexual relations. It isn't clear whether the prosecution's insinuations refer to the absence or infrequency of such relations or to coitus interruptus. The term "consideration," obviously charged with irony here, can accommodate any one of these interpretations. As we said, the terms employed were always most chaste. Thus, when the public prosecutor, in the heat of oratorical eloquence, asked the president if he might refer to certain sexual details that had been discussed behind closed doors, the president uttered a heartfelt "No!" and all but choked. However, the captain's consideration had emerged only from Polimanti's confidences to his friends, which depicted the captain (presumably in mocking tones) as a strict "Malthusian." Precisely. A "Malthusian," according to the orderly's own words. And the term must have seemed somewhat alien to his audience, requiring elucidation. Moreover, isn't it likely that he had acquired it, together with its implications, from the contessa's lips, rather than chanced upon it himself?

The hearings lasted from May 26 until June 2. Words, words, from which the odd island of concrete facts occasionally surfaces, circumstantial evidence for one party or the other. The defense plead that the accused acted in self-defense and to protect her reputation and that of her family (although once this was established, it was prepared to admit that the contessa was in a disturbed, exasperated, and overwrought state at the time of the incident); the prosecution plead that the crime was the result of cold-blooded premeditation, which did not exclude the fact that the contessa's desire to safeguard her reputation and that of her family had played its part. However this reputation was a spurious one since, in fact, she had already made nonsense of it by seducing the orderly—or being seduced by him. And the prosecution was willing to accept as an "attenuating circumstance" her worthy impulse to save appearances and avoid a scandal, so long as the verdict was one of premeditated manslaughter.

And ever present in all this was the Gentiloni Pact, which was then rising up as a bulwark around the family and against the threat of a frantic pursuit of pleasure—and among its staunchest supporters were those most frantic pursuers of pleasure, the members of a newly established, amorphous, numerically indeterminate but securely dominant bourgeoisie. Nor had the pact emerged from the void; it possessed an ancient, vast, and varied heredity, hereditarily dedicated to the cult and celebration of appearances, to the need to save them even at the expense of truth.

The prosecution had no lack of substantial arguments and circumstantial evidence to expose and elaborate. But it preferred to concentrate on the passion a beautiful woman of thirty-five, married for twelve years, had experienced for a handsome, vigorous, and naturally passionate youth of twenty-two. Even the evidence of the disappearing locket, which the accused herself admitted she had seen and had tried to take from Polimanti, was lightly passed over: since the military authorities, who had immediately taken charge of the orderly's belongings, were responsible for its disappearance, how, in that heroic moment of patriotic and military enthusiasm, could anyone in Italy voice any criticism of the army? Indeed, the public prosecutor was careful to avoid mentioning the evidence of the locket. He left it to the lawyer for the prosecution, who made little use of it. As to the defense, its only clearly pertinent allegation, consistent with equity and common sense, was that expressed by Professor Conti: even a prostitute is entitled to refuse intercourse and to defend herself, even by resorting to murder, if constrained to it by violence; and any woman is free to break off a relationship when—out of remorse, convenience, or tedium—she decides to do so; and in view of such freedom, if the other seeks to force her by violence to continue this relationship, and her physical strength alone and on equal terms is insufficient to contain his (which is inevitably greater), the use of a weapon becomes entirely legitimate. Obviously, he was careful to add, neither of these examples can be applied to the contessa, who, even in the eyes of her vilest detractors, is most blatantly not a prostitute, nor can she be sullied by the suspicion—expressed by the prosecution in their distortion of evidence and their trust in slanders based on Polimanti's vile fantasies and boasts—that she had resorted to premeditated murder in order to terminate a relationship that was becoming irksome and risky.

This allegation didn't seem to make a notable breach in the well-established opinion, shared even by the women, that between prostitutes and adultery the boundary is imperceptible and very fluid, and that once a woman has crossed this uncertain frontier and entered that territory, she cannot and must not kill a man simply because he asks her for what, at other times, he has obtained. And this is certainly what even adulterous wives maintained, since they obviously adorned their own adultery with the sanctity of a passion "as violent as death" and capable of eclipsing the sanctity of marriage, whereas they condemned any other woman's adultery as neither more nor less than prostitution. And it isn't hard to imagine how much more such a view would appeal to adulterous husbands.

But everybody was awaiting Raimondi's speech for the defense. He spoke at last. And for hours. Nor did he let his audience down. He was moving, indeed inspiring. His hair and his beard tempestuously agitated by the storm of his eloquence, he delivered one of those empty speeches that, in those days, served to establish a lawyer's reputation (and even today, that of a politician who speaks on television, when all that remains in the viewers' memory an hour or so later is that "he spoke well"; and it's pointless to ask what he said, since he will have spoken all the better if it was about nothing). I read Raimondi's speech without being able to find the slightest trace of emotion in it, or anything persuasive or convincing. Yet in the law courts of Oneglia the public wept that day and the applause was frenetic and prolonged. The accused wept, of course. Moreover, the president of the court also wept (which is more surprising, in view both of the impassivity proper to his status and of habit, which inures against any emotion one might experience on hearing moving speeches). He was in tears as he called the public to order.

A lawyer who defended a woman charged with killing a man to whom she has not yielded, or has yielded only after promises—later unfulfilled—of lawful marriage, had to overcome the many and persistent voices within him, echoes of old prejudices and conventions that had come to constitute a theoretical apparatus, a system of beliefs and related attitudes, overt or ignored, exposed as virtues or hidden as vices. And this would equally be the case if the woman was the plaintiff suing because of violence done to her—cases incurring by law sentences of three to ten years' detention, substantially increased if the victim happened to be under age or if the act had been perpetrated in "violation of authority or trust or family relationships"—that is to say by a Don Bartolo on a Rosina (*Barbiere di Siviglia*), if Don Bartolo had been less concerned with money and more passionate; by a Rustico on an Alibech (*Decameron*, third day, tenth tale); or by a man on his housemaid or on a young relative living under his roof and surprised in bed during her afternoon nap. Obviously, although the civil code made no mention of the fact, the "virginity" of which the victim is deprived by the act of rape was a more or less accepted *sine qua non*, a definite advantage for the plaintiff—whence the humiliating medical examinations, official and private, to certify her virginity prior to the event, its loss, and the time of this loss. How medical science could prove the last point is one of its unsolved mysteries, but then, throughout the ages medical science has had its share of mysteries; Magalotti lists a number of things doctors once prescribed and then forbade; and Savinio tells how, during his life, medical opinion on the virtues of the tomato changed no less than four times. And all the worse for us. But to return to virginity: when it wasn't a point of dispute and the victim didn't claim to have been deprived of it, the outcome of the affair was doomed to such questionings and disbelief that rape victims—and especially their families—preferred to forgo any attempt at redress. Almost always. And it seems things haven't changed in this respect.

But despite the civil code's leniency toward the woman who had committed murder to save her reputation, and its harshness toward the rapist, when a lawyer was defending such a woman or pleading the rights for the rape victim against the rapist, he was always beset by hesitations and doubts. I refer here to lawyers of the past. And not to lawyers as such, of course, as a race apart; but as members of a society, a culture, a system of more or less universally held beliefs (of which traces can still be found, unexpected out-crops discovered). The firm belief, for instance, that in cases of rape the woman is always to blame, that she is always, wittingly or unwittingly, the instigator, was deep-rooted and instinctive. There was an anecdote in circulation that served to illustrate this theory, a myth or fable reflecting the truth. It was attributed in turn to any one of the many famous lawyers of the period, but more particularly to a Neapolitan. In this anecdote, a lawyer defending a man accused of rape asks one of the carabinieri adorning the law court to un-sheath his sword and to hand him the sheath; the carabiniere then holding the sword and the lawyer the sheath, the former is told to try and put it back into the sheath, which the lawyer is slowly and almost imperceptibly swaying from side to side. The carabiniere is of course unable to resheath his sword, and the lawyer obtains his client's acquittal. And this meta-phor was always most persuasive whenever anyone had re-course to it in proving that rape was impossible (and I seem to remember that a similar image recurs frequently in the *Arabian Nights,* but farcically). However, it's highly unlikely to have convinced the judges, who were probably aware of the obvious fact that the rapist's offense consists not simply in the act illustrated by the metaphor but in all the incalcu-lable terror and violence that precede it. Moreover, it is most improbable that the little scene ever took place in a law court, since, according to regulations, a carabiniere would not have been allowed to give in to the lawyer's whim (for such it would have seemed, if not a sudden fit of madness, until its significance as a pertinent metaphor emerged); since the judges and the public prosecutor would have forbidden it; and finally, since the lawyer could not have been so carried away by enthusiasm for the case as to overlook the fact that the carabiniere, first in his bewilderment and later in his absorption in the game, was likely to nick with the tip or the edge of the blade, the hand that held the sheath. Nonetheless, the metaphor is popular to this day, even if it is ostensibly evoked as an oddity from the past.

That a woman is to blame for the violence she has suffered and has in some way provoked it is a notion that, as we saw, is reflected in the chronicler's sympathy for Polimanti at a given point. But it is also reflected in the lawyer Raimondi's speech when, absolving the contessa of any guilt whatsoever, he declares that until her death she will have to endure the remorse of seeing, "ever renewed, a shadow of ridicule cast upon her husband," and dismisses her with these words of doom: "This is the burden of your sin, which you will bear upon your shoulders when, after your vacillations, you go on your way with lowered brow as one who has stumbled, before the merciful and unerring judgment of God." Not to mention (that is, mentioning it) the near lapsus or blunder he commits when referring at a given point to Roman Lucretia, who killed no one but herself to atone for having had to give in and for the consequent and imperious need to blame and punish herself: a myth men have held up as an example to women throughout the centuries and perhaps the most antifeminist myth ever conceived. A myth and an example that recurs persistently among the few myths the Italians recall. And just as Lucretia stands for virtue, so Messalina, her mirror image, stands for vice. Thus how could Raimondi not have realized that by evoking the image of Lucretia in the Tiepolo affair, he would suggest that other of Messalina? And indeed, we read in the press: "She is a true Messalina, who enjoys the gladiator and then has him put to death."

Rossi, the prosecution lawyer ("Oh, Rossi, my friend!" Raimondi addresses him, in his endeavor to persuade him of what he himself is not persuaded), had an easier task. He could openly state what the defense lawyer secretly believed. He could accuse, deride, even slander. In fact, allege what Montaigne indulgently declares, albeit with good-natured levity, as though all were for the best in the best of possible worlds: as to women, where love and lovemaking are concerned, "there isn't a word, a pattern, or a gesture they don't know, as a science that runs through their veins, better than can be learned from books." And this theory of Montaigne's was, indulgently, regretfully, or obscenely, shared by all those who were gathered in the Oneglia law courts. And not only by those in the law courts. And not only the male contingent. And indeed, who can tell if it didn't temper—with regret, remorse, fear—even the contessa's thoughts? Thus we can imagine the general approval—malicious, winking, and nudging (winking and nudging one's neighbor to show that a malicious insinuation hadn't passed unnoticed)—that greeted Raimondi's question, during the hearings, to the mother superior of the Suore della Misericordia of San Remo, in whose convent the contessa had taken refuge, and according to whom the contessa's behavior had been "an example both to the nuns and to myself." The lawyer had asked: "But men were excluded from the convent, were they not?" and the mother superior, with resentful innocence: "Men are not allowed into nuns' convents."

N ineteen thirteen is the year of universal suffrage; of the Gentiloni Pact; of the guerrilla warfare in Libya (which, once the war itself was over, provided most Italians, far more than the war had done, with a sense of colonial possession, of "We've got you, Africa!"); it is the year when the more experienced and acquisitive Western states share out colonial territories among themselves; and it is furthermore the year in which Italian nationalism is stirred and startled into quite different channels from those dictated by foreign policy. But there is yet another innovation: the "definitive text of the code of criminal procedure" is enforced. Through reports on the Tiepolo affair the public can get some idea of what has been altered in the "formalities" of a criminal trial. But the penal code is still that of 1889: no one would take the risk of altering it lest the whole thing collapse.

Thus, to come back to the Tiepolo affair, what exactly is "premeditation"? Premeditation is neither more nor less than premeditation. Just as everybody (according to a witty *incipit* of Croce's) knows what Art is, so the penal code assumes that everybody knows what premeditation is, and especially and precisely the judges. Article 364: "Whoever, with intent to kill, causes a person's death is sentenced to eighteen to twenty years' detention." But Article 366 adds that long-term sentences are enforced in six cases, the second of which is when the crime has been committed "with premeditation." And that's that.

There's a novel by Simenon—*Maigret hésité*—that envelops (rather than develops around) Article 46 of the French penal code; and true to the magic of numbers, this article corresponds to Article 64 of the Italian code: "He who at the moment of committing the act was of unsound mind such as to deprive him of the consciousness and freedom of his actions is not punishable." The French code states that: "Neither crime nor offense is imputable when the accused . . . ," which amounts to the same thing, although the "wording," as Manzoni would have said, is different. Now, premeditation is the exact and total opposite of what these articles define— only it is never itself defined. Thus almost always, and sometimes very liberally interpreted, a defendant has to suffer the additional charge of premeditation *if he has had time to reflect* on his decision to kill a fellow human being. Time, that is, to calm down sufficiently to see that he had better desist from his homicidal intention. And if he hasn't calmed down (a process that anyway takes more or less time according to the individual), the decision to kill is seen as cold-blooded and premeditated—no consideration being accorded to the fact that time for reflection, however long, may even serve to aggravate passion, excitement, and fury.

In the case of Contessa Tiepolo, what made premeditation plausible or even indisputable was, according to the prosecution, besides the time she had had to reflect, the obvious advantage she had in putting an end to a relationship that had become inconvenient and irksome; and furthermore her unexpected, unwelcome, and compromising pregnancy, pregnant (aptly) with inevitable consequences for the family. Instead of the desired advantage, all she had achieved was arrest, detention, and trial; and above all the result that, with Polimanti dead, nearly all Italy believed what few would otherwise have believed: that she had been his mistress. Thus anything but premeditation. Indeed, whether or not we believe he was her lover, the contessa shot Polimanti in a fit of despair and passion, however superficial or deep, concerned with appearances, or willful these feelings may have been. Nothing could have been more unfair than to accuse her of premeditation. And unfair too—though not too unfair—was the fact of acknowledging legitimate defense: considering the silence that preceded the shot; the distance at which it was fired; the fact that the safety catch had been released, and the unerring accuracy of her aim, obviously intended neither to intimidate nor to wound, but to kill.

Thus, apart from criminal gangs, whose crimes are planned with as much premeditation as declarations of war or acts of repression, almost all offenses sentenced as premeditated ought to be considered under Article 46. The only really premeditated crimes are those that are not committed.

There were eleven questions for the jury to answer: (1) Is it a fact that on the morning of November 8, 1913, in San Remo, Corso Umberto 2, and more precisely at the flat occupied by Oggioni Ferruccio, captain of the First Bersagliere Regiment, and his family, a shot was fired at the orderly Polimanti Quintilio, the bullet, having struck him in the face and penetrated deeply, being the sole and immediate cause of his death? This fact being incontrovertible, the query is superfluous, not to say stupid, and the answer is "Yes." (2) If the answer to the preceding question is in the affirmative (as if it could be otherwise: indeed, in that eventuality it would be necessary to call for an ambulance and straitjackets for the jury who had pronounced it!), did the accused Maria Tiepolo Oggioni commit the act of firing the shot at the orderly Polimanti Quintilio, causing his immediate death? How could this be doubted, since she had admitted it herself from the start? (3) Is it a fact that Maria Tiepolo Oggioni committed the act in self-defense and in order to restrain violent and unjustified aggression? The answer is not unanimous: five say "Yes," four "No," and one abstains. But this suffices for the eight remaining questions to be dropped and for the contessa to be acquitted.

The contessa is released. And her husband unexpectedly turns up to embrace her. Had he been hanging around waiting for the verdict before deciding whether to show himself or to remain "far away"? It has been said that Pirandello had already begun to explore this little-known sphere of amour propre (La Rochefoucauld had said there were many others), which according to Savinio is a "reaction to real or imagined cuckoldry, an emotion which, especially in Sicily, can attain cosmic proportions." But there is much in the Tiepolo affair that savors of Pirandello: the proliferation of truths, the conflict between appearance and reality ...

The sentence resounded throughout Italy, commented on everywhere, more condemned than approved. But before the month was out, Archduke Franz Ferdinand and his wife were murdered at Sarajevo. Shots once again, as well aimed as the contessa's. And by the first of July the Tiepolo case was no more than a distant memory. As armies gathered around frontiers, ready for the great massacre, someone mentioned it—but only because in France Madame Caillaux, who had killed Calmette, editor in chief of *Le Figaro,* had been acquitted—observing ironically that perhaps it was the latest fashion for ladies who had murdered gentlemen, whether orderlies or journalists, to be acquitted.

T he trouble about living and dying is that God exists but we'll know less about him dead than alive— since, as Borges says, alive we at least make him the subject of our best works of fiction (and although it may not be of the best, that's what I'm doing here). Alive we do nothing but pronounce the name of God in vain. Dead we shall most likely no longer pronounce it. And we believe, as living human beings, that by implanting in ourselves and in the deeds of our fellowmen words such as "truth," "justice," "poetry," we come closer to him. But as we approach death, we gradually realize through unexpected and fleeting reminders that, on the contrary, they distance him—almost as if they conspired against him, were the passwords of a ceaselessly and vainly prearranged outrage. Being is. Nonbeing is not. And what if they were the same thing? But already the word "thing" rebounds, void in the void, a nothing in nothingness. Something crosses our minds, which we can't decipher, and it isn't fictional writing. But everything else is. And we go on writing it. And God, who in a Borges tale can't tell the Orthodox Theologian from the Heretic—not because he's confused, which would be inconceivable for God, but because nothing human can affect him—probably can't tell the killer from the killed, the executioner from the victim, the torturer from the tortured, pleasure from pain. "Where is the executioner, where the victim?" The question already reechoed in the land of the gods, and men asked it in the name of the gods. In a theater, arrogantly and uselessly seeking to disturb the gods.

Let us therefore imagine a place where the name of God is not pronounced: a Victorian drawing room, elegant, with dark mahogany furniture, landscapes and hunting scenes on the walls, bone-china figurines, and silver knickknacks. A drawing room where light conversations occur, where never a misplaced or questionable word is spoken. This is the hereafter. But it resembles the here and now of "The Gioconda Smile," that short story by Aldous Huxley to which I appositely referred earlier. A story that could be called a detective story, except that the name of God is not pronounced, whereas in detective stories it's always pronounced in connection with "Justice." A simple tale: A woman believes she is loved by the husband of a friend but doesn't know that this man already has a young mistress who is about to give birth to his child. One day the sickly wife invites her friend Miss Janet Spence to lunch; and suddenly, just after the meal, she is taken ill, goes to bed, and dies—of arsenic poisoning, for which the husband is accused, sentenced to death, and hanged. Some time later, however, in Miss Spence's drawing room, Dr. Libbard, who had been the deceased lady's doctor and is also Miss Spence's, says, as though he were discussing the weather, lightly, vaguely: " 'I suppose it was really you who poisoned Mrs. Hutton.' . . . 'Yes.' After that she started to cry. 'In the coffee, I suppose.' She seemed to nod assent. Dr. Libbard took out his fountain pen, and in his neat, meticulous calligraphy wrote out a prescription for a sleeping draught."

And the following flight of my imagination is to be understood as pure fantasy: In this place where the name of God is no longer pronounced, as they pass the time of day discussing this and that, some Dr. Libbard (perhaps Professor Conti rather than Senator Raimondi) unexpectedly and vaguely says to the contessa: "There's just one thing I didn't understand at the time. That open suitcase on the bed, which you said you were packing to go away?" And the contessa, like Miss Spence, absentmindedly replies: "It was so that he'd suspect nothing; it was the best excuse I could think of for opening that drawer and taking out the revolver."

NOTES

Last year I wrote and published a brief tale (how else to define it?) intended as a homage to Manzoni: a modest tribute, I pointed out, among the notable contributions to the commemoration of the two hundredth anniversary of his birth. This year, the fiftieth after Pirandello's death, I happened to write another, equally brief, that could be seen as a homage to Pirandello—but this time not deliberate, not intended as such from the start. And having finished writing, I ask myself what link exists for me between these two almost equally beloved writers. But it would take pages and pages to find an "exhaustive" answer (as they say). The short answer, which comes to me here and now, is that the link is perhaps Pascal. A Pascal differently read by Manzoni and by Pirandello and with very different results. For Manzoni it is the reasons of the heart that reason wishes to select and incorporate; while for Pirandello, it is these same reasons that elude reason and merge with universal dread.

But as I began to write, I was not thinking of Pirandello.

I was thinking rather of a rambling stroll through time, through a brief stretch of time in the history of Italy. And thus I chose as epigraph the two first and the two last lines of that poem of Palazzeschi's which is called, precisely, "The Stroll" *(La Passeggiata)*. But then, in my story (again, how else to describe it?), other things intervened, and especially the Pirandello I was in the process of revisiting.

As ever—and ever more as I advance (or perhaps regress) in years—I seek concision: an old ideal I keep encoded, as it were, in the definition of that aspect of the terms "succinct, precise, concise" which more expressly concerns the art of writing in the *Dizionario dei sinonimi* by my old friend the unsurpassable Tommaseo, a definition I have made my own. And I think it's only fair to entertain the reader with it: "No writer can be concise who is not precise, because if he has no exact understanding of things he will always err in that correct use of terms which is the source of brevity and clarity, that is, of the noble style to which nothing can be added and from which nothing can be subtracted without loss of quality. Alfieri is a concise but not a precise writer; for he failed to realize that the brevity or length of a work is measured not by the number of words but by the time required to understand them; and that brevity which is only on the page is a false brevity. Alfieri in his affected brevity is often longer than Metastasio. He uses less essential epithets in his desire to make them apter and more tripping. But I wouldn't call Metastasio concise. Neither one nor the other is parsimonious. And parsimony is a quality which involves words and things, ideas and emotions; it is most desirable because it is most directly conducive to honesty." I have sought concision—whether or not I have achieved it is another matter. It's not for me to decide.

I didn't want to weigh down this text (not to call it a tale), cluttered as it already is with quotations, references, and allusions, by adding explanatory and bibliographical notes. I wanted it to flow smoothly and not to obstruct the reader's vision and mind with all those little numbers or ciphers that clutter "scholarly books," an obligation to which writers apparently submit with a certain relish but which is less pleasing for the reader when numbers and ciphers rain down on the page. Thus I decided to relegate here, without any number or cipher relating them to the text, the few notes that might be of interest to the reader.

Among my books is one of the fifty copies on *papier de Hollande* of D'Annunzio's *Martyre de Saint Sébastien.* It is inscribed by hand "à Fernand Charles Ecot. 'Chaque flêche est pour le salut' Gabriele D'Annunzio. 7 Juin 1912 + 1." Inside the book is an invitation for the *"répétition générale"* of the play. Proof that in Paris at that time Ecot was somebody. I have been unable to discover who.

The exchange between Renard and Blum can be found at the precise date of January 21, 1905, in Renard's *Journal,* obviously.

Marinetti's Manifesto against the tango and *Parsifal* is a handbill dated January 11, 1914. So as not to be accused of unjustified intolerance for Marinetti and Futurism, I give it here in all its quirky integrity:

Last year I answered a questionnaire in *Gil Blas* by denouncing the tango's subversive poison. This epidemic swaying is gradually spreading throughout the world and threatens to corrupt every nation, reducing them all to jelly. Therefore we see ourselves compelled once again to violently attack the imbecility of fashion and to divert the sheeplike flood of snobbishness.

Monotony of romantic haunches amid flashing glances and Spanish daggers out of Musset, Hugo, and Gautier. Industrialization of Baudelaire; *Fleurs du mal* swaying in Jean Lorrain taverns for the benefit of impotent *voyeurs* à la Huysmans and homosexuals à la Oscar Wilde. Final hysterical tremors of a sentimental, decadent, and para-lytic romanticism for a papier-mâché Femme Fatale.

Clumsiness of the English and German tango, me-chanical spasms of skeletons and frock coats incapable of externalizing their emotions. Plagiarism of the Parisian and Italian tango, shellfish couples, feline Argentinian savagery stupidly tamed, drugged, and powdered.

To possess a woman is not to rub oneself against her but to penetrate her.

—Barbarian!

One knee between her thighs? Come now, there must be two!

—Barbarian!

All right. We are barbarians! Down with the tango and its modulated swoonings. Do you really find it such fun to stare into each other's mouths and ecstatically pick each other's teeth like a pair of delirious dentists? To snatch? ... To pounce? ... Do you really find it such fun to bend desperately over each other in the hope of recip-rocally unbottling an orgasm, but never succeeding? ... My Own Beloved, do you really wear size 4? ... How beautifully you are shod, my Dreeeam! ... You tooo! ...

Tristan and Isolde holding back their orgasm to tit-illate King Mark. Drip-fed love. Pocket-size sexual torments. Candy floss of desire. Public lechery. Delirium tremens. Alcoholic hands and feet. Intercourse aped for the cinema. Masturbatory waltz. Ugh! Down with skin-deep tactfulness. Long live the brutality of a passionate possession and the noble frenzy of a muscular, exhilarating, and invigorating dance!

Tango, pitch and toss of a sailing boat at anchor in the deeps of cretinism. Tango, pitch and toss of a sailing boat soaked with lunatic morbidity and silliness. Tango, tango, nauseating pitch and toss. Tango, slow, patient funeral of dead sexuality. Oh, it's not by any means a question of religion, ethics, or modesty! These three words mean nothing to us! We shout *Down with the tango* in the name of Health, Strength, Will Power, and Manliness.

But if the tango is evil, *Parsifal* is worse because it injects dancers tottering with boredom and lassitude with an incurable musical neurasthenia.

How shall we evade *Parsifal* with its cloudbursts, its puddles, and its floods of mystical tears? *Parsifal* is the systematic devaluation of life! Cooperative factory of sorrow and despair. Unmelodious contractions of weak stomachs. Poor digestion and bad breath of middle-aged virgins. Whimperings of fat, constipated old priests. Instant wholesale of regrets and elegant cowardice for snobs. Bloodlessness, ailing kidneys, hysteria, anemia, and chlorosis. Genuflection, degradation, and collapse of Man. Ridiculous trailing of wounded and defeated notes. Swooning of drunken organs wallowing in the vomit of bitter leitmotifs. False tears and pearls of a Mary Magdalen in low-cut dress at Maxim's. Polyphonic festering of Amfortas's wounds. Sniveling drowsiness of the Knights of the Round Table. Absurd Satanism of Kundry ... Traditionalism! Traditionalism! Enough!

Kings and queens of snobbishness, know that you owe total allegiance to us, the Futurists, the living innovators! Abandon to the bestial lust of the mob the corpse of Wagner, that innovator from fifty years ago, whose works, now superseded by Debussy, Strauss, and our own great Futurist Pratella, have no longer any significance. You helped us defend him when he needed defending. We shall teach you to love and to defend something alive, dearly beloved slaves of Snobbishness.

Furthermore, you overlook *this final and for you persuasive argument:* to worship Wagner and *Parsifal* today when he is performed everywhere and especially in the provinces, to hold Tea Tangos today like every good bourgeois all over the world IS NO LONGER CHIC!

Huxley's story "The Gioconda Smile" was published in the volume *Mortal Coils* by Chatto & Windus, London, 1922.

On misprints in James Joyce's *Ulysses* see *Il corriere della sera* of June 17, 1986 (and voluminous correspondence in the *New York Review of Books,* 1988 —Ed.).

The painter Julio Romero de Torres has a whole museum to himself in Cordova, where he was born in 1874 and died in 1930. A visit to Torres's museum provides enchanting moments in a city that is full of enchantments.

The play *La signora senza pace* (and not, as reported at the trial, *La donna senza pace*) is by Regina Winnge, a writer who, apparently, today enjoys the tranquillity of oblivion.

The trial of Maria Tarnowska, Nicholas Maumoy's accomplice in the murder of Count Paul Kamarowsky, was held in Venice, May 4–20, 1910. A rather turbid case, which enthralled all Italy. Arturo Vecchini and the young Francesco Carnelutti were lawyers for the defense. Annie Vivanti based her novel *Circe* on this affair.

Raimondi's speech was published at the time in all the papers and received more publicity than any other speech in the Tiepolo affair. Ten years ago, it was anthologized in a gift edition published by Giuffrè under the title *La parola della difesa*, together with three other examples of the eloquence of "former times." The others are by Enrico Ferri, Enrico Pessina, and Genunzio Bentini. The volume is adorned with illustrations by Mario Maccari. Most appropriately.

Madame Caillaux, former wife of the minister Joseph Caillaux, in 1914 killed Gaston Calmette, who had made *Le Figaro* the organ of French nationalism and had patriotically accused the minister of corruption. But Madame Caillaux claimed to have murdered Calmette because he had published a very intimate letter of hers. Thus, to defend her honor.

The fact that God's existence is within the competence of the best fictional writers has been stated by Borges in a number of interviews. The story to which I refer, "The Theologians," is included in Jorge Luis Borges, *Labyrinths*.

AFTERWORD

It was a matter of some surprise when, late in his life, Leonardo Sciascia returned to fiction, and no one seemed more
surprised than Sciascia himself. For some time, although his
output had remained prolific, he had limited himself to works
of a different type, including book-length interviews, books
on aspects of Sicilian life, collections of essays and articles
that had originally appeared in newspapers, as well as several
works in that idiosyncratic genre which has no standard name,
but which it will be convenient to tag "investigative essays."
About half of his output falls into this category, and although
it is common enough for writers to divide their time between
fiction and nonfiction, the "investigative essay" was something Sciascia had made his own. None of his contemporaries
produced anything in exactly that style, and his only precur-
sor in the field was Alessandro Manzoni, the nineteenth-
century novelist, whose pamphlet *The Column of Infamy,*
denouncing and exposing the machinations of an Inquisition
tribunal in Counter-Reformation Milan, provided Sciascia
with a model and an inspiration.

Even if he takes an incident from history as his starting point, these investigative pieces of Sciascia's are not orthodox historical works. He generally preferred to use publicly available documents, and was more interested in analysis and comment and in observations, which could be arbitrary or whimsical, than in reconstruction. The approach is reminiscent of Borges—whose presence in Sciascia's writing became ever more marked—but where Borges would mix invention with fact, Sciascia would intertwine public event and private speculation. He reveled in the looseness of structure of his adopted genre and in the freedom it afforded him to roam at will through his material, intervening, speculating, and, constantly, making an implicit contrast between, on the one hand, an order that could be given only by reason and, on the other, the disorder of history and the Machiavellian nature of human conduct. Perhaps the best-known work in this style was *The Moro Affair*, on the kidnapping and imprisonment of the ex–Christian Democrat prime minister by the Red Brigades. The work entitled *1912+1*, published in 1986, is of the same type. In it Sciascia recounts the known facts of a celebrated murder case in the decadent high society of pre–World War I Italy, when King Umberto was monarch of the nation and Gabriele D'Annunzio monarch of letters. D'Annunzio worshipped the Nietzschean superman, that ambiguous figure who, in his dealings with other men—or women—viewed himself as exempt from the laws of all conventional morality (or "the code of the slave"). His novels are impregnated with a Swinburnean sensuality, and Sciascia, in addition to exposing what to him seemed an evident injustice in the case in question, explored the links between the D'Annunzian culture of the time and the actual conduct of men and women.

It was D'Annunzio, with his superstitious refusal to use the number 13 even in reference to the year, who provided him with a title. Sciascia did not regard *1912+1* as a novel, and in the notes dubs it a text ("not to call it a tale"). The central theme—of justice frustrated—recurs in many of his works, and while it emerges forcefully from the account of the trial that provides the heart of the present writing, it is perhaps best to regard the book as an eighteenth-century-style occasional book, packed with jottings and reflections, or as the literary equivalent of an album of fading daguerreo-types. Through a multiplicity of stills of individual incidents, Sciascia builds up a portrait of a year, but he does not at-tempt to force parallels with the present or to imply that the year under review was in some sense a turning point. The assassin's bullets in Sarajevo were too close to make any such endeavor plausible.

By no means do all the events chronicled in the story have connection with the trial. Although the prophet par ex-cellence of reason, Sciascia was endlessly amused by the spec-tacle of human stupidity. There is no overwhelming reason why F. T. Marinetti, the founding father of that monument of harlequinade and self-aggrandizement which was Futur-ism, should be recalled in this context, except that Sciascia so clearly relished recording Marinetti's extravagant denun-ciation of the new rage for the tango. Who but Marinetti could have linked this dance with Wagner's *Parsifal,* and who but Sciascia would have cared?

The same year saw such diverse events as the rediscovery of the *Mona Lisa* after its theft from the Louvre, Italy's fal-tering imperialist campaign in Libya, and the Gentiloni Pact. Ever since the seizure of Rome by the forces of united Italy, the Pope had lived as the "prisoner of the Vatican," and

Catholics had been banned, under pain of excommunication, from participating in the affairs of the new Kingdom of Italy. Although an obscure figure, Count Gentiloni proposed a compromise whereby the Italian state would guarantee to respect all that Catholics held most sacred in the social sphere, thus preparing the way for an eventual agreement between Church and state. One of the clauses underlined the centrality of the family, the indissoluble unity of marriage, and the consequent "absolute opposition to divorce."

Sexual practice has always made nonsense of sexual moral precepts, and there was no doubt a touch of ironic malice in Sciascia's decision to counterpose the Gentiloni Pact with the case that made headlines that year, the murder by Countess Maria Tiepolo of her officer husband's aide-de-camp, the unfortunate Quintilio Polimanti. The case had the indispensable ingredients of scandal—sex, money, uncertainty, and the alluringly decadent atmosphere of high-society vice. Did the countess dispose of an ex-lover whose demands were becoming inconvenient, or did she ward off by the only means available unwelcome assaults on her person and her virtue? When the mass media were coming into their own, Italy was given the chance of being divided over the case. It retains its own intriguing mystery, but Sciascia was no yellow-press voyeur, and his aim was to probe the workings of the system of justice and to investigate the wellsprings of human behavior. Did D'Annunzio, or Gentiloni, construct the values that made the conduct of these people explicable? Sciascia digresses as frequently as he reconstructs, intervening with ironic asides or wandering off in directions dictated by his own fancy. Literature is as important as historical fact or speculation, and even his own judgment on the countess's guilt is given obliquely, if unmistakably, via a short story by Aldous Huxley.

According to his own account (in a conversation in Siracusa, in eastern Sicily), when he sat down with the documents he had accumulated on another murder case in Palermo during the years of fascism, Sciascia had every intention of writing the same kind of book. He followed a fixed routine, collecting his material in winter and writing over the summer months. He insisted that he never thought in advance about form and that he never found it necessary to rewrite. *Open Doors* only became a novel once he started to write. It was published in 1987 and was his first work of fiction since *Candido*, ten years previously. It also represented a return to the detective story, the form he had used for his first four novels but abandoned after *One Way or Another* in 1974. He subsequently produced the two other detective stories contained in this volume: *Death and the Knight* the following year and *A Straightforward Tale* in 1989, a few months before his death, in November of the same year.

Since the return to fiction was haphazard, there is little point in attempting to build an ideology into it, but it is intriguing to note the extent to which in his last novels Sciascia re-covers old ground, re-examines familiar topics, analyzes again the themes that have always obsessed him, but from a different perspective. It was always facile to view Sciascia exclusively as a survivor from the Age of the Enlightenment, as the upholder of the concept of Law in a land that despised it, as the solitary hero engaged on a quest for Justice and Truth, or the intrepid adversary of violence and mafia in Sicily. Gore Vidal pointed out that from his Sicilian experience Sciascia forged something unique, which spoke to all European peoples, and it seems clear that in his last novels, he was attempting to widen his canvas, to use his subject matter as metaphor. He remains close to history, and as he again recounts episodes associated with fascism, terrorism, and mafia, there is at times a real tension between history and metaphor. These had been familiar topics in his principal works, but here life itself is seen by an old man who knew he was dying. At times, in these books, the world seems to be glimpsed through a hospital window, and nothing is more moving and striking than the cosmic pity and compassion with which these novels are imbued. Sciascia had not been a notably compassionate writer at other times, but all his life he shadowed his fellow Sicilian Luigi Pirandello. In the nihilistic worldview Pirandello adhered to—most forcibly expressed in his essay *On Humor*—a sense of compassion for the ultimate plight of the human being was the one positive, life-enhancing value that survived. It is this quality which emerges most tellingly in Sciascia's final phase.

Fascism, terrorism, and mafia intrigue feature in the three final novels. *Open Doors* is set in the Fascist period, as had been the first of his writings, *The Parishes of Regalpeira.* He was always contemptuous of Mussolini's fascism as well as of what he judged "the eternal Italian fascism," and many of the characters in his works are presented as coming to maturity at the moment they free themselves from it. *Death and the Knight* has evident links, both thematic and stylistic, with the sinister, tangled political society depicted in *Equal Danger,* while the posthumous *Straightforward Tale* can be seen as a return to and an updating of the mafia world of his first novel, *Day of the Owl.*

Although *Open Doors* is set in 1937, the Fascist period, by openly making reference to the year of writing, 1987, Sciascia introduces an element of movement between fictional and real time. There is no demand for the "willing suspension of disbelief," but there are few of the other customary attributes or features of traditional fiction. This work is halfway between the novel and the "investigative essay" of the sort Sciascia had in mind when he started writing, but in form and approach it is also in line with novels produced by such contemporary writers as Kundera and Vargas Llosa. The leading character is in reality Sciascia himself. It is odd that at the moment when the pundits of postmodernist criticism have declared the author dead, novelists have made themselves more visible than at any preceding time. Discussing the "little judge" whom he had apparently created, Sciascia suddenly announces that when he had seen him in life, he was not in fact "little" at all, at least not in stature, but in some imprecise way made an impression of littleness on Sciascia. This physical "littleness," Sciascia explains, was a mere invention to emphasize his moral and human grandeur. At times, Sciascia puts his reflections into the mouth of one of the characters, but just as frequently he talks *in prima persona.*

Sciascia was never strong on description, and at no time in this novel does he spend a word in re-creating period atmosphere or providing any kind of physical background. He never provides any description of his characters, apart from a few somewhat cloying, florid words on the women. His fictional world is a purely intellectual construct, inhabited by intellectuals. The characters are given no names. None of them have any life outside what is strictly required for the development of the central conflict. They have no emotional life, in the sense of affections, friendships, sexual relations. They are ciphers, or creations drawn, like Cubist sketches, on a deliberately flat surface. Anonymity is preferred, perhaps because anonymity crushes individuality. In the Book of Genesis, names are given to creatures so that they can be distinguished one from the other.

Is it then possible to arrive at some understanding of

what fiction was for Sciascia? Years previously, he accused himself of not having a "great creative imagination," adding that for his characters, unlike those of Pirandello, "the distance between life and the printed page is minimal, the gap very slight." Fiction in Sciascia is not creation *ex nihilo*, nor is it the manufacture of a parallel world. He never was a writer who set out to create an alternative universe, where the rules of physics, of time and space relationships, could be suspended at will. Unlike the South American exponents of magical realism such as Marquez, he never had the inclination to rebel against existing conditions by allowing his fantasy to manufacture a dimension where recognizable and purely invented elements become one. He adhered to certain conventions. It is not too much to say that his creativity is essentially realistic, yet in these novels he strains at the leash.

The novella *A Straightforward Tale* is the most evidently realist of his later works. The title is clearly ironic, and if it does not have the multilayered richness of the other stories, it is a masterly exercise in narrative. Indeed, it is as expertly plotted as any work of Sciascia's. On this occasion there is no temptation to go beyond the conventional bounds of the novel into territory more usually assigned to the essay. The land is Sicily, the characters are Sicilian, and the villains are, although the word is never used, the modern mafia of drug dealers. Behind them lurks that complex network of corruption and double dealing involving Church and police which makes this tale a tour de force of detective fiction, and life in Sicily such a nightmare. The reality depicted is anything but straightforward.

The strength of Sciascia's fictional world comes from the power of the intellect that created it, from the decency (in the sense Orwell attached to the word) of the values advocated rather than from the richness of imagination called into play. More and more the two styles of his books came closer together. It would be curious to know if he would have written *Open Doors* differently if he had adhered to his original intention of presenting it as an investigative essay. Perhaps it is a novel only because he says it is. In it Sciascia is engaged on a quest, and it is not a search for the inner life of individual characters but a quest for public values. He unites in a unique way a relativism over fact reminiscent of Borges or Pirandello with a moral absolutism that is as rigid as any Counter-Reformation Jesuit would have wished. As a writer, he proclaims the need to stand by a notion of the value of a truth that at first sight finds no response in his own skeptical treatment of history. The truth in question is, of course, moral truth.

In *Open Doors* the facts of the case are provided by history, but they are briefly, even cursorily and contemptuously, reported inside a framework of debate and discussion. The novel opens with a discussion between the two legal figures over the prospect of actually imposing the recently reintroduced death penalty, and it closes with a discussion between the same two characters over the value of the outcome of the case in the court of first instance. The prosecution will undoubtedly appeal against the decision not to apply the death penalty. There is only one other extended dialogue in the work, between the judge and the farmer, and that, unsurprisingly in Sciascia, concerns bookish matters. The three murders committed by the "Beast" are given in a rapid journalistic summary, but only when Sciascia is almost halfway through his tale. Information about the presumably anxious debates in the jury room is conveyed in one paragraph, which is so restrained and spare as to be almost laughable.

Considering the nature of the crimes, anything further from what John Buchan would have called a "shocker" is hard to imagine.

The central fact is not the crime but the potential punishment: the death penalty. The focus of Sciascia's attention has shifted onto the criminal, but only inasmuch as the criminal can be in his own way a victim. The accused, the Beast—and the enormity of his crime or the fact of his guilt is never in dispute—is by now a captive, a prisoner, a human being who might well be torn apart by the machine. Whatever his tenaciously held abstract position on Law and Justice founded on Reason, Sciascia never can bring himself to regard the actual judicial machinery with any tenderness. He was too much of a Sicilian to regard the judge charged with discharging the law with anything other than uncomprehending distaste, or to regard the living human being who faces the rigors of the law with anything other than fellow feeling. In some ways, the accused is in the same position as Aldo Moro, or as those of Sciascia's heroes who face death or pain at the hands of the Inquisition, of terrorists, of the mafia, or of any tyrannical force that has arrogated to itself the power of God over the destinies of other humans. There is in this complex standpoint a mixture of an attitude born of centuries of Sicilian history and a more universal, liberal distaste for the taking of life whatever the circumstances.

Fascism had always been the very synonym for the forces of unreason, the antithesis of any life-enhancing value, or even of life. In this work, the metaphorical sense of fascism is as significant as the strictly historical. Fascism reintroduced the death penalty, but fascism itself is a death force. All that counts against it is the commitment of the individual, but plainly that commitment is doomed to failure. The splendid closing dialogue between the two lawyers, by now reconciled on a human level, is a discussion of how to confront and cope with the inevitability of defeat. The prosecutor believes that the judge wasted his time in opposing the death penalty, not so much because the sentence will undoubtedly be overturned on appeal as because the decision will merely expose the guilty man to an extended period of anxiety and a longer period of futile hope. Against this, the judge urges that all life is transient, that no hope is ever futile, that the individual in whatever desperate circumstances will invariably find consolation in even the most illusory of hopes, and that ultimately the principle of the final, intrinsic value of life itself must be asserted, always and everywhere, against the forces of death.

Figurative elements become the determinant, essential element of the style and approach in *Death and the Knight*. The novel is a meditation, infused with elements of poetry, on life and death. The theater of action is presumably Rome, but the city is given no name and it is part of a Kafkaesque planet from which all coherence has fled. Sciascia operates here on the verges of history, for if the terrorist-dominated society is not entirely unfamiliar from recent Italian experience, the division between terrorist activity and legitimate government action is blurred. It is no longer clear where power resides, any more than it was to K, but it is a sinister force, which can construct an opposition as shady as itself, and can destroy capriciously. Society is a moral quagmire, where the idealistic preach slaughter, where the weak-minded execute these teachings out of a desire for status, excitement, and acceptance, while behind them lurk cynical, gray men who manipulate both groups, drawing from the anarchy they have unleashed comfort and justification for their own domination. The authoritarianism of established power of whatever hue—old divisions into right and left have lost all sense—bases itself on the disorder it has itself created. In this labyrinthine world, Machiavelli and the mafia blend. Principles are matters for public consumption, but there is never any savor of them in practice.

The print that gives the novel its title is the property of the deputy, who once again is given no individual name. The theme is a reprise of the topics Sciascia developed in an earlier novel, *Equal Danger,* and if he subtitled that novel a "parody," he subtitles this later work a *"sotie."* A *sotie* is defined as a satirical farce from the fifteenth and sixteenth centuries, but it was adopted by André Gide as a description of *The Vatican Cellars.* The term *"sotie"* does not suggest, any more than the term "parody," that Sciascia was intending to write what Graham Greene dubbed an entertainment. Nor is it a pastiche, although that term has now acquired more respectable connotations in certain critical circles. Sciascia's purposes were always fundamentally serious. It would be flippant and otiose to attach $x = y$ type equations to the three figures from the engraving, but the sense of death hangs over the book, and the devil is, in a purely humanistic sense, required as the counterpoint to forces that wish to present themselves as the forces of good and right. The battlefield for this modern Pilgrim's Progress is of course politics, but the action is seen from the perspective of a man who knows he is dying.

In some ways this is a work that is as much put together from preexisting sources as Umberto Eco's *The Name of the Rose.* For those with a taste for such matters, the novel is a thicket of what are now called intertextual references. The images from Dürer's etching haunt the deputy's mind, but the identical print was in the possession of another celebrated fictional detective, Inspector Barlach of the Bern police, and was used by his creator, Friedrich Dürrenmatt, for the same purposes in *The Judge and the Executioner*. Similarly, Sciascia pays homage to the greatest of all Italian detective stories, C. E. Gadda's *That Awful Mess on Via Merulana*, by introducing references to its hero, Inspector Ciccio Ingravallo. He is equally generous to R. L. Stevenson's *Treasure Island* and quotes copiously from writers ranging from Feydeau to D. H. Lawrence. Hand in hand with these references to literary antecedents go a series of throwaway remarks which imply that the whole plot was a joke. The initial encounter between Aurispa and Sandoz at the banquet before the murder was intended, according to Aurispa, as a joke. The young man who is arrested after making the telephone call in which he passed himself off as a terrorist protests that he was only playing a joke, leading the deputy to conclude that "we are tied up inside a *sotie*."

These references both shadow and shape the development of the action. They are not intellectually clever exercises in counterpoint, nor do they signify that the novel is intended as no more than a purely literary construct. They are something of both, as the novel itself is much more. The "artificial" nature of the novel, its tendency to keep history at arm's length, to see the events of the book through a prism, reflects the very nature of the events recounted. As is invariably the case with Sciascia's detective stories, the case is not solved inside the confines of the novel, but the reader will have no doubt of who is responsible. The dilemma is resolved by reference to a wise man—in this case Dr. Rieti, who followed the affairs of the two rival industrialists but who himself will end up a victim of murder squads for talking to the deputy. The final victim is the deputy, killed by some unknown group who could be the Children of Eighty-nine, by this time brought into existence. Death is the only victor.

Whatever the truth about Power and the Children of Eighty-nine—this is Pirandellian territory, where illusion and reality overlap—the world is ruled by a system of self-perpetuating corruption. All power is ultimately mafioso in its operations, but not all activities can be covert. A devil of some sort is essential. If the old-style devil is no longer serviceable, a newer model must be summoned up, and fortunately there are always enough weak-minded individuals prepared to offer themselves for the task in return for fifteen minutes' celebrity. The self-proclaimed activist in the Saint-Just cell serves the purpose here. The police leap on both the man and this confirmation that their work was along the right lines. His arrest proves that all is right with the world, that the old order was fundamentally sound—precisely the standard ending of the classical detective story. No doubt the wrong man has been—almost certainly—unmasked, but he can act as a very modern devil, allowing real evil to continue unchecked.

As always, the detective protagonist is a highly cultured intellectual, and at a certain point Sciascia seems to lose interest in his plot and to turn to the dilemma and character of the deputy himself. The last sections—from his quitting the police station on temporary leave until his murder—provide prose of the most refined, limpid, and perspicacious order. At times, Sciascia attains that level of meditative prose which is the distinctive quality of the supreme essayist, and this passage, where the deputy reaches the "threshold of prayer," displays a quality of mercy, a measure of open-hearted benignity toward humankind, worthy of Montaigne.

Like Sciascia, the deputy knew he was dying, but his dying was not embittered by hatred for life. Death itself may be the ultimate absurdity, but Sciascia never reaches the point of believing that the absurdity of death makes the living that precedes it senseless and vain. The central drawback of modern criticism is that in concentrating on scientific or linguistic aspects, it loses sight of the quest for and assertion of values that are as intrinsic to certain works of literature as they are fundamental to life. To overlook that feature of quest and assertion in Sciascia is to diminish him.

JOSEPH FARRELL

A NOTE ABOUT THE AUTHOR

The late novelist and essayist Leonardo Sciascia (1921–1989) was one of Italy's greatest contemporary writers. His critically acclaimed fiction has been translated into a number of languages and has also been turned into films, the most recent of which, *Open Doors,* based on the novella contained in this quartet, was nominated for an Academy Award for Best Foreign Film in 1990.

A NOTE ON THE TYPE

This book was set in Bodoni Book, a type face named after Giambattista Bodoni (1740–1813), a celebrated printer and type designer of Rome and Parma. Bodoni Book is not a copy of any one of Bodoni's fonts, but a composite, modern version of the Bodoni manner. Bodoni's innovations in type style included a greater degree of contrast in the thick and thin elements of the letters and a sharper and more angular finish of details.

Composed by Creative Graphics, Inc.,
Allentown, Pennsylvania

Printed and bound by Arcata Graphics,
Martinsburg, West Virginia

Designed by Cassandra J. Pappas